"What is it that you think I know about your sister?" Clay asked.

"Nothing."

He raised an eyebrow and Tessa shrugged. "Renee explained that you were involved, so it's possible you have some insight into what she was thinking during those last few months."

Clay stared. "Tessa, there was nothing like that between us. We didn't interact more than I do with any other guest."

"You were the guide on almost every trip she took."

"That isn't unusual. If clients like a certain guide, they often try to schedule trips based on who might be leading it or make a special request, but there was nothing going on with Renee. I have a personal rule about that sort of thing."

"You weren't happy about Patrick Frazier flirting with me. I wondered if it was because..." She stopped and seemed to shake herself. "I guess not."

Dear Reader,

When I was writing the first manuscript in my Hearts of Big Sky series, my heroine mentions a boy who broke her heart when she was in the second grade. And just like that, Clay Carson came into being. I thought, What happens to all those little boys who carelessly break little girls' hearts? Are they still breaking hearts? Did they turn into bankers or doctors or something more unconventional?

One of the nice things about being a writer is that I can answer some of those questions.

Naturally, Clay grows up to be a decent, hardworking guy. He's a determined bachelor who owns a successful outdoor adventure company near Glacier National Park. Everything is going well until a reckless client drowns on a white river rafting trip. He isn't at fault, but he still feels responsible for the young woman's death. Then the client's sister shows up, wanting answers of her own.

I enjoy hearing from readers and can be contacted on my Facebook page at Facebook.com/julianna.morris.author. If you prefer writing a letter, please use c/o Harlequin Books,
22 Adelaide Street West, 40th Floor,
Toronto, Ontario Canada M5H 4E3.

Best wishes,

Julianna Morris

HEARTWARMING

The Man from Montana

—

Julianna Morris

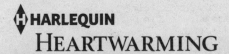

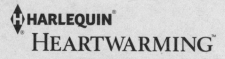

HARLEQUIN®
HEARTWARMING™

ISBN-13: 978-1-335-17993-7

The Man from Montana

Copyright © 2021 by Julianna Morris

Recycling programs for this product may not exist in your area.

This is a work of fiction. Names, characters, places and incidents are either the product of the author's imagination or are used fictitiously. Any resemblance to actual persons, living or dead, businesses, companies, events or locales is entirely coincidental.

This edition published by arrangement with Harlequin Books S.A.

For questions and comments about the quality of this book, please contact us at CustomerService@Harlequin.com.

Harlequin Enterprises ULC
22 Adelaide St. West, 40th Floor
Toronto, Ontario M5H 4E3, Canada
www.Harlequin.com

Printed in U.S.A.

Julianna Morris barely remembers a time when she didn't want to be a writer, having scribbled out her first novel in sixth grade (a maudlin tale she says will never ever see the light of day). She also loves to read, and her library includes everything from history and biographies to most fiction genres. Julianna has been a park ranger, program analyst and systems analyst in information technology. She loves animals, travel, gardening, baking, hiking, taking photographs, making patchwork quilts and doing a few dozen other things. Her biggest complaint is not having enough hours in the day.

Books by Julianna Morris

Harlequin Heartwarming

Christmas on the Ranch
Twins for the Rodeo Star

Harlequin Superromance

Bachelor Protector
Christmas with Carlie
Undercover in Glimmer Creek

Visit the Author Profile page
at Harlequin.com for more titles.

To first responders and medical personnel—
thanks for everything you do.

CHAPTER ONE

TESSA ALDERMAN PARKED in the Carson Outdoor Adventures lot and gazed at the rolling hills and snowy mountains beyond. It was so beautiful, she wished a vacation was the only reason she was in Montana.

She flipped down the SUV's sun visor and felt the familiar drop in her stomach at seeing her twin sister's picture, which she'd taped next to the mirror.

Renee.

A selfie, taken a few weeks before her death, with a defiant, almost angry look in her dark eyes. But why those particular emotions? Her divorce had been long over and she'd received a cash settlement from her ex, outside of the community-property division. She'd been published. On top of that, she'd just become an associate professor in Renaissance and Gothic art at the private college where she taught, so her career had been on track. Brilliantly on track, as a matter of fact—she'd been the youngest professor in the college's history.

Then suddenly, Renee had taken a leave of absence and left for an extended vacation in Montana, which was strange, because she'd never liked to travel. Just as strange, the college had believed she was in Europe, doing research to finish her second book. It was the only reason they'd allowed her to take the time when she was so new to her professorship.

Tessa pushed the visor back up and squared her shoulders. She'd searched for answers at Renee's apartment when she and her parents had cleared it out, wanting to understand what had happened and why, yet she'd just ended up with more questions.

Now, Montana was the only place left to search, and Tessa was afraid there wouldn't be any answers here, either.

A hotel courtesy van arrived as she got out. Six passengers disembarked and took backpacks from the cargo area. Tessa retrieved her own pack and gauged the weight. According to the information on the Carson Adventures website, a few pounds of food and equipment would be distributed to each person going on the trip. But that wouldn't be a problem; she'd gone on many hikes in the past that required much heavier packs.

"Hello," called a man's voice. "Welcome to the Carson Outdoor Adventures Ranch. I'm Clay. Presuming you're here for the four-day wilderness hike, I'll be your guide."

Tessa gave him a long look.

So *that* was Clay Carson, owner of the company and the man her twin had supposedly been dating on her extended vacation. He'd also been the guide on the rafting trip when Renee had died.

He was striking, with a strong bone structure, piercing gray eyes and dark brown hair. The image of a rugged outdoorsman. It was easy to see why her twin sister would have been attracted to him, less easy to understand how a woman as shy as Renee would have caught his notice.

Tessa sighed. She missed her sister terribly. Though not identical twins, they had been close, or at least she'd believed they were close until Renee had suddenly left Arizona and started participating in high-risk sports, sending bright little group emails to the family about everything she was doing. It didn't make sense. As a kid she wouldn't even jump off a high dive or go horseback riding, so how had she ended up dying in a whitewater rafting accident?

The others members of the group introduced themselves to Clay, and when Tessa didn't step immediately forward, he turned toward her with an inquiring expression.

"Are you part of my group?" he asked.

"Yes. Tessa Alderman."

Clay gave her a friendly smile. "It's nice to meet you, Tessa. Everyone, let's head over to the staging barn. We'll go over your gear, discuss the guidelines, sign the paperwork and divide up the food and common equipment. Then a company van will take us to the trailhead and you'll have the next four days to enjoy an incredible wilderness area."

Though Tessa had mostly backpacked with friends and youth groups, she'd taken a few guided trips and knew the first order of business was getting the liability releases properly signed. But they'd also want to be sure everyone had brought the basics listed on the website.

"Do I really need the tent?" she asked when Clay reached her. She'd laid everything from her pack on the table. The other women had kept their personal items out of sight, but Tessa refused to be coy about the scraps of underwear she'd stowed in ziplock plastic bags.

"I'm afraid so." A hint of a frown creased his brow. "You're from Tucson, Arizona, right?"

She tensed. Tessa wasn't keeping her relationship to Renee a secret…*exactly*, but she also wasn't advertising it. However close, they'd been as different as two sisters could be. Not only that, Renee had kept her married name after getting divorced, so it seemed unlikely that Clay Carson would make the connection based on the city where they'd both lived. Actually, not even the same city, since Renee's apartment had been in a little community outside Tucson.

Also, the accident had happened almost eight months ago. Tessa's parents hadn't brought a lawsuit against the company, so unless Clay Carson had been serious about Renee, he'd probably put it in the past. But it wasn't in the past for her family; Renee's death was a wound that refused to heal.

"I was born and raised in Arizona," Tessa said, pushing the thought to the back of her mind. "The main reason I use a tent in the Southwest is to keep scorpions out, and they aren't too common here, right?"

"That's right, but the weather can change quickly in this part of the world, so you'll need to bring it. Is the extra weight a problem?"

"No, I just wondered." Tessa enjoyed camping and hiking, but she was careful. If a local guide told her a tent was advisable, she'd go along.

She'd researched Carson Outdoor Adventures and their safety record was excellent. Even when she'd called the sheriff's office to ask about Renee's accident, she had been assured there was nothing to suggest the guides or equipment were in any way to blame. To the contrary, the guides had gone above and beyond in the effort to rescue her. Yet, however nicely he'd expressed his sympathies, the sheriff's responses had seemed guarded, as if he was holding something back. So maybe her next step would be requesting a copy of the report.

Surely she was entitled to see it as a member of the family.

CLAY ASSESSED HIS current group with a practiced eye.

The three couples had readily admitted they were new to backpacking. A few ounces here and there added up to pounds, so he'd recommended leaving various items behind in the lockers he provided for situations like this. They were cooperating. Nobody was allowed to dispose of anything on the trail, so except for food being eaten, if an item started out with a hiker, it stayed with the hiker.

As for Tessa Alderman?

She was a question mark. Her backpack seemed new, but her sleeping bag and tent had seen heavy use and she hadn't brought more clothes and supplies than she needed, which suggested she was an experienced backpacker.

His biggest concern was her looks; two of the wives were already eyeing her with a hint of wariness. Having a striking single woman on a trip with couples had caused tension in the past, but other than giving a cordial nod to the others, she seemed to be keeping to herself.

"Rrrf," barked his golden retriever, reminding Clay that he needed to find out if she could go along on the hike.

"Everyone," he called to get the group's attention. "This is Molly. If you're allergic to dogs or have another concern for any reason, feel free to let me know and she'll stay at the ranch, spoiled rotten by my aunt and uncle. They'll love you for it, so if you have any hesitation, speak up. I *will* say that she carries her own food, water, bowls and other supplies in a doggy backpack, so no worries there. She even has her own bear bag."

Laughter came from the group. "She's okay with me," one of them said, and the rest agreed with pleased smiles. As a rule, Molly was popular with his clients, especially first-timers who felt more comfortable going into the backcountry with a dog.

It was a good time to talk about encounters with predators, so Clay did a quick review of how to respond if a bear or other animal crossed their path.

One of the women shifted her weight from one foot to the other as he finished, looking nervous. "How often does that happen? I know bear attacks are rare, but what about wolves and mountain lions?"

"Hey, I'd love to see a wolf," her husband said. She dug an elbow into his side. "From a distance," he added hastily. "But don't worry, hon, you can run a lot faster than me."

Clay waited until the chuckles had died down. "Actually, as I mentioned, running generally isn't the best response." He gestured to the can attached to his belt. "This is bear spray, and I carry a backup can, as well. Groups are safest out there because we talk and make more noise, which alerts animals to our presence. But I've never had a problem, even with all the times I've gone out alone. I'm not saying that nothing can happen, but the truth is, most wild animals are shy of humans. Especially wolves. We just need to keep a close watch. If we see any predators, it will likely be from a distance."

"Zz-z-zro-o-o-om, zoom," a child's voice interrupted and Clay looked up to see his three-year-old nephew run into the barn.

"Whoa, pal." Clay grabbed him before he could careen into one of the guests. "What are you doing out here?"

"He wanted to give one of his pictures to Uncle Lee and now he's running away from a bath," Aunt Emma said breathlessly. "Derry, you little scamp, you're covered in finger paint."

Derry giggled as Clay swung him high in the air and into Emma's arms. She and Uncle Lee had moved here to help his brother with Derry. Having more family on the ranch was great, though he felt bad for Andrew, who'd never expected to be raising a child alone.

Clay did what he could, but Aunt Emma was the real lifesaver.

"Sorry for the interruption," Aunt Emma apologized to the group. "We're going, Derry. Tell everyone goodbye."

"Bye-bye," Derry said over her shoulder, waving his little hand.

He received waves and a chorus of "byes" in return.

Clay grinned at his clients when they were alone again. "All right, let's divide the food and common equipment and get going. When you repack everything, be sure to put the heavy items at the bottom so the weight rides on your hips. Like this."

He demonstrated with the contents of his own pack. They set to work and were soon returning to the parking lot.

Uncle Lee met them at the large passenger van. He'd become one of Clay's drivers, delivering groups to trailheads and picking them up. After thirty years in the US Navy he didn't like being idle, so in between he supervised the kitchen staff as they prepped for the backpack trips and the evening ranch barbecue, which were part of several afternoon day hikes and horseback rides. Aunt

Emma helped, too, though Derry kept her pretty busy.

"I see our Derry has marked you," Uncle Lee said, grinning.

Clay shrugged at the finger paint, which had rubbed off on his sleeve, and the small, faint handprint on the front of his shirt.

He noticed that Tessa sat in the back of the van with Molly next to her. Molly often had her favorite guest on a hike, and today it seemed that she'd picked Tessa Alderman.

It was interesting. Not that Clay disliked Tessa—they'd barely met—but there was an expression in her cool blue gaze that he didn't understand. At least she hadn't fought him on the question of bringing her tent along. Tents weren't optional at any time.

They ate an early lunch at the trailhead, then Clay gathered the group together and went over the remaining rules.

"I know I'm repeating what's on our website," he explained, "but this is a protected wilderness and Carson Outdoor Adventures is committed to being ecofriendly. So don't discard any wrappers or other items. We take our trash out with us, and anything with a scent, even something like soap or toothpaste, needs to be placed in bear bags and suspended in the air at night. But don't worry, I'll take care of getting it up there. Let's go."

Clay took the lead.

Though Tessa Alderman didn't have a hiking partner, she didn't try to stay with him. Instead, she remained at the rear of the group with Molly, who he'd carefully trained to be voice-command obedient. At regular intervals, he stopped and talked about the sights they were seeing or to answer questions. It helped him assess how the group was doing without being too obvious, and gave individuals who were less fit an opportunity to rest.

He hadn't made up his mind about Tessa. She seemed watchful, reminding him of the corporate representative who'd come out to evaluate Carson Outdoor Adventures. Gunther Computer Systems had been interested in a long-term contract to send their executives on backcountry retreats, but they'd pulled out of negotiations following the rafting accident the previous September.

On the other hand, maybe it was just wishful thinking to wonder if they were interested again. Still, they hadn't completely shut the door on doing business with him, even saying they'd look into it again "next year."

Clay let out a harsh breath.

The worst part was that he felt responsible for the accident. He'd run it over and over in his mind, trying to think of what else he could have done.

There had been other problems since, including from the insurance company, which was still doing spot audits of his liability releases. They'd just done an audit, in fact. It frustrated Clay, and yet how could he blame anyone for wanting to be sure that he and his company were good risks?

"What's that?" asked Ginny, breaking into his thoughts. She was the guest who was especially nervous of large predators. They were at a promontory and she was pointing at something a hundred feet below in a small meadow.

Clay admired Ginny's willingness to try something new, despite her fears. Truth be told, he'd rather have someone who was cautious and watchful, than a guest who was cockily certain nothing could happen to them. But he also didn't want her to be so afraid she didn't enjoy the trip.

"Good eyes, Ginny," he said approvingly. "That's an elk. You can take a closer look through my binoculars."

He showed her how to adjust the lenses

and glanced around the group. Everyone was looking down the slope, except Tessa, whose gaze was fixed on him.

It wasn't feminine awareness—it was something else. He just didn't know what.

Clay returned his focus to the other guests as they continued on. Ginny and her husband had sometimes stayed close behind him, other times dropping back to talk with the other couples when the trail was wide enough. For the last hour the three husbands had been engaged in a lively discussion about renewable energy production.

They were an interesting group and he tried to dismiss his other concerns. It was only right for them to receive his full attention.

THAT EVENING TESSA decided one of the nice things about taking a commercially guided trip was having someone else cook.

The couples erected their tents with Clay's assistance and then he began preparing dinner. He chose a spot that was well away from the campsite, which was standard practice in wilderness areas, because the odors from cooking could attract scavenging bears. The air turned crisp as the sun dropped lower in the sky and jackets were pulled out.

Tessa put up her own tent, though she would have preferred sleeping in the open. Her sleeping bag was rated to five degrees Fahrenheit, so warmth wasn't a problem. On the other hand, tents provided some privacy, and dressing and undressing inside a sleeping bag were overrated activities.

Across the clearing, the woman who'd mentioned wolves was surreptitiously rubbing her neck. In a way she reminded Tessa of Renee and she couldn't resist going over.

"Hey, I'm Tessa. You're Ginny, right? Is there a problem?" she asked softly.

Ginny bit her lip and looked ready to cry. "The straps rubbed my neck all day and my shoulders hurt. Please don't tell anyone. My husband and I have talked about doing this for years and I don't want to spoil it for him."

"Try loosening the strap across your chest tomorrow," Tessa suggested. "That should help your neck. And I noticed you moved the contents of your pack around at one of our early stops. Did you leave the heavier items at the bottom?"

Ginny sighed. "Probably not. I was looking for something and in a hurry to put everything back. I never realized there was so much to know about backpacking."

"It'll get easier. I promise."

"I hope so. My husband and I worked hard to retire early. We wanted to be young enough to still do this kind of thing, and now I'm worried about every rustle in the leaves."

Tessa gave her a reassuring smile. "Give yourself a break, this is new to you. It's natural to be leery. But I've been backpacking and camping since I was a small kid and never had any trouble with animals. Well, except for the raccoon who peed on my head. It was up a tree."

Ginny giggled and relaxed. "Oh, dear. I don't think I'll sit under any trees."

"I didn't for a long time afterward. You'll be fine, Ginny. Honestly."

"Thanks. Um, is it okay if I hike with you tomorrow? My husband keeps debating stuff with the other two guys and their wives are getting chummy, talking about kids."

"Sure, I'd like that."

Just then Clay called everyone over to eat and somehow Tessa ended up sitting on a log next to him, so close she could feel the heat from his body.

The food was surprisingly tasty—mild

chicken enchiladas prepared in a skillet, loaded with melted cheese and a salad on the side. Not gourmet cooking, but considerably better than freeze-dried beef stew, which was what she'd expected, despite claims on the Carson Outdoor Adventures website about quality meals. Dried red-pepper flakes had been included in the supplies as a seasoning, so she spiced her meal with a liberal sprinkling.

"I never thought a backpack meal could taste this good," one of the women declared.

Clay grinned comfortably. "I can't claim all the credit. My uncle used to be in charge of food prep on a navy aircraft carrier. Now that he's retired, he runs our in-house kitchen, which supports the guides with their cooking efforts. Uncle Lee is the one who drove us to the trailhead."

"Was that your little boy who came into the barn?" Tessa asked when the conversation lagged, though she'd planned to watch Clay from a distance to get a sense of him. Following this trip, she was going to schedule a rafting tour where he was the guide and then go from there.

Okay, it wasn't the best plan, but it was a work in progress.

"That was my nephew. Derry is a great kid."

Tessa glanced at him. It was a mark in Clay's favor that he didn't seem self-conscious about the handprint his nephew had left on his chest, or the colorful streaks on his sleeve.

"You all live on the Carson Outdoor Adventures Ranch?"

"Officially it's the Carson Double C. But yeah, we all live there, along with a few wranglers and guides in the bunkhouse."

"Must be a big bunkhouse."

"Actually, there are two for crew quarters, along with a couple of homes on the property. I bought the ranch several years ago when I wanted to expand to horseback riding trips. Do you ride?"

"Since before I can remember. I love horses. They're remarkable animals. My grandparents have a boarding stable in the desert outside Tucson."

Clay nodded and got up to refill his coffee cup. "Anyone else?" he asked. "It's still a bit warm. I make decaf in the evening, so it shouldn't keep you awake."

Ginny's husband yawned. "Doesn't matter. Pour away. After today's hike, nothing will keep me awake."

A couple of the others accepted, as well,

and the group chatted for another hour. Tessa thought about offering to help when Clay went to deal with the dishes, but there was something almost intimate about doing cleanup with another person. She and her mom talked about everything under the sun when they were cleaning the kitchen. The same with her dad.

But right now it was all Tessa could do not to ask Clay outright about Renee, and it was the wrong time and place for those questions.

Would it have made a difference if he'd come to the memorial service? Perhaps. They wanted to believe Renee had been in a good relationship before her death, but his absence seemed to contradict that. Or maybe not. The world was changing. Quite a few people were opting out of traditional rites, believing they didn't help. In all honesty, Tessa didn't think the memorial service had given her closure any more than it had for the family. It was just a lot of words that were supposed to be comforting, yet left them wondering how well they'd known Renee, after all.

And wondering if they'd failed her.

The thought occupied Tessa over the next couple of days, though hiking with Ginny was a helpful distraction. Ginny became less concerned about wild animals as the trip progressed and proved to have a fun sense of humor.

For the most part Tessa avoided any additional conversations with Clay and tried not to participate in group discussions where he was actively involved. So it was a surprise when he came over on the third afternoon as she splashed her face with water from a stream.

"I need to ask you something," he said, crouching to dip a hand in the current, too.

Her nerves went on alert. "Oh?"

"Are you from Gunther Computer Systems?"

She blinked. "No. Why would you think that?"

"Sorry, it's just the way you're acting. I've dealt with a wide variety of clients since starting my business, and you don't seem especially interested in the scenery or the wilderness backpacking experience. You also didn't bring a camera and haven't taken any pictures with a phone. Gunther sent someone out last summer who behaved similarly. She was acting as a scout for the company—like a headhunter, except for executive retreat locations."

Tessa tried not to wince.

Normally she would have been thrilled to take a trip like this. She picked a different vacation destination each November and loved the adventure of seeing a new place and trying new things. She'd gone scuba diving in the Bahamas eighteen months ago, but hadn't been anywhere since.

She thought fast, trying to come up with a believable reason for everything. So much for thinking she'd been discreet, or maybe Clay was just too observant.

"The thing is, I thought some of the outdoor adventure companies around here might be hiring seasonal employees," she said. "Taking this trip was an unconventional way of demonstrating I have the right outdoor skills. Sort of a job interview. I want to spend more time in Montana, but to do that, I need to find work. While I have some savings, I don't want to wipe them out entirely."

The skepticism grew on Clay's face. "Other jobs are available in the area, especially during the summer, when we get more tourists. Why go to these lengths?"

"A good number of seasonal positions are for restaurant servers, which doesn't appeal to me. My résumé is limited. I'm a landscape architect as well as a restoration specialist for swimming pools—you know, where the minerals have built up or there's algae or rust stains and that kind of thing. Unfortunately, while you have swimming pools here, it's nothing like Tucson. I doubt there's much need in Elk Point or Kalispell for my particular knowledge."

Tessa hated prevaricating, though most of what she'd said was true. Her father's construction business specialized in building swimming pools, and people also hired them to restore and repair their old pools. Both restoration and doing sustainable poolside landscaping were her specialties. She'd even thought about starting her own business before losing her twin.

It was one of the last things she and Renee had talked about.

CLAY NARROWED HIS EYES, not entirely sure he believed Tessa. On the other hand, there *weren't* many swimming pools in northern Montana compared to places famous for their hot, dry weather. Maybe he'd wanted her to be a representative from Gunther Computer Systems because it meant his reputation was recovering.

Molly let out a small "rff" and he rubbed

her neck. She'd begun sharing her time between the guests, but still had a preference for Tessa.

"I don't have any openings for guides, though I need someone in the office for a few months," he told Tessa. "No promises, but after we get back, give me the information I need for a background check, along with a couple of references, and I'll consider hiring you on a trial basis."

"Thanks."

While Tessa's quick smile reminded him of someone, he couldn't place the memory. But it didn't matter—if she did okay in the office, he'd save time looking for someone.

And these days, time was a valuable commodity.

CHAPTER TWO

TESSA DID HER best to look pleased, rather than shocked. But that's how she felt—completely and utterly flabbergasted.

Saying she was looking for work had just been something to explain why she didn't seem to be acting like the rest of the group. A job offer was the last thing she had expected. And now she'd have to give Clay references. She had people who would vouch for her, that wasn't a problem, but it would be tricky since she didn't want them revealing too much.

Perhaps she could provide her pastor's name and number, and the same for her dad's foreman in the building division. But first she'd have to ask them not to mention Renee. Family shouldn't be discussed in a reference check, but most of the people she knew were chatty. If she didn't warn them ahead of time, they might speculate aloud whether she was looking for a change after her sister's death. Most prospective employers probably wouldn't dig for additional personal details, but she didn't know enough about Clay to be sure of what he'd do.

Being friendly and conversant was his public persona as a guide. The individual underneath was an unknown. So while she hadn't intended to get a job under false pretenses, working for the company might help her understand more about him and how his business operated.

"Right now you're still a paying client," he said, standing up. "And we have a few miles left to hike before reaching our campsite."

"Of course." She stood, as well, pretending not to see the helping hand he'd extended. "This area is amazing. I can see why you love it so much. Did you grow up around Glacier National Park?"

"Nope, in a little Montana ranching town called Shelton. It's southeast of Elk Point, on the other side of the Continental Divide. Shelton is a great place, but the family would come up here on long weekends and for vacations. As time passed, I just couldn't see living anywhere else. Don't get me wrong, I like my hometown, but I'd rather hike mountain trails than look at cows. And there are a whole bunch of cows there."

Tessa suspected there was more to the story, but didn't see how it could affect anything related to Renee.

"And yet you own a ranch," she said lightly.

"Not to raise cattle—it supports my outdoor adventure business. I don't even breed horses, I just make sure the ones we keep for trips are properly looked after. We have quite a few, so it's a big job. By the way, are you going to need a place to live, or do you already have an apartment?"

Tessa thought about the hotel where she'd been staying before the backpack trip. While it was midrange in price for the area, it still wasn't cheap. She didn't want to touch her inheritance from Renee's estate, but she had the money she'd saved to start her pool-restoration business. She'd gladly use every penny to get some answers, but living in a tourist hotel wouldn't fit her claim of needing work in order to remain in northern Montana.

She lifted her backpack and settled the straps on her shoulders. "Yeah, I need a place. Any ideas?"

"As I mentioned, I have two bunkhouses. One is for women and it's empty at the moment. You could camp there for a couple of days while I do the reference checks. Then, provided everything works out, lodging would be part of your pay."

"That sounds fine. But we should get back to the group. I wouldn't want them to think they've been abandoned."

"That sounds like something a guide would say. Still hoping for the job?" he asked, raising his eyebrows.

"Nope, I'm just anxious to reach our campsite and find out what you're whipping up for dinner." She headed up the trail.

"You're hungry? We just had lunch," he called after her.

She waved a hand and continued to where the rest of the group was putting items into their packs, getting ready to leave. Ginny gave her a welcoming smile.

There were a few good-natured complaints as the others lifted their packs, but it hadn't taken long for them to settle into the routine of being on the trail. By this evening, they'd probably start bemoaning that the trip was ending tomorrow.

"Is everything okay?" Ginny asked. "You and Clay seemed to be having an intense discussion. Was he warning you not to drink the water…just in case you didn't hear his two hundred other warnings?"

Clay's regular reminders that water in the backcountry wasn't safe to drink without filtering had become a point of sly humor in the group, though the reminders weren't a bad idea. The larger waterways were unappealing due to silt from rapid snowmelt in the higher mountains, but the sparkling clear water in the smaller streams and creeks looked far too refreshing to someone hot and thirsty from hiking.

"Nothing about water, but I may have gotten myself a job," Tessa said lightly.

"Oooh, you'll be a great guide. We'll stay in Elk Point longer so we can go on your first tour."

The warm friendship in Ginny's face made Tessa's eyes burn briefly. Ever since losing Renee, her emotions had been even closer to the surface. Sad movies prompted tears, poetry had a deeper meaning, music wove itself around her heart with a particular intensity, and the kindness of someone she barely knew could make her cry.

"I wish you could," she said. "But just my bad luck, Clay only has an opening in the company office. Anyway, I'd have to learn more about the area before guiding a group. Tell me, where are you and your husband headed next?" Tessa asked to change the subject.

"We're going to explore more of Montana, then head for Alaska. Have you ever been there?"

"I wish."

Tessa thought Alaska would be a fabulous place to visit, but since she took her vacations in November, she generally chose warm, southern destinations with longer winter daylight hours. And sometimes she just relaxed around her parents' pool to save money. Their backyard was comfortable enough to be a destination spot of its own, with a fountain, spa, sauna and loads of Spanish tile.

Being there also gave her a sense of accomplishment. While getting her degree in landscape architecture, they'd let her dig up the place and put in a whole new design as part of a class project.

"How about you, Clay?" Ginny called to him. "Have you ever been to Alaska?"

"It's hard to get away when you own an outdoor adventure company. Do you plan to climb Denali?"

"You mean the mountain they used to call McKinley?" Ginny scrunched her nose when he nodded. "Fat chance. If you think I was concerned about wolves and mountain lions on *this* trip, how do you think I feel about Kodiak bears? Those things are humongous. On the other hand, since I can still run faster than my husband, I'm not going to worry."

Her spouse groaned and appreciative snickers went around the group. Tessa happened to catch Clay's gaze and caught a hint of amusement in his eyes, so he was probably enjoying the joke.

Tessa would have preferred seeing more wildlife than she had so far. It was difficult to connect with nature around people who were energetically discussing every subject under the sun.

Clay had helped moderate between the husbands, only offering his opinion when pressed, and often directed their discussions to more neutral topics. And Tessa had spent most of her time with Ginny, who enjoyed travel, but also loved to be at home, growing flowers and vegetables in her garden, a pursuit they both enjoyed.

"I'm sure we'll find a balance," Ginny had said that morning. "We had to do that with work, putting in extra hours so we could retire early and still have a life at the same time."

It was a good reminder.

Ever since Renee's death, Tessa had lost her balance. It was why she was in Montana now, and why she might end up working for the man who'd been there when her sister died.

CLAY WAITED UNTIL Monday morning to call the people whom Tessa had provided as her references. He ran an online background check immediately. It came up clean, but he sent a message to his payroll company which offered an impressive array of services—to do a more intensive check. He also looked for her on various social-media sites and found nothing under her name. It seemed odd until he reminded himself that the only social-media networking *he* did was to promote the company.

Tessa's pastor gave her a glowing recommendation, saying he had known her since she was born and regretted that she might relocate to another state. In Clay's experience, pastors tried to be positive about their parishioners, but they weren't bound by the regulations that could restrict what a former employer might say. Reverend Hathaway sounded genuinely dismayed that Tessa could be leaving Arizona.

Clay dialed the second number.

"Alderman Pool Company," answered a crisp voice after several rings.

Alderman, as in Tessa Alderman?

"Er, yes, is Mr. Garcia available?" Clay asked. "I thought I was phoning his cell number."

"Mr. Garcia's calls are forwarded to the company line when he's unable to answer within a few rings. Is there something I can do to help?"

Clay tapped the tip of a pen on his home-office desk. "No, but will you ask him to return my call? The name is Clay Carson, of Carson Outdoor Adventures in Elk Point, Montana."

"Of course, Mr. Carson. I have your number from caller ID. Is that the one you want him to use?"

"Sure, it's my private line."

"Then I'll text him a message. Have a good day."

Clay disconnected and rubbed his jaw. Alderman wasn't the most common name in the United States, so it seemed a good possibility that Tessa had been working for a family business.

He poured himself a cup of coffee and returned to his computer. When he found the website for Alderman Pool Company in Tucson, he saw a picture of Tessa with an older man's arm around her shoulders. The caption read, Keeping it in the family—Chuck Alderman and daughter Tessa. The text below talked about the company's award-winning pool designs and landscape architecture. Landscape architecture appeared to be Tessa's area. Her work had won numerous awards and been featured in various magazines on Southwest living.

Her father's name rang a bell in the back of his mind, but he couldn't quite figure out why. The picture of Tessa and her mother showed where Tessa had gotten her blond hair and complexion. But before he could dig deeper, the phone rang. "Carson Outdoor Adventures," he answered. "Clay Carson speaking."

"Hello. This is Javier Garcia, returning your call."

Clay sat back. "Yes, Mr. Garcia. I'm doing a reference check on Tessa Alderman. What can you tell me about her?"

"Tessa is a wonderful young woman," his caller said warmly. "I've known her for years."

"I see. Were you her supervisor?"

"She doesn't have a supervisor. I'm in the pool construction and repair division of the company, while she developed our restoration and landscaping department. We did some of that work before she started here, but she made it a critical part of the business."

Clay gulped the rest of his coffee. "If she's so valuable, I don't understand why she isn't employed there any longer."

"I never said *that*," Mr. Garcia retorted in an indignant tone. "Tessa is on a leave of absence. She has a position whenever she chooses to return."

"Leave of absence?"

"For personal reasons that have nothing to do with her abilities or reliability." Mr. Garcia sounded reproving, as if Clay didn't have the right to ask anything further. He was probably right. "Personal reasons" covered a gamut of possibilities and Clay had already been assured that Tessa was employable.

"That's all I need. Thank you for your time," Clay said and put down the receiver.

Molly let out a "rrrfff" to catch his attention and he got up to stroke her head. She was eager to be out on the trail again, but he wasn't taking an overnight group out this week, so she'd have to be content with day hikes.

Tessa had guessed right that outdoor adventure companies often picked up seasonal employees, but they weren't fully into the busiest season yet. While he wished he could keep his people on the payroll year-round, it wasn't feasible.

Luckily, all of his guides were returning this summer. He'd expected a few to leave after both the sheriff and the insurance company had grilled them about safety procedures following the accident. It couldn't have been pleasant to be put under a microscope because of a tragedy they hadn't even witnessed. But each had indicated they would return when he needed them. It was good for the business. Repeat clients often requested a specific guide, and though it wasn't guaranteed, he tried to accommodate their requests whenever possible.

"Come, Molly," he told the golden retriever. "Let's go see Tessa."

He was convinced Molly understood more than most dogs, because she raced to the women's bunkhouse and barked at the door. It opened before Clay got there. Molly was too well-mannered to jump on someone, but she danced around Tessa, who bent to pet her.

Tessa had moved into the bunkhouse upon their return from the backpacking trip, keeping to herself except for trips to the barn to visit the horses. He wasn't sure why he'd offered lodging to her, aside from knowing it wouldn't cost him anything and could save time in finding someone to work in the office. His office manager had left unexpectedly when she began having problems with her pregnancy; he hoped she would return at some point, but her plans were still in the air.

"Yes?" Tessa asked, straightening as he approached.

"I've finished checking your references. Will you meet me at the office in a few minutes? The entrance is around by the parking lot."

She nodded and Clay turned, realizing he should have just called her cell phone to set up a meeting time. This situation was more unusual than with his normal hires, but Tessa checked out and he understood her wanting to stay longer in Montana.

He also understood why someone might want to get away from parental expectations.

In the office, Clay looked at the booking requests that had come in overnight. The website has just been redesigned to make it easier for people to read descriptions of the various trips, along with prices. Booking wasn't fully automated, but the system let customers know which dates remained tentatively available, along with other information. Private trips could also be requested. If he'd gotten the contract with Gunther Computer Systems, all of the corporate retreats would have been handled on a separate schedule.

The door opened a few minutes later. "Hi," Tessa said. She gestured to her jeans and T-shirt. "Sorry. If this is supposed to be a formal interview, I don't have any traditional office clothing with me."

He shook his head, gesturing to a chair by the desk. "It would look odd if people came in here and saw someone in business attire, so casual is fine. The job is yours on a trial basis, though I should have asked if you have any office skills."

"I can use a computer and answer phones."

Clay sighed. He needed a whole lot more than that, but maybe she could learn.

TESSA RAISED HER CHIN, refusing to be embarrassed because she didn't have a long list of office skills. She didn't cook much, either, although Renee had liked to tease that her twin sister was a disaster in the kitchen, which wasn't true.

Clay took some papers from a desk drawer. "When I phoned Mr. Garcia, the call was forwarded to the Alderman Pool Company. That's your father's company, right?"

"It belongs to my parents, they're partners." Tessa had known giving Javier as a reference might mean Clay would discover her family owned the business. "The Aldermans have been building pools in Tucson for over thirty years. My mom does the designs, and Dad builds them."

"Well, I understand why you'd need time away from all of that," Clay said, surprising her. "I'm an escapee from my father's career plans for me. He's a workaholic banker and expected me to go into the field as well, with the idea I'd eventually take over as president of the Shelton Bank when he retires."

Tessa barely knew Clay, but she couldn't imagine him in a suit and spending his days behind a desk. Her dad didn't like doing that, either. Chuck Alderman still preferred to be out on a job, running a backhoe or other equipment. It frustrated the site supervisors, even though they knew he trusted their work. He just wanted to be in the middle of the action.

Her mother, on the other hand, was a whiz at designing swimming pools to fit unusual spaces, getting permits and doing other paperwork. They made a terrific team.

"My folks are great," she said. "I just wanted to get away from Tucson for a while."

"As I said, I understand. I suppose most parents hope their children will follow in their footsteps." Clay held out the paperwork. "Go ahead and complete these. I have an external payroll company, which handles withholding and stuff, so most of the information is for them, aside from the list of emergency contacts. I already know where you'll be living."

Emergency contacts?

Tessa was briefly concerned, recalling the emergency contacts she'd provided for the four-day hike. What if he compared them to the information from her sister?

Stop, she ordered.

If Clay started comparing forms for two people with different last names, from two different years, then so be it. Besides, it was one thing not to tell him about her relationship to Renee, another to make a serious attempt at concealing it.

She plucked a pen from a cup on the desk and began entering the information. It felt odd, because she'd never needed to apply for a job before.

She'd just finished when the door opened and she saw a man enter who bore a close resemblance to Clay. He was just as tall and strongly built, but he had lighter brown hair and his eyes were more blue than gray. He also seemed warmer and more boyish.

"Oh, hi," he said. "I didn't realize anyone else was here. I'm Andrew Carson, Clay's brother. Are you the Tessa Alderman I've heard about?"

"That's right."

"Pleased to meet you. I understand my son disrupted the start of your backpacking trip last week."

Tessa recalled the little boy who'd run into the barn covered with finger paint. "I wouldn't call it a disruption. He's adorable."

"And a handful. But, uh…luckily I have help with him." Andrew locked gazes with Clay. "I didn't mean to interrupt. Can we talk later? It's about Derry and his mother."

Clay's face seemed to tighten. "Sure. I

need to show Tessa a few things to get going, then I'll catch up with you." When they were alone again he gave her an apologetic look. "I should have asked if you wanted to start today, or wait until tomorrow."

"Today is fine, unless it would be easier for your payroll people if I wait."

"No, it'll be good to have somebody answering the phone, at the very least. Customers are frustrated when they keep getting a recording."

He spent the next hour giving her a swift overview about ordering supplies and other paperwork requirements, along with showing her the company's social-media pages. They were interrupted several times by phone calls from clients, mostly asking general questions, though one was from a repeat client who wanted to book a three-day horseback riding trip in July.

Tessa's head began to ache.

"You're an experienced backpacker, so it's fine if you talk to callers about what they can expect," Clay said after showing her the computer system. "But don't confirm any reservations. Check several times a day for reservation requests, then send an email that acknowledges it was received. Somebody else will handle the rest until you know the process well enough."

"Um, okay."

Clay glanced at the clock. "I need to leave now, and this afternoon I'm taking a group on an afternoon hike, so I won't be in for the rest of the day. I don't ask employees to follow a rigid schedule when it isn't necessary, but I'd like you to be in the office no later than nine o'clock. If you want to flex your work hours around that to get off earlier in the afternoon, it's fine. Lunch and breaks are when you need to take them. Also, you don't have to do a full eight hours today."

"All right."

When the door closed behind him, Tessa sagged in relief. Clay seemed like a fine person to work for, and while the view out the front window looked mostly onto a parking lot, beyond it was a beautiful vista of trees and rolling grassland dotted with cows and horses. So if she had to be in an office, it was a fairly decent spot.

At the same time, she was already feeling claustrophobic, though maybe her uneasiness was due to Clay. She was used to being around people she'd known and understood for years, but Clay Carson didn't reveal that much of what he was thinking or feeling. His pleasant, tour-guide face had been switched for a no-nonsense, business-owner face, and neither one was especially revealing.

The phone rang and she shook the sensation away. For now, she was an employee of Carson Outdoor Adventures, and she intended to do her best.

ANDREW WORKED ON inventorying supplies as he waited for Clay, his stomach churning.

Was his ex-wife really back in the area?

And if so, why?

Of course, Aunt Emma had only met her a couple of times, so it could be a case of mistaken identity. Mallory had colored her hair an artificially brilliant red and Emma might have simply spotted someone with the same dye job. On top of that, there was no reason to think his ex was still a redhead. She might just as easily be a blonde or brunette, or have purple hair, for all he knew. His grim musings were interrupted when his brother came in.

"What's going on?" Clay asked, looking concerned.

"Aunt Emma thought she saw Mallory in Elk Point this morning. I hope she's wrong, but I wanted to warn you in case Mallory shows up at the ranch."

"Didn't she say she never wanted to see Elk Point or Montana again?"

Andrew shrugged.

The possibility of having his ex-wife back in the area bothered him because he didn't want her anywhere near his son. While Derry was too young to understand that his mother had abandoned him as a small baby, someday he *would* understand.

Andrew hadn't known where she'd gone beyond a plane ticket to Los Angeles, and then out of the blue she had contacted him, saying she wanted a divorce. She had offered him full custody in return for a large check. He'd agreed, even though it had seemed highly unlikely she could get custody under the circumstances. So, what trouble could she make now? On the other hand, she might be hoping for another big payoff.

They'd met when she'd come up to work as a seasonal employee for one of the hotels in town. *I've always lived in cities like Miami and Atlanta and New York. I thought it would be a lark. But it's boring*, she'd declared when they were chatting in line at the market.

Montana…boring?

That should have been the only warning sign Andrew needed that they weren't compatible, even on a casual basis. Instead he'd sympathized that she was so far from family and friends and had asked her out. They'd had fun together, too.

He marked the amount of coffee left on the supply shelf and shifted to evaluate how much tea was in stock. Clay bought top-quality products to serve guests on trips and they kept everything as fresh as possible. That meant keeping a close eye on the amounts on hand with frequent orders.

"I don't see how Mallory could do anything," his brother said, echoing Andrew's own thoughts. "She emptied your bank accounts, took a taxi to the airport and flew away, leaving Derry alone for hours until you got back to your apartment. And we're fairly certain it wasn't the first time she'd left him alone. No judge is going to overlook that. Heaven knows what could have happened to Derry before you got home."

"Don't remind me."

Andrew had gotten cold chills too many times about the possibilities. His six-month-old son had been left for a full day without food or care, possibly more than once, and it horrified him. How could a mother, much less *anyone*, do that to a child?

It wasn't that he'd married for love; he had proposed to Mallory when she got pregnant, which wasn't the best foundation for a marriage. But he had thought they were doing all right. And when he'd held his son for the first time, all of his uncertainties about being ready for fatherhood had vanished. If he accomplished nothing else in the world, being a good dad was enough.

He would do anything for his son.

CLAY WISHED HE could help his brother, but right now they'd have to wait and watch. Anyway, Mallory might be in town for purely innocent reasons. While she'd done her best to profit from the divorce, that didn't necessarily mean she'd come back to make mischief.

Though from what Clay had seen of his former sister-in-law, mischief was a distinct possibility.

CHAPTER THREE

"SHE ORDERED *HOW* MUCH?" Clay clenched the phone in his hand so hard it was a wonder it didn't break. "We don't use four hundred pounds of coffee in a year, much less in a month. You know that, Hans."

"Yes, I know and it's all right," soothed Hans Garrett, the manager from the local coffee company. "The amount was so much higher than your usual telephone orders, I told the sales rep that I'd verify it with you."

"I appreciate it. Just send twenty pounds of the Special Reserve regular coffee beans, and twenty of the decaf in our usual eight-ounce packages."

"Sounds good. I'm going down to Kalispell tomorrow, so I can run the order by the ranch in the morning."

Clay disconnected the call. It was the third purchase Tessa had messed up in less than a week. The other two errors had been fixed just as quickly and were sort of understandable, but this one? It would have cost the company a huge amount. Good coffee wasn't cheap.

He rubbed his throbbing temples, grateful that the Elk Point Coffee Company provided a high level of personalized service. It had been a bad week, not that Tessa was totally responsible for everything that had gone wrong. For example, she'd had nothing to do with one of his guides breaking an ankle while playing basketball with his kid brother.

When Clay's injuries from the rescue effort he attempted during the accident had sidelined him for a few months, he'd been covered by worker's compensation. But that wouldn't help Oliver. The doctor had said he'd be in a cast at least eight to twelve weeks, which meant no backpacking and no horseback riding. After that, Oliver would still have a long period of recovery and physical therapy, so he was going to be out of action for the whole season.

Still, maybe there was a partial solution.

Clay walked over to the Carson Outdoor Adventures office and saw Tessa on the phone. She glanced up when the door opened and nodded to acknowledge him, then re turned her attention to the caller.

"I'm happy to help," she said, typing something into the computer, after which she explained the general climate conditions in northern Montana for July. Then she reminded the caller to keep in mind that the weather was unpredictable and to come prepared. "I hope you have a beautiful wedding. We look forward to seeing you on your honeymoon," she added.

"Honeymoon?" Clay asked after Tessa had hung up the phone.

"She's one of the clients whose trip you confirmed on Tuesday. I gave her weather advice, courtesy of the internet. It wasn't anything she couldn't have looked up herself if she wasn't drowning in wedding details. I remember when my sis—" She stopped and seemed flustered. "Sorry. Never mind."

Clay hesitated. He didn't enjoy telling someone they'd made a mistake, but it was part of owning a business. And he also needed to remember that he had thrown Tessa into the job with almost no training. "I just spoke to the sales manager over at the Elk Point Coffee Company. He says you called in a total order of four hundred pounds of coffee beans. It should have been twenty pounds of regular, and twenty pounds of decaf. That's a difference of over twenty-five hundred dollars."

Dismay darkened Tessa's blue eyes and she glanced at a piece of paper on the desk. When she looked back, the emotion had vanished. "I'm awfully sorry. I must have misunderstood."

"Yeah, well, you're excellent with clients, but paperwork and other details don't seem to be your forte," he said carefully.

Her chin went up. "I never claimed to be trained for this kind of work. Do you want my resignation? You don't have to pay me for the week and I'll move out of the bunkhouse immediately."

"That isn't what I'm saying. The error was caught in time, so no harm done, but making a change is a good idea. One of my guides has been sidelined with an injury. I'm going to see if Oliver is willing to take over here, and then you can become a trainee guide and general helper." Clay held up a hand when he saw relief in Tessa's expression. "Don't get too excited. General helper means you'll do odd jobs, which could include scrubbing down the guest barbecue area or cleaning out horse stalls."

"That isn't a problem. I told you that my

grandparents board horses. I've been helping them with chores practically every weekend since I was a small kid."

"You mentioned being a longtime horseback rider. Do you have experience riding in the mountains? I'm not prying, I just need to know your skill level if you're training as a guide."

Tessa nodded. "I often ride in the desert, but also in the mountains around Tucson. And unlike what some people think, desert terrain can be rugged, which it is around my grandparents' property."

"You seem to have an ideal situation down there," Clay said, realizing there was an underlying question in his statement. She obviously loved her home, so why *would* she need to get away for an extended period? "Aside from dealing with parental expectations," he added.

Tessa tucked a lock of dark blond hair behind her ear, looking uncomfortable. "I'm just taking a break. Look, I shouldn't have let you assume my mom and dad put pressure on me to work with them. They didn't. I have a degree in landscape architecture and my focus was on developing sustainable landscapes. I'm sure eco issues are just as important here in Montana, but the desert is far more fragile than many people think, and I wanted to do my part to protect it. I still do, so that hasn't changed."

Clay measured the emotions in her face. Strangely, he thought this was the first time Tessa had been completely up front with him. Not only that, her concern about the environment resonated with his own views. It was the reason the vehicles used by Carson Outdoor Adventures were hybrids, and why there were solar panels on each of the buildings, including the barns. Solar panels didn't fit the traditional atmosphere of a ranch, but savings on the power bills had already paid for the upgrade.

"How does all of that connect to the pool business?" he asked.

"Because it makes more sense ecologically to restore existing swimming pools and put in landscapes around them that don't suck up huge amounts of water," Tessa said. "It's more economical, too. Mom and Dad let me come in and do what I wanted. They even encourage people with fixable pools to consider restoration, instead of replacement. Not that they've ever tried to convince customers to go the most expensive route."

"They sound supportive," Clay said, feeling almost envious. His father was still struggling to accept that neither of his sons was following in his footsteps.

Tessa's smile was rueful. "They've been great, though I don't think they realized what I do would become such a big part of the business."

"I get it—you're worried about them feeling displaced. That makes sense. Being away for a while might help, but have you considered becoming an independent contractor? That could help resolve the situation."

She glanced away. To hide what was in her eyes? Clay didn't know, except he was becoming a little too intrigued by Tessa. He appreciated strong, self-assured women and he sympathized with her frustration over things going poorly in the office. Plainly, she was the kind of person who succeeded at what she tried to do, and she'd probably *still* succeed if he gave her enough time. He just couldn't afford to do it when there was a workable alternative.

"I've considered starting my own business, but I'm not ready," she explained finally. "You know, I've been reading about the wilderness complex around Glacier National

Park. I see some of the trails allow horses, and other don't. That must make it easier for backpackers."

It was a deliberate change of subject, shutting the door on further personal discussion, however minimally personal that discussion had gotten. Still, the emotion in her voice when talking about the fragility of the desert had been revealing.

She cared deeply about the place where she'd grown up, the same way he cared about Montana.

"Um, right," Clay said. "I'll loan you material on the region, along with maps that show the various trails. Also books about our animals and plants and geology. Try to absorb as much as possible, though no one expects you to become an expert overnight."

"I'LL START STUDYING IMMEDIATELY," Tessa promised.

She was excited, even though she'd never considered being an outdoor adventure guide before. Not that she was going to abandon her career; she loved what she did in Arizona and was actively involved in creating the landscapes she designed. But guiding would be interesting and different, despite her true reasons for coming to the area.

"Great. I'll phone Oliver. Maybe he can start next week."

Tessa wanted to dance a jig in relief as Clay went outside to make his call. After five days in the Carson Adventures office, she was exhausted. Some people had a gift for this type of work—she just wasn't one of them.

Nonetheless, she wasn't entirely at fault for the coffee mix-up. It had been based on a note from Clay's brother, saying how much was needed. Someone with experience might have known those scribbles meant twenty pounds of regular and twenty of decaffeinated, but it had looked like twenty cartons of each. She should have clarified the amount when the coffee sales rep said, *You mean boxes, not cartons*, but she'd thought it was just a difference in terminology.

Besides, Carson Outdoor Adventures seemed to use lots of coffee. And not being a coffee drinker herself, Tessa didn't know how much was a reasonable amount. But she didn't mind taking the blame for it, since she *should* have double-checked before confirming the order.

As for some of her other errors and prob-

lems getting things done? They were embar-
rassing.

She made a copy of Andrew's note about
needed supplies, then dropped it in the coffee file, where it should have gone in the first
place. That was one of the challenges of running an office. You needed to put all the parts
together to make everything work out right.
While Tessa had always respected her mother's
talent for record-keeping, her admiration had
skyrocketed over the past few days.

She slipped the folded photocopy into her
pocket, just in case she needed it in the future.
Luckily the copier hadn't messed up on her
again. Practically every time Clay had come
into the office this week, she'd been clearing
a jam in the mechanism.

"Are you using an unusual setting or something?" he'd asked on the third occasion. "The
machine is old, but we've rarely had an issue
with it."

"I'm just pressing the button," Tessa had
declared, trying not to sound hostile. Anyway, for a supposedly ecofriendly company,
Carson Outdoor Adventures seemed to rely
heavily on paper.

She had to stop letting the stress get to her.
Trying to do a foreign type of work, on top

of worrying how Clay might react if he discovered her connection to Renee, made her feel as if she was performing a high-wire act without a net.

Worst of all, she'd only learned a small amount about her sister's visit to Montana. Ironically, what she *had* discovered was because Clay had asked her to sort the company's digital photos into folders. A make-work project, Tessa had suspected, trying not to roll her eyes. But in the process of sorting the picture files, she'd found a large collection of group photos, some of which included her twin. The guides shot them before each adventure tour and Renee had obviously taken quite a few trips before her accident, even more than she'd told the family.

Tessa's throat tightened at the memory of her sister's face in those photographs. Renee's obvious trepidation begged the same old question—why had she suddenly started doing extreme sports? Was it to make her new boyfriend happy?

The office door opened again and Tessa tried to compose herself.

It was Clay, looking pleased. "Oliver will start in the office on Monday. He's familiar with how we do things, so the new plan should work out okay. I'll have to juggle the schedule, but it shouldn't be too hard. You'll go on trips with me where a support employee is needed—that way I can do training and evaluate your progress. When you don't have a trip, you'll be assigned to other work around the ranch."

Tessa nodded, both pleased and bothered about spending so much concentrated time with Clay. While he could have the answers she needed, he was dynamic and compelling. In any other circumstance, she might find him attractive.

Any other *circumstance?*

Tessa gave a mental shrug. Okay, Clay was attractive no matter what. But he was connected to Renee and her death, whether or not they'd been romantically involved. The reminder would be too hard to handle.

Luckily she was done for the day and Tessa left him at the computer, reviewing reservation requests.

Outside, the air was softly warm and she tried to shake off her mixed emotions. The green, tree-studded hills set against the backdrop of the mountains were inviting, and she went to the bunkhouse to change her clothes and shoes for a walk.

So far, she was still the only resident in the bunkhouse. The building was designed to have small individual bedrooms with private bathrooms, and a common area with couches and a television on one end, along with a communal kitchen and laundry utility room on the other.

Before leaving she made a face call to her mother.

"Hello, dear," Melanie Alderman answered with an eager smile. "It's good to see you."

"It's good to see you, too, Mom." Ordinarily Tessa didn't bother with the phone's video feature, but while in Montana she was using it for every call home. Her folks loved it.

"You look tired. How was your day?" Melanie asked.

Tessa stifled a yawn. "I honestly don't know how you do this stuff, week in and week out. But I've gotten a reprieve. One of Clay Carson's other guides was injured playing basketball and is going to work in the office, while I become a trainee guide and general odd-jobber. I'm sorry he was hurt, but it works out well for me."

Though Melanie smiled again, her expression was strained. She'd dropped weight since they'd lost Renee and spent too many hours at the company, rather than deal with her memories at home. It was the same with Tessa's father.

"Running an office isn't difficult. It's partly a matter of paying attention," Melanie said.

"It's more than that. This stuff is *hard*. Why do you think Dad and I leave most of it in your hands?"

"Patience helps. Isn't that what you tell your landscaping clients?"

Tessa wrinkled her nose and then grinned. "My landscaping clients don't realize how expensive it is to install fully grown desert plants until I show them the prices. They're usually okay with the smaller ones once they see the cost difference. I dread the day someone insists on a full-grown saguaro cactus. If I could even find one that's legal to move. Those things are over a hundred years old and deserve to be left where they started life."

"Mmm, I agree. It must be strange to be in Montana, where everything is so green."

"It's green around Tucson, too," Tessa said stoutly. The shades of greens were subtler at home, but that just made the wildflowers appear brighter. And how could anything be as peaceful as a dawn horseback ride in the desert?

The sound of a child's high-pitched laughter broke into Tessa's attention and she glanced out of the open window. It was Andrew Carson's little boy. She hadn't had much contact with him, though she often saw him playing in the large fenced yard shared by the two main houses. Now *that* was a yard begging for attention. The scraggly grass had been mowed and there were sticks along the fence that might be trees, but that was all she could say for it.

"Who is that?" Melanie asked.

"Derry Carson." Tessa turned the phone around to show her, then turned it back again. "He's playing with his uncle's dog. That is, Clay's dog. Clay isn't married or even engaged, as far as I know."

Her mother swallowed visibly. "Have you spoken to Mr. Carson about your sister? Renee seemed really taken with him."

"No. And nobody has mentioned Clay having a girlfriend, though I'm not sure they would. Gossip doesn't appear to be a big thing here. He seems to be very private—conversant about nature with his clients, but closed emotionally. Anyway, I feel strange about the situation. I didn't intend to get a job and now..."

"I know you're doing this for us as well

as yourself, but you could just come home," Melanie said quietly. "No matter what you find out, it won't bring Renee back. Besides, you already have customers waiting for your landscape designs. They want you and no one else."

Tessa sighed. She appreciated being in demand, but this was something she needed to do, and she thought her parents needed answers almost as much. They were tearing themselves up over whether they could have done anything to change what had happened.

"Ask Freddie to take pictures, videos and 3D scans of the different sites," Tessa said. "He knows what I need in order to work. There's Wi-Fi on the ranch, so I can check emails and access the company website whenever I'm not on a hike or something. I'll talk to the clients by phone and create the designs here."

"Should I send your drafting tools up there?"

"I should be able to get what I need in Elk Point or Kalispell." Tessa did most of her initial work on paper, though she had computer-aided design software on her laptop. "Give my love to Dad," she told her mother. "And don't worry, we're going to figure things out.

As soon as I get a chance, I'll go to the sher-iff's office and ask for a copy of the accident report."

Melanie bit her lip. "I just don't understand how Renee could have been on that raft in the first place. She disliked outdoors activities and was scared of rivers. It's why we started letting her stay with your grandparents when we went camping or hiking as a family. So the accident report won't tell us what Renee was thinking or why she was in Montana."

"Maybe, but it seems as if something is missing."

"We feel the same. It's just…we just don't… How can you stand being around Mr. Car-son?" Melanie asked in a rush.

Tessa gulped and pressed a hand to her stomach. She understood wanting someone to blame, and Clay was the logical person, whether or not he was at fault for Renee's death. Grief was hard and they were all mud-dling through the best way they knew how.

"Mom, being around Clay isn't going to make me think about Renee any less. And from what I've seen, he's competent and safety-conscious. I want to stop being angry about what happened. This might be the best way."

Some of the tightness eased from Melanie's face. "I know. We're angry, too. Reverend Hathaway keeps saying we need to move on."

"That's what I'm trying to do up here. Give my love to Dad, and I'll talk to you both again soon," Tessa said, even though seeing their pain made hers worse because she hadn't been able to do anything that helped.

"Good night, darling. We miss you. I won't tell you to be careful, since I know you're always careful."

Tessa collected her daypack and put a can of bear spray on her belt, but as she headed past the main horse barn, Clay came through the double doors.

Drat.

She still wasn't accustomed to running into him at odd moments, something that happened regularly with her living on the ranch. He seemed to be on good terms with the wranglers and guides who lived in the men's bunkhouse, so it probably wasn't an issue for them. But in her case, a whole lot more was going on than just trying to prove herself as a valuable employee.

"Oh, hi," she said awkwardly. "I was just going for a hike."

"I'm pleased to see you remembered to

bring your bear spray. Where are you headed?" he asked.

"Higher into the hills. I've never lived in a place where I can walk out into nature without driving for miles first. I'm cashing in on the advantage." She shifted her feet uncomfortably. "Um, is there a particular trail you'd recommend?"

"Several. Most of our shorter day hikes originate from the ranch."

"Right, the trips between one and four hours long. I read about them on the website," she explained when he looked surprised. "I thought knowing about the various excursion packages would be a good idea while working in the office."

"Of course. If you'd like, we can hike together. I could show you some of the trails and start explaining how the trips are handled."

"Sure, sounds great," Tessa said, though she would have preferred getting away for quiet reflection and to consider her next steps. Clay, on the other hand, probably wanted to accelerate her training as quickly as possible. She wished she could tell him that she'd just work for her lodging, but it would raise too many questions.

"Then I'll be right back."

Clay returned in a few minutes with a day-pack of his own and they set out.

A measure of Tessa's tension eased with the steady pace. Though Clay topped her by a number of inches, she didn't have trouble keeping up. He also didn't talk every single minute, just pointed out various features in the landscape, along with tidbits of natural history.

The crisp scent of evergreens suffused the air as the altitude rose and Tessa inhaled, letting it fill her senses. After forty-five minutes, they crested a ridge and saw a small lake, set like a jewel among the trees.

"This is Bull Moose Lake. It's where the two-hour hike turns around," Clay explained. "Always keep an eye on the time. If the group has lagged, there's a shorter trail back. I'll show you that next."

"It's beautiful," Tessa said, drinking in the scene. There weren't any hidden lakes in the desert around her grandparents' property, though there were several arroyos with year-round water. Water was precious to a desert dweller. "Are we still on the ranch?"

Clay shook his head. "I wish. This land is managed by the forest service. My ranch is so small it can barely be called a ranch, but it's adjacent to protected wilderness. That makes it ideal for an outdoor adventure company. The former owner had the same idea, but overextended himself building the different facilities. Then his wife passed and he lost interest."

"That's too bad."

"Yeah. Luckily I was in a position to expand my business at the time." Clay took off his pack. "Hungry? I grabbed food from the kitchen. Just leftovers from yesterday's ranch barbecue, if you don't mind. A small way to show my appreciation for letting me combine your hike with training."

"There's nothing wrong with leftovers."

While they ate, a Steller's jay landed on a rock nearby and let out several loud squawks.

"He's either hoping for part of our meal or scolding us for being here in his territory," Tessa said. "My apologies, we don't feed animals or birds," she told the inquisitive jay as it hopped back and forth and cocked its head at them. She could see why some Native American mythology portrayed blue jays as nosy gossips or tricksters.

"Not feeding animals can be one of the hardest things to help guests understand,"

Clay remarked. "They often think it's unkind to withhold food from birds and other animals. Even when the reasons are explained, they don't always believe them."

"I bet they don't feel that way about a five-hundred pound grizzly."

"Not if they have any sense, though you'd be amazed at some of the stories I've heard. By the way, I should have thanked you for helping with Ginny on the backpacking trip. You may have been trying to prove yourself to me, but she needed reassurance and you provided a nice level of support to her."

"I would have done it regardless."

CLAY THOUGHT THAT was probably true. He'd tried talking to Ginny on the first day of the hike because she seemed to be having trouble, but she'd assured him that everything was fine. It would have been wiser to do what Tessa had done—speak with her in private when her husband or no one else could hear. He never stopped learning how to be a better guide.

Working with inexperienced clients was probably the most challenging part of guiding for him. They had to be warned regularly about risks and they sometimes pretended to know more than they actually did. Or in Ginny's case, she'd been trying not to reveal too much fear and discomfort to her husband. Tessa's handling of the situation had earned her high marks.

Perhaps he should have considered hiring her as a guide from the beginning, but until Oliver hurt his leg, there hadn't been any openings. Admittedly, Clay also preferred guides who already knew the trails. It would be a while before he was comfortable sending Tessa out solo, and then only for shorter day hikes since she wasn't a wilderness EMT.

"Is this what you expect to do for the rest of your life?" she asked, breaking into his thoughts. "Run an outdoor adventure company?"

"Why not? I started as a guide for someone else. It was a good outfit, but I wanted more choice over how things were done. Becoming my own boss was the only way to do that."

Tessa's faint smile seemed to communicate volumes, but he wasn't sure what it was saying. Sometimes her emotions seemed crystal clear, other times so much seemed to be churning inside of her that he didn't have a clue what to think. Complicated women baffled him.

"So now you have vans, horses, a ranch

and barns full of equipment," she murmured. "You even have your own commercial kitchen and staff to prep food for overnight trips. From the outside looking in, you seem to be as ambitious as your father. Maybe more."

Clay stared. "That's absurd. I'm not the least bit ambitious. Anyway, like I said, most of the facilities were here when I bought the ranch."

"Aren't you fooling yourself? Not that I'm criticizing, but you appear consumed by your company. Don't you ever think about the other things that life has to offer?"

"If you're talking about marriage, I'd rather be single," he said firmly. "I've never wanted the traditional route. Life as a guide is much easier when you don't have a spouse or children. I like my freedom. Anyway, I have too much going on to want any distractions."

"I see." Tessa wiped her fingers. "Oh, I meant to tell you about a woman who came into the office this afternoon, but then everything else happened. She wasn't interested in the trips you offer, instead she kept asking about the ranch and the people who live here. She got rather pushy, especially when I wouldn't say anything beyond what the company does. I didn't think it was any of her business who lived on the property or what their social lives might be."

Clay's senses went on full alert. "What was her name?"

"She simply introduced herself as Mallory, almost as if she expected me to recognize her. It made me wonder if she could be a reporter from a Montana newspaper or television station. Or a local celebrity of some kind. Anyway, I gave her your card and said to direct any questions to you. She seemed annoyed, but didn't argue."

"Did she have bright red hair? That is, practically fluorescent red?"

Tessa nodded and Clay gritted his teeth. Apparently, his brother's ex-wife *was* back in the area.

"That was the best way to handle her. Notify me immediately if she returns. Or Andrew or my aunt and uncle. If we aren't here, call us, no matter where we might be."

"Since I won't be in the office, I can't imagine I'll encounter her. Unless you've changed your mind about where I'm going to be working."

"No, I haven't. But I doubt Mallory will respect the private areas of the ranch."

Curiosity filled Tessa's face. "Exactly who *is* she?"

"Trouble," Clay said succinctly.

CHAPTER FOUR

"I UNDERSTAND," TESSA SAID, though she didn't understand in the least. But the expression on Clay's face was forbidding and she decided it was better not to ask for clarification.

Instead, she focused on the lake, wishing she could absorb some of its peacefulness. Unfortunately, there was too much suppressed energy radiating from Clay.

"It's getting late. Maybe we should head back," she suggested after a few minutes.

"Right." With jerky movements, he gathered the containers from their meal and began stuffing them into a bear bag, using none of the careful attention she'd seen during the four-day backpacking trip. She frowned, even though the chances were low of them running into a hungry predator on their return hike.

"Maybe we should close everything up more tightly," she suggested. "And the bear bag should be rinsed since there's barbecue sauce from the chicken on the outside. You don't want that on your daypack."

"What?" Clay looked down at the leftovers he was handling so carelessly. He muttered something she couldn't decipher. "I'll take care of it."

He walked away from the lake and trail with the bag and a bottle of water as Tessa closed the other containers and made sure no crumbs of food would be left to attract animals, bears and other predators being the biggest concern.

As a rule they didn't see bears in Tucson, though a few wandered down from the mountains or lived in riparian washes. Mountain lions were a little more common and she often spotted bobcats around her grandparents' ranch. The past few years a mama bobcat had been having her kittens behind the hacienda. Tessa's grandfather had set up a video camera near her favorite den, though the mama moved the family around quite often.

A brief, intense homesickness hit Tessa and she gulped. She didn't miss Tucson; it was her family and the desert that called to her, with its quiet, subtle beauty. Even the blistering hot days were in her blood, when the heat made the air shimmer in waves and blur the outlines of the mountains beyond. Sometimes she had the fanciful thought that time and space might intersect on afternoons like that, explaining the mirages people were reputed to see.

The crunch of boots nearby made her shake herself. She would be home again soon enough. In the meantime, she had the mountains of Montana, which were nice, too.

Clay crouched, packed the food containers into the bear bag and put it in his pack.

"I apologize, I'm usually more careful," he said. "It isn't unknown to see bears, coyotes and other animals close to Elk Point or the ranch. I don't blame them since we're intruding on their homes, but we need to exercise caution."

"You mean this wasn't another test of my skills?" Tessa asked, trying to lighten the moment.

He met her gaze squarely. "I don't try to trick anyone, but if it had been a test, you would have passed with flying colors. I'm also pleased you didn't hesitate to say something. I don't want any of my guides or wranglers to worry about calling me out when I'm wrong. It's important."

His sincerity impressed Tessa. Some people couldn't tolerate being wrong and would go to absurd lengths to avoid accepting responsibility. But Clay seemed confident and secure enough to admit when he'd made a mistake.

He gestured to another trail leading down from the ridge. "That's the short route back. We'd better get moving."

The pace he set on the return hike was even faster than the one they'd taken earlier. He was silent, as well, but Tessa didn't mind. She had even more to think about now than before.

Working with Clay meant she was starting to see him in a much more personal light. He wasn't putting on an act as a rugged, impassive guy. That was simply who he was. If Renee *had* fallen for him, she must have quickly realized he wasn't the kind of man who settled down. And her rival wouldn't have been other women, but the lure of the mountains and forests.

The freedom Clay craved was the freedom to go into the backcountry as he pleased, without having to consider a wife or children. In another day and age he might be a mountain man or an explorer, like Meriwether

Lewis and William Clark. Instead he was a backcountry guide.

Tessa was so lost in thought that she didn't realize Clay had stopped walking until she practically ran into him. So much for being alert and watchful herself. Luckily, he didn't seem to notice, or was being polite. She shook her head at the second possibility; he wasn't the type to be polite when it came to backcountry safety.

"That's one of the advantages of this particular trail," he said, pointing. "We see moose here quite often. Eating plants and shrubs doesn't provide all the sodium they need in their diet, but they can get it from aquatic foliage."

A hundred yards away Tessa saw a large moose standing up to its knees in the water. His rack of antlers had to be nearly six feet across. He was still somewhat thin and angular from the ravages of winter, though dedicated eating would resolve that soon enough.

"We don't have any of *those* in Arizona," she murmured. "He looks positively primeval. As if he was put together from spare parts of other animals."

A low chuckle came from Clay and his taut expression eased. "Spare parts? I'll have to remember that. Is this the first one you've ever seen?"

"Other than in nature programs and documentaries."

THOUGH CLAY WANTED to get home so he could speak to his brother and the rest of the family, he waited awhile to let Tessa watch the moose feeding. After all, he wouldn't have hired her in the first place if she wasn't a nature lover. He didn't believe somebody could be a top guide without loving the places they were sharing.

It was good that Tessa didn't constantly feel the need to say something. She might be better than him at knowing when and when not to talk to a group about the sights they were seeing. On his first trips as a guide, he'd been so enthused about sharing his knowledge that he'd gone overboard telling guests about every tree and plant and rock formation. He still struggled to strike the right balance. It didn't help that each group of people was different.

After a while, Tessa turned. "What a remarkable animal."

"I agree. Just don't let clients get too close—twenty-five yards is the absolute minimum, and more if the animal seems aware of the group. A moose may give the appearance of being clumsy, but it's fast and can be aggressive if it feels cornered. We also don't let clients leave the trail for photographs."

Clay motioned to the path and Tessa fell into step with him. When they got back to the ranch, she murmured "good night" and headed for the bunkhouse. He watched the gentle swing of her hips for a long moment, also appreciating how the long rays of the sun glinted on her hair.

It was a distraction he didn't need.

He shook himself and took out his cell phone to see if his former sister-in-law had called while he was out of range. *Nothing.* He strode to the ranch house where his brother lived and knocked on the door.

"Hi, dear," said Aunt Emma as she opened it. "Come in. Are you hungry?"

"I grabbed some leftovers from the main kitchen, so I hope nobody was counting on them. Look, I need to talk to Andrew, along with you and Uncle Lee."

Her smile faltered. "That sounds serious."

"It's about Mallory."

Now she looked as concerned as he felt. "Derry is already in bed. He wore himself out playing with Molly. Andrew and Lee are out in the shop. Go into the den and I'll get them."

Molly ran over to greet Clay, though she seemed to realize he wasn't in the brightest of moods. She whined softly and leaned against his leg as he ran his fingers through the ruff of fur on her neck. She loved children, so he frequently let her spend the day with his nephew. Now he thought it would be best to leave her at home until they learned what was going on. Molly wouldn't let a stranger near Derry, and that's exactly what Mallory was—a stranger.

"What's up?" Andrew demanded as he arrived, followed by Uncle Lee and Aunt Emma.

"Your ex came into the business office this afternoon and started asking questions about the ranch."

"Did she say what she wanted?"

"No, but Tessa said she was being pushy and told her to contact my number. I haven't gotten any calls or messages, though."

ANDREW'S JAW CLENCHED.

Over the past few days he'd tried to dismiss the possibility that his ex-wife was back in Elk Point. After all, why would Mallory return to a place she'd professed to hate? She didn't have any ties here aside from Derry, and her son obviously meant nothing to her—she'd never even bothered to ask how he was doing.

Uncle Lee clasped him on the shoulder. "Don't let it get to you. You're a fine father and you have all of us to help."

"I appreciate everything you're doing."

"We're the ones who are grateful," Aunt Emma said quietly. "Derry is such a joy. No one could dispute how happy and healthy he is. He's our little ray of sunshine."

Andrew was tempted to say it would be a lot more reassuring if everyone else didn't look as worried as he felt. They all knew how complex custody issues could be and that unfathomable things could happen in family court. But what Mallory had done, leaving Derry alone that way, was on public record.

"I need some air," he told the family. "I'll be back later."

They didn't argue and he went outside. The sun was dropping low on the horizon, tingeing the air with gold. The lights were on in the main horse barn and he headed over there automatically.

"Hey, Andrew," Jillian called to him as he went inside.

He and Jillian Mahoney had been friends since they were kids, when his parents started coming to Elk Point for vacations. She knew too well what it was like to have her life dragged through a meat grinder, though in her case it was from losing her fiancé in a convenience store robbery. Michael had stopped for a cup of coffee and gotten caught in the crossfire.

"Is everything okay?" Andrew asked. "You're here late."

"I don't feel right about how this mare is doing, so I'm spending the night."

Jillian had grown up in a ranching family that bred and raised some of the finest horses in Montana. With the possible exception of her father, she was the top expert in equine care around Elk Point, so it had been a coup when Clay talked her into being his head wrangler.

"Colic?"

"Maybe." Jillian patted the mare and stepped out of the stall. "I caught one of the clients feeding her a pail of grain earlier, which could have put her system out of balance. They meant well, but unfortunately,

Shadow Girl never turns down unauthorized snacks. So, what's bothering you?"

That was Jillian—straight to the point.

"My ex-wife. She showed up earlier at the business office and talked to Clay's new employee, but didn't say what she wanted."

"I realize it's hard, but try not to borrow trouble. She may not be here for negative reasons. Wouldn't it be better for Derry if his mother showed genuine interest in him?"

Andrew shrugged. "Mallory exchanged full custody for a big chunk of money. She didn't even want visitation rights. On top of that, she told me not to bother sending pictures, because she wasn't interested. And don't get me started again on the way she left him alone in the apartment. I still have nightmares."

"I know."

Jillian sank down on a bale of hay, rubbing the back of her neck, and it struck him how tired she must be. During the busy season, she put in long hours between the Carson Double C and her family's spread. Now was especially hard because her father had broken an arm and a leg, along with seven of his ribs, while doing roof repairs on their foaling barn. The doctor had said it would be a long, slow recovery. Until he was better, she was trying to cover his work on the horse ranch as well as her own.

"I should have asked about your dad," Andrew said belatedly. "How is he doing?"

"Fairly well, but he hates being inactive. He shouldn't have been up on that roof at his age. If only I'd insisted we bring in a roofer."

Uh-oh.

Andrew had seen that expression on her face before. Jillian had a fierce sense of responsibility. She'd needed a change after her fiancé's death, so she had taken the position at Carson Outdoor Adventures. Her parents were fine with it, but with her father being temporarily incapacitated, she felt guilty that she wasn't putting in more time at the Mahoney Horse Ranch.

He sat next to her. "I think your dad would balk at you claiming he's too old to repair a roof. And he's still in charge over there, so you couldn't have insisted anything. Besides, you have two brothers. It isn't your fault that you're the only Mahoney who inherited any horse sense."

She let out a weak laugh and shoulder-bumped him. "I guess. How did we end up here, Andy? It isn't what we talked about as kids."

"Hey, nothing is over yet. We're still young. I'm not counting myself out."

"I suppose. Though at the moment I can't even remember what my dreams used to be."

"As I recall, you were going to be a professional kitten cuddler, while I was going to join a traveling carnival so I could ride a roller coaster every day."

JILLIAN SMILED, HER spirits lifting.

It seemed like forever since she and Andy had first met. The Carsons had started renting the Mahoney guesthouse when they were both six. The two families had quickly grown close and she and Andy had become the best of buddies.

"That was a long time ago," she said.

"Almost twenty-four years. And I'm riding a roller coaster every day, just like I planned. Only it's called fatherhood."

Ah. Andy was a great dad. He adored Derry and his son adored him. His ex-wife's attitude had been a huge disappointment, but things didn't always go as planned. Anyway, Mallory had put on a good show in the beginning.

"Well, I'm not a professional kitten cuddler," she said.

"No?"

Jillian glanced down and realized she was absently petting one of the barn cats that had jumped onto her thighs. Mittens was purring and flexing her paws in contentment. "I just cuddle cats as a sideline. There isn't any money in the job."

Andrew gave her a serious look. "Look, if dividing your time between Carson Outdoor Adventures and your dad's ranch isn't what you want, then quit. Here, there, or both. Do what makes you happy."

"Don't let Clay or my father hear you saying that. Besides, it's only full-time at the Carson Double C during the summer. More to the point, it would help if I knew what I wanted. Everything was so clear before Michael died. It was going to be love, marriage and a baby carriage, along with working with Dad and eventually taking over someday. What could be better than raising horses and babies and being in love with the finest doctor in Elk Point?"

Andy squeezed her hand. "At least you had the love part for a while."

"Yeah, but I expected to have sixty or

seventy years with Michael." She blew out a breath and lifted her chin. "Jeez, I sound maudlin. I don't know what's wrong with me. Sorry to be a wet blanket when you're the one with a problem."

Sensing the tension in her body, Mittens jumped to the floor. She was a great cat, mostly black, with white feet, a white throat and a white tip on the end of her tail. Clay had offered to let her take Mittens—Jillian now lived in her parents' guesthouse—but she was at the Carson Double C more than she was at home.

Andy leaned down and scratched around Mittens's ears, then straightened. "Nothing is wrong with you. You're just tired and concerned about your dad. And as you pointed out, I don't even know if Mallory is a problem yet. She might simply want to find out how Derry is doing. Knowing what I know about her now, I doubt it, but there's always a chance she's discovered a shred of maternal instinct."

Jillian nodded and went to check on Shadow Girl. The mare still seemed restless. "I'm going to take her out for a walk. Want to come?"

"Sure."

The sun had dropped below the horizon, but there was plenty of light left. They walked up and down, not getting too far from the barn in case Shadow Girl tried to lie down or roll. Gradually the mare seemed to grow more comfortable and they took her back to her stall. Perhaps the extra ration of linseed oil she'd been given and the walk were helping. Shadow Girl was gentle and excellent with new riders, especially kids, but her intestinal system was extra touchy. Because of it, they only sent her out on day trips.

"Thanks for keeping us company," she told Andy.

"Anytime. Are you still sleeping here tonight?"

"I think it's best. But if you're going to suggest I ask one of the wranglers to do it instead, it's my turn in the rotation. Anyway, I'll probably get more sleep here than at home. I've been staying at the house to help Mom out and it can get a little tense. She'll call if she needs me to run over for a few minutes."

"That's hard on you."

"You're sweet to be concerned, but I'm fine."

He began to leave and mumbled, "Guys

don't want to be called sweet. Haven't you learned anything from me?"

Jillian laughed. He'd once explained that men wanted to be seen as strong, bold and decisive, not nice or sweet. It had become a running joke between them.

She set up the camp cot the wranglers used when spending the night in the barn, thinking how fortunate she was to have Andy Carson as a friend.

He'd helped get her through the worst time of her life. Now she was in a kind of limbo, neither particularly unhappy or happy, and she didn't know how to get out of it.

THE NEXT MORNING Clay was surprised when Tessa showed up in the staging area with her backpack.

"Hi," she said breezily. "I asked the kitchen staff if it was a problem if I went on your trip today for training purposes. Your uncle said it was fine and he could add to the food supplies easily, but to let him know if you're okay with me going."

Clay frowned. "You've already put in a full week of work."

She waved her hand. "I already know being a guide isn't like a regular nine-to-five job.

Besides, I love backpacking and don't mind learning something along the way. I wouldn't expect to be paid for the trip. That's the last thing I had in mind. If I had enough money, I'd just pay to go on one trip after another, all summer long."

She made it sound quite reasonable and her attitude fit with how a number of his other guides felt—some of them claimed they'd take people out for free if they didn't need an income. He saw it that way himself.

"All right," he agreed. "But you'll just be observing, not working. I'll give the kitchen a call."

"No problem," Uncle Lee assured him when they talked. "Tessa is a fine choice. She should be a good addition to your guide roster. Emma is especially pleased. She says you should have more—"

"I know," Clay interrupted hastily. His aunt was always talking to him about hiring more women as guides. He was all for doing it—the women on his roster were outstanding—but he needed the right people to apply when he had openings. "I'll be over to get the food in an hour."

"It'll be ready."

Clay disconnected and looked at Tessa. "You've already seen how we verify that clients have brought everything needed on a hike, so you'll want to memorize the inventory of required equipment or else work off a checklist."

The corners of her mouth twitched. "I remember, tents aren't optional. If you want to check before anyone gets here, I brought mine."

"That won't be necessary. You should be aware we have equipment clients can rent for a reasonable price if needed, including one-, two- and three-person tents."

Her eyes darkened to a deep well of blue. "I'm sure the two-person tents come in handy for couples."

Clay didn't believe for a minute that Tessa was flirting with him, yet the comment raised images he didn't want to consider.

Cozy, intimate images.

He was far more intrigued by her and what she was thinking than he ought to be. Perhaps it was natural. She was beautiful and seemed considerate of other people. On top of that, he hadn't done much socializing for a while.

Quite a while.

He enjoyed spending time with women, but dating had been low on his list of priorities over the last several years. Buying the ranch and adding horseback tours had required a substantial bank loan. He was accustomed to taking risks, but now the ranch had become home to his brother and nephew, along with his aunt and uncle. If his company failed, it would affect more than him and his employees.

He cleared his throat. "The larger tents are good for families, as well as couples, and it means less weight overall to carry. Of course, most of our trips don't allow kids under fifteen, and at that age they usually prefer being in their own tent."

"I see. I hope it was all right to wear shorts. I have jeans and sweats in my pack, but the weather report said it was supposed to be warm during daylight hours."

Clay reluctantly focused on Tessa's legs and the modest khaki shorts she wore that were neatly cuffed above the knee.

"Uh, yeah. Shorts are fine."

He swiftly turned and began laying out his own gear on a table. His standard procedure was to clean his equipment and do needed repairs immediately following a trip, so it was ready to go the next time. The common equipment—stove, fuel, eating utensils and so on—was already spread out on a center table.

Yet the image of Tessa's legs lingered in his mind…silky smooth, tanned and toned from walking and hiking. He couldn't help thinking he was being inappropriate in some way, yet it wasn't as if he'd ogled her.

"The information you completed on the employee form shows you have first-aid training," he said, staying focused on the equipment. "Along with CPR certification. But if you want to remain a guide beyond this summer, you'll need to be certified in wilderness first aid at the minimum."

"Oh, well, right now I'm just on a break from the pool and landscaping business." The discomfort in her tone was unmistakable. "But that doesn't mean I won't give guiding my best."

"I'm not worried about it."

The things they'd discussed the day before kept running through his head, along with the flashes of sadness haunting her eyes and the affectionate way she spoke about her parents. He was curious about what was going on in her life, yet he already knew more than he needed to as an employer, strictly speaking.

And it wasn't as if he didn't already have enough challenges in front of him.

CHAPTER FIVE

TESSA SMILED AND talked with everyone on the backpacking trip, all the while trying to observe Clay.

The depth of his knowledge was astounding. It seemed as if whatever question the clients threw at him, he knew the answer. Yet she couldn't help thinking that he needed to show more emotion about the land and animals he was talking about. She was sure he was passionate about his mountains and forests, yet he sounded like a professor spouting facts from a lectern.

"Are you really a trainee guide, and how do I get a summer job like this when I come back home?" asked one member of the group, a teacher who was there with his parents, a sister, two brothers and their wives. Patrick was leaving almost immediately for Peace Corps training and this would be their last family outing together until he returned from his overseas assignment.

"Yes, I'm really a trainee," she told him. "As for how to become a guide, I can't offer any advice. It happened by accident."

He winked. "I'll take that kind of accident. Especially if I have someone like *you* along when I'm working."

It wasn't the first flirtatious comment Patrick had made. They were around the same age, but she doubted it was a good idea for outdoor guides to get distracted, regardless. Still, she hadn't gone out since Renee's death and it was flattering that Patrick found her attractive.

"What do you think?" he prompted.

"I think you're trying too hard," she said with a smile.

"Everyone, it's time for a break," Clay called. She noticed he was frowning.

The family stopped and shed their backpacks, teasing each other about who was keeping up the best. Tessa drank from her canteen before going over to see what might be bothering him.

"Is something up?" she asked softly.

"No."

Tessa hadn't been able to sleep the previous night, so her instincts weren't at their best. Nonetheless, she wasn't convinced. "We don't know each other well, but I suspect something is on your mind."

His frown deepened. "Fine. I was going to wait before saying anything, but you should know it isn't unusual to have guests hope for a fling on vacation. The situation can get awkward if you don't discourage it from the beginning."

"That isn't a problem, because I'm not interested in a fling and I'm not flirting in return."

Clay regarded her for a long minute. "All right. But you also need to tell me if you're being harassed. I won't put up with that. Patrick Frazier may be a paying client, but he's still expected to behave appropriately."

She blinked. "Even if Patrick was bothering me, I could handle him myself. But he's just letting off steam before heading to his Peace Corps training. I don't know much about the Peace Corps, but he's probably wondering if romantic possibilities will be few and far between until he gets back. He's fine, really. Everything's fine."

"If you're sure?"

"I'm positive."

Clay's concern was charming, if misplaced. And it just made her feel guiltier. He'd taken a risk by hiring her in the first place, and now she was a trainee, which meant she wouldn't be productive for a while. Not only that, she hadn't planned to spend the entire summer in Montana. Through June, perhaps, but not July and August or later. Now she felt she should stay.

Anyhow, remaining in Montana was the only way she'd be able to go on a whitewater-rafting trip and observe Clay as the guide, and she'd discovered that all of the Carson Out-door Adventures rafting trips were booked through June.

"By the way," she said, trying to sound casual, "I don't think I mentioned that I'm an experienced rafter and kayaker. I also have lifeguard certification."

"The guide you've replaced doesn't do raft-ing trips since it requires specialized training, but if there's an extra slot at some point, I'll consider bringing you along as an observer," Clay said.

She nodded and stepped away, not want-ing it to look as if she was monopolizing his time…or to reveal how much she wanted to go on one of those rafting trips. When work-ing in the office, she had planned to watch the upcoming whitewater excursions and book one that Clay was leading. It wouldn't be possible now.

"Are you enjoying yourself?" she asked Patrick's mother.

"We're having a great time. We're proud of what our son wants to do, but it'll be hard not to have him with us for the next couple of years. That's why we planned this weekend. Camping and hiking is a Frazier family tradition and a couple of days are all we could manage between everyone's schedules."

They talked until Clay reminded the group they still had a ways to go before stopping that night. When the hike resumed, he subtly maneuvered things so she found herself hiking with Patrick's sister, Brianna. The high school junior chattered away, requiring only an occasional nod of agreement or brief comment, which gave Tessa time to muse about why Clay had reacted how he had about Patrick Frazier. With someone else, she might have wondered if a hint of jealousy was involved, but Clay hardly seemed the type.

The question that *did* nag her was whether he was concerned about guide-and-client romances because something had gone terribly wrong with Renee.

THAT NIGHT TESSA watched Clay prepare the meal—largely a case of putting prepared ingredients together—and then offered to handle the cleanup after everyone had finished eating.

"No, because you aren't working," he said.

"I'm getting a free guided trip. I should contribute."

"I'd love to help," Brianna volunteered.

Clay gave her a friendly smile, though he also appeared uncomfortable. "That's nice of you, Brianna, but at Carson Outdoor Adventures we pride ourselves on letting guests enjoy their time without having the housekeeping chores around meals. Go visit with your brother, I'm sure he'd appreciate it."

"Oh, right."

"Better let me take care of the dishes," Tessa told him softly. "You already told them I was a trainee guide. How will it look if I don't do anything?"

Clay regarded her for a long second. "Fine, you can help."

Helping wasn't what she'd intended, but she couldn't object too strenuously without it sounding strange. He probably wanted to ensure she knew the proper procedures to keep bears and other animals from getting used to the presence of people. Being cautious wasn't just for the safety of the current group, it helped protect future campers and hikers.

"You didn't have to maneuver Patrick Frazier away from me earlier," she said as they waited for the rinse water to heat.

"Is that what I did?"

"Yes, as you well know." Tessa yawned and stretched. Her restless night was catching up with her physically, in addition to mentally. "Will anyone else be living in the women's bunkhouse this summer?"

"A couple of postgrad students, Grace and Nadia. They have family locally, but wanted to be freer to come and go this year. The bunkhouses have been convenient in getting and keeping employees. Rentals can be in low supply in Elk Point during the summer, so being able to offer lodging works out to everyone's benefit."

"You seem to employ a good number of people."

His face tightened. "Unfortunately, I don't have work for all of them year-round. Mostly I keep staff to take care of the horses during the off-season."

"And your brother."

"Of course. Andrew is an expert cross-country skier, so we both lead trips in the winter. Snowshoe trips are also popular."

Tessa shivered. She'd heard stories about northern Montana winters. The Going-to-the-Sun Road that crossed Glacier National Park wouldn't even open until after the middle of June, or possibly later.

Carson Outdoor Adventures only offered trips outside the national park, but the snow situation probably wasn't that different in the surrounding wilderness areas, at least in the upper elevations. Only the lower trails were being used for backpacking at present, and even so, she'd seen a few patches of white in deep shade.

"I'll be able to hire more guides if Gunther Computer Systems decides to use my company for their executive retreats. Those trips would be outside of the regular posted schedule," Clay added.

"Have you heard from them?"

"Nope. They may have gone elsewhere. Though not locally, or I would have heard about it."

His expression was so stern and forbidding that Tessa didn't want to ask anything else. She could see why a contract for corporate retreats would be profitable, and also that it would help the local economy. Perhaps he had mixed feelings because it would require a change in how he did business.

She gazed at the pine trees on the edge of the cleanup area Clay had chosen. It was a natural clearing due to the rock outcroppings.

"What are those?" she asked, pointing to a bush she'd seen quite often. Small, pink lantern-shaped blossoms grew along stems with glossy serrated leaves.

"It's a huckleberry bush, one of my favorite August treats," Clay said. "The berries are delicious in pancakes."

"When I was driving through Montana I saw all sorts of signs for huckleberry ice cream and other products. I don't think we have them in Arizona. What do the berries look like when they're mature?"

"Similar to small blueberries when ripe, though huckleberry enthusiasts will tell you they have much more flavor. Just a few handfuls are needed for a batch of pancakes. My aunt is partial to putting them in muffins."

"The aunt who looks after your brother's son?"

"That's right."

Tessa waited for him to say more, but she'd already discovered that he could be tight-lipped about anything personal, and this appeared to be one of those times.

Curious, Tessa crossed the clearing to examine one of the bushes. She could see that many of the blossoms were drying and berries were forming. When she returned, the pot on the camp stove had begun steaming.

After they'd dealt with the dishes, Clay scattered the rinse water over a broad area; he was meticulous about the leave-no-trace travel guidelines in the backcountry.

When the Frazier family had finally retired to their tents, Tessa crawled into her own and took off her boots and shorts. She scooted inside her sleeping bag and drew it close around her neck. The temperature had dropped and was expected to get down into the thirties. It might even frost. Quite different from Tucson, where they'd already had a number of days well into the nineties.

She lay awake for a while, exhausted more from stress than lack of sleep and the hike.

Snippets of conversation mixed with laughter came from the other tents, but she didn't mind. The Fraziers were nice people, enjoying their last get-together as a group for the next two years. Anyway, how could she begrudge a family their time together? She knew all too well how that time could be cut short with no warning.

As they gradually settled down, small noises from the woods around the tent became audible. The rustle of the breeze through spruce branches. An owl hooting. And there was the whisper of small feet padding nearby, perhaps a raccoon or other nocturnal creature.

Tessa yawned. Now that she'd made her decision to stay in Montana for a longer period, it should be easier to sleep.

But just before she drifted off, she thought about Clay, lying in his own tent on the opposite side of the campsite. She doubted he was cold—he seemed as strong and self-sufficient as anyone she'd ever met.

While hiking together, Brianna Frazier had sighed over Clay for at least an hour, her eyes wide with appreciation as she watched him from a distance. If they'd been on a longer hike, she'd probably come down with a first-class crush. It was amusing that Clay almost seemed embarrassed by the girl's starry-eyed admiration, even though he was an experienced guide who must encounter this sort of thing on a regular basis.

Tessa had known a few guys who saw

themselves as a real prize and it was nice that Clay didn't seem to be one of them. And in his case, he actually *was* a walking, talking example of a sexy, experienced outdoorsman.

Sexy?

Drat.

Now she was wide awake.

Tessa shivered as she unzipped her sleeping bag and sat up. She was just starting to learn yoga and meditation, so she decided to give it a try. Head space was limited in the small tent, but she tucked her legs into the proper position and began concentrating on her breathing.

In. Out. In. Out.

Meditation wasn't supposed to be a cure-all for life's problems—her instructor was very clear about the goals—but it couldn't hurt.

THE NEXT DAY Clay invited the Fraziers to join the ranch barbecue at the end of the trip as his guests. It was a small gesture considering one of their sons would be spending the next two years of his life helping others.

He'd phoned Uncle Lee ahead of time to advise him that there would be extra unplanned people for the meal. Lee had just laughed and said the kitchen was always prepared for last-minute additions. They were, too. He was an efficient manager after all those years in the navy.

"Come eat with us," Lee urged Tessa when they arrived back at the ranch.

"Oh, I don't—"

"Please, Tessa," Brianna said and the rest of the family chimed in with their agreement. It wasn't unexpected. Groups enjoyed having their guides join them. Even a trainee guide who hadn't been officially working.

"All right, but I need to put my backpack away first." Tessa smiled and walked toward the bunkhouse.

She'd demonstrated impressive people skills with the Fraziers. Though it had been a short trip, she had interacted with each of them in a low-key manner that hadn't intruded on their family time. They'd clearly enjoyed her company and she didn't seem guarded with them, the way she was with him.

The contrast was annoying, and he was annoyed with himself for being annoyed. It wasn't as if he was particularly open himself. Sometimes his family teased him, claiming that they could stand a stuffed bear in the corner and it would be as much company.

In a short period of time, Tessa had gotten under his skin. At the moment, he wasn't even certain why he'd hired her, or kept her employed after she'd proved less than satisfactory in the office. Unsatisfactory in the short term, at least. He was certain she would have figured things out if he had been able to wait long enough.

It would be nice to believe he wasn't susceptible to an attractive pair of blue eyes and a mass of sun-kissed hair, but there were no guarantees.

As for how he'd felt when Patrick Frazier was flirting with her? Clay wouldn't mind developing a case of amnesia over *that* part of the trip. *Jealousy* was too strong a word to describe his reaction, but he hadn't enjoyed seeing it.

Tessa returned and joined the group of guests beneath the covered picnic area. Come June, the number served would double, with even more on weekends. It was almost like having a block party every night on the property.

While it was called a ranch barbecue, Uncle Lee had added dishes that weren't necessarily associated with traditional ranch life. Hamburgers were always on the menu, but some dishes, such as beef and chicken shish kebabs—which included mushrooms, onions, cherry tomatoes and peppers—had been a huge hit, along with his teriyaki chicken and grilled pineapple.

"Over here, Clay," called Brianna Frazier after he'd filled a plate. He looked and saw that the only vacant seat at the table was next to the teenager.

"Why don't you take my place instead?" Tessa suggested, standing up as he approached. "I'm left-handed and I keep joggling elbows with Patrick because he's right-handed. Is it okay if I move over by you, Brianna?"

"Uh, sure."

Clay appreciated Tessa giving him her seat. While Brianna was a nice kid, she'd asked if he was married and whether she could "friend" him online. He'd gently discouraged her—she just hadn't gotten the message. But soon she and her family would head for their hotel and he wouldn't have to keep avoiding her innocent attempts at flirtation with a man twice her age.

He was just starting to enjoy his dinner when a flash of red caught his attention.

It was Mallory, walking toward the picnic area from the parking lot. He got up and muttered an excuse, hurrying over to prevent his former sister-in-law from disrupting everyone's evening. He didn't know if that was her intention, but when she'd been married to Andrew, making a scene had been one of her favorite activities.

"What are you doing here, Mallory?"

"I want to see my little boy."

"We haven't heard a word since you signed the divorce and custody papers, now all of a sudden you're concerned about Derry? You were very clear you didn't want visitation rights and that we weren't to 'bother' you with news about him or even any pictures."

She shrugged, a hard expression on her face.

For what must have been the hundredth time, Clay wondered what his brother had seen in Mallory. Beauty didn't count for much when someone had a cash register instead of a heart. He'd always suspected her pregnancy had been deliberate because she'd believed Andrew owned part of Carson Outdoor Adventures. If so, she hadn't done her homework. Clay had offered his brother a partnership in the business several years ago, but Andrew had declined, saying he'd rather stay a guide without having the hassles of management. Clay hadn't pushed, too aware of how hard their father had pressed them both to go into banking.

"I repeat, what are you doing here, Mallory?"

"That's what I want to know," affirmed a voice from behind him. It was Andrew, with Uncle Lee bringing up the rear.

"My, my, aren't you the family that sticks together," she said snidely. "Fine. I have to wonder if my son is being properly cared for by his father. You go out for days at a time while guiding trips, Andrew. What kind of father can you be?"

Andrew stepped forward angrily and Clay put a restraining hand on his arm.

"Derry has excellent care. Far better than a woman who would abandon him the way you did," Clay said sharply.

Mallory put a dramatic hand to her throat. "I was overcome with the stress of being a new mother. Only the most hard-hearted person wouldn't understand and sympathize with my situation."

"AND YET FOUR months after you abandoned him you asked for fifty thousand dollars in

exchange for a divorce and uncontested custody. *Four months*," Andrew said harshly,
disgusted by the single crocodile tear rolling down her cheek. "Surely that was long
enough to get yourself sorted out."

She'd once told him she had cried her way
out of a dozen traffic citations and two jury
summonses. Her pride at being able to ma-
nipulate people with false tears had bothered
him at the time, but they had just gotten married and he hadn't wanted to think badly of
his pregnant bride.

Mallory dashed away the tear, probably
recognizing it wasn't having the intended ef-
fect. "So what? I needed cash to get started
again. By the way, where is my car?"

Disgust filled him. "*Your* car? You mean
the one I bought for you to use after you to-
taled your own? The car was in my name, so
I sold it to help pay off the credit card you
used for your plane ticket out of here. Along
with everything else you charged in the week
before you left."

"Selling the car wasn't very nice," Mallory
said, ignoring the rest of his comments. "And
you canceled the credit card. I was counting
on that."

He stared. "You emptied the bank accounts

before you left, took over twenty thousand dollars and you still expected to keep using my credit card? One you'd maxed out, by the way."

Mallory shrugged again.

It boggled Andrew's mind that she could be the mother of his sweet, loving child. How could he have failed to see her utter self-absorption from the very beginning?

"Well, Derry is fine," he said. "My aunt and uncle are here, helping take care of him while I'm working. He couldn't be in better hands."

"An aunt and uncle aren't the same as a mother."

"Don't worry about that. Derry is going to have a mother." It was Jillian, and Andrew had trouble hiding his surprise as she slid her arm around his waist. He hadn't realized she'd followed him. They'd been in the barn talking when Tessa Alderman came in to say that Mallory was there.

"Who are *you*?" Mallory demanded.

Jillian lifted an eyebrow. "Jillian Mahoney, soon to be Carson. Andy's fiancée. You must have a short memory—we met a number of times before you abandoned your husband and child. Of course, I should thank you for leaving, because I'm getting a terrific guy. And I absolutely adore Derry."

Mallory's brow creased. "Mahoney..."

"That's right. Don't you recognize the name? My father owns the Mahoney Horse Ranch and my aunt is the mayor of Elk Point. Gosh, Mahoneys have been in the area for ages."

Frustrated anger flew across Mallory's face before she could conceal it. She wasn't stupid. Jillian was telling her that she had roots here—family and loyal friends throughout the community.

"When are you getting married?" she demanded.

Jillian rose on her toes and kissed Andrew's jaw. "We haven't announced our engagement yet, so we haven't talked about possible dates. But not too long. I've always liked the idea of a summer wedding. What do you think, Andy?"

"Uh, autumn might be better," he said, trying to contribute to his part of the charade. "Your father will want to be fully recovered from his fall and it'll be quieter after the major tourist season ends. Much nicer for a wedding."

"You're right, though I hate waiting that long."

Mallory's eyes narrowed. "You don't have a ring."

Jillian gave her a cool, unruffled look. "I work with horses and prefer not to wear it around them. But I keep it with me."

Andrew was even more astounded when Jillian slipped a finger beneath the gold chain around her neck and pulled out the engagement ring that Michael had given her. She'd worn it since his death, hidden beneath her clothing as a reminder of love lost but not forgotten.

The circlet swung back and forth on the long chain, while the long rays of sunlight flashed red on the gold, almost hypnotically.

Without a word, Mallory turned and stomped toward the parking lot. She got into an old car with mismatched paint and gunned the motor.

Andrew hugged Jillian as the vehicle screeched out of the parking lot. "You're a lifesaver. How did you think of that so fast?"

She laughed. "After the last time we talked, I kept thinking how fortuitous it would be if you'd gotten remarried. But, to be honest, it was my ring that gave me the idea. The clasp on the chain came open today. I didn't notice right away and spent a good part of the afternoon going over every inch of ground where I'd worked. It was still on my mind when Mallory got here, and I suddenly realized a fake fiancée might do the job, almost as well as a real wife."

"The look on her face was priceless. She thought my job as a guide and me being single would sound like the perfect argument in a custody suit, though I'm sure her real goal is to get more money."

Jillian nodded. "She'll probably be back, so we need to keep up the pretense for a while. We'll have to explain to our parents, and Emma should know. When it's safe, we can have the most amicable broken engagement in the history of romance."

"I agree." Andrew looked over at his brother and uncle. "In case you didn't follow that, we aren't getting married."

"I figured," Clay said. "How did you know Mallory was here?"

"Tessa Alderman alerted us. You haven't told her anything, have you?"

CLAY SHOOK HIS HEAD. "Of course not."

Whatever questions he had about Tessa, she'd proven her ability to swiftly evaluate a situation and take action. She must have spotted Mallory, as well, and remembered what he'd said about letting the family know if she showed up. He was impressed, especially since Jillian had devised a workable plan to discourage Andrew's ex.

It was too bad the engagement *wasn't* real. Clay would have welcomed Jillian as a sister. Other ranches in the area had wanted to hire her, but she'd come to work for him. He figured it was mostly because of the family friendship. It helped that the Mahoney spread was just down the road, so she could live there and still get over quickly to the Carson Double C if a problem cropped up. Her father was the one who'd told Clay that a neighboring ranch was going to be sold; his bid had been accepted before the property could even hit the market.

"I'd better go back to the guests," Clay told the others. "In the meantime, get together with Aunt Emma and come up with a plan for telling people. We don't want any surprises."

"Any *more* surprises," Andrew affirmed, grinning at his pretend fiancée.

Clay returned to the picnic area and found the Fraziers and Tessa were already eating dessert—homemade ice cream and cake that the kitchen baked in huge pans. Someone had thoughtfully covered his plate with a sheet of aluminum foil.

"You left so abruptly, and then Tessa disappeared for a while, we wondered if there was a problem. Is everything all right?" Mrs. Frazier asked as he sat down.

"Sorry it seemed abrupt. I was just taking care of some business. It's a relief to get out on the trail with understanding people like yourselves."

Mrs. Frazier beamed at the sideways compliment, but when he glanced at Tessa, her eyes were coolly thoughtful.

Though his appetite was gone, Clay dug into his meal again. His clients were here to enjoy themselves, not to be drawn into someone else's problems. It was important to him that he provide an atmosphere for relaxation and fun. The need for rest and stress relief was why the Carson family had started visiting Elk Point in the first place. His father had been diagnosed with an irregular heartbeat and Dr. Wycoff had ordered him to stop drinking coffee, lose ten pounds, get more exercise and relax regularly.

Or else.

Mom and Dad had taken the *or else* to heart.

Dad had followed the doctor's orders faithfully and was in better shape now than twenty-four years ago. He just hadn't realized that the family vacations and getaways would end in his sons finding something to do with their lives besides the world of banking and corporate finance.

CHAPTER SIX

TESSA WOKE AT her usual early hour the next morning and went over to the large horse barn to visit the animals. She'd loved horses since before she could remember; they were such intelligent, sensitive creatures. As a child she'd always confided her secrets to the horses at her grandparents' ranch—secrets she couldn't even tell Renee. There hadn't been many of them, but a few.

"Hey," she murmured to Coal Dust, a mostly black Appaloosa gelding she'd grown particularly fond of. It was interesting that at least half of the riding horses owned by Carson Outdoor Adventures were Appaloosas. She'd heard they were popular with rodeo contestants, but knew little more about the breed.

Coal Dust put his head over the stall door and she stroked his nose. His calm eyes blinked at her.

"I thought I'd find you here," said a man's voice.

Tessa turned her head and saw Clay at the barn door. "Why did you want to find me?"

"You let Andrew and Uncle Lee know that Mallory had shown up last night. I appreciate the quick thinking."

She squirmed, uncomfortable with the praise. She'd guessed that Mallory was Andrew's ex-wife and Derry's mother. The family tension over the woman's appearance suggested a custody fight was brewing. Tessa didn't know the rights and wrongs of the situation, yet she hadn't gotten a good impression of the redhead, and her instincts told her that Derry was already in the best place for him.

"I just did what you asked if she showed up. What do want me to do this morning, wash down the picnic area?"

"Already done. It's scrubbed with soap and water as soon as guests leave to discourage ants and larger pests."

Tessa had noticed the barbecue center was designed with concrete flooring and drains where food traces could be flushed away. There hadn't been any of the usual long-term grease stains or sticky spots on the colorful aluminum tables. She admired Clay's attention to detail, which made it seem even more unlikely he'd acted irresponsibly on her sister's rafting trip.

But it wasn't the question of fault keeping her in Montana.

Tessa still didn't have a clue about why Renee had told the college where she worked that she was going to do one thing, then done something completely different. She'd put her academic career at risk to come to Montana, to do things she'd always avoided in the past.

"Take the morning off," Clay said, breaking into Tessa's grim musings.

"I'm happy to work."

"I know you are, but there's a four-hour hike this afternoon with seventeen guests. I usually don't allow that many in a single group, but they're retirees who caravan by RV each year. They asked to stay together for the hike, rather than split up, so I want someone else along to ensure they all stay on the trail as agreed. We leave at one."

Tessa nodded. "I'll be at the staging area by twelve thirty, unless you need me earlier."

"Twelve thirty is fine."

Having the morning free was an opportunity she hadn't expected. She got her keys and purse and drove to Elk Point. The architecture lacked the Spanish influence popular in Tucson, along with palms, giant saguaros and bougainvillea, but it was a pleasant town, with large old brick homes and a profusion of flowers and other trees. Some were Douglas firs and aspens, others were the deciduous western larch that Clay had pointed out on various hikes.

At the sheriff's office, she squared her shoulders and went inside. A young deputy was at the front counter and she gave him a pleasant nod.

"Hello, I need a copy of an accident report. Th-the victim was Renee Claremont and she died while on a commercial rafting trip on September twenty-fourth last year. The online information I've found is minimal, so a more complete report must be available."

"I see." The officer wrote Renee's name and the date on a sheet of paper. "Are you the family's lawyer, or is there another connection?"

Tessa swallowed. "Renee was my sister. Surely, it's considered a public record."

"I'll have to speak with Sheriff Maitland. Give me your name and contact information. Also, may I see your identification?" he asked politely.

She produced her Arizona driver's license and then took the paper and wrote down her name, cell number and email address.

"If needed, I have our birth certificates," she explained. "Claremont was my sister's married name, but the death certificate shows our parents' names. I can obtain a copy of her divorce decree, too, and other documents."

"I'll let the sheriff know about your request. He'll determine what documentation is needed."

There seemed little else Tessa could do or say at the present time. Elk County was a small place and might operate by its own rules. Regardless, they probably wouldn't release personal data on witnesses or other individuals, so the full report would have to be edited before they could give her access. If necessary, she could speak with an attorney, but she suspected that would just antagonize everyone and make things harder.

She managed a smile. "I'll look forward to hearing from whoever is able to speak with me."

Tessa was turning to leave when the deputy cleared his throat. "If you don't mind my asking, why do you want to see the report?"

She tried to keep her eyes from tearing.

"Renee was my twin sister. My family and I are having a hard time dealing with her death. It might help if we learn more about what happened."

"Twin? Jeez, I'm really sorry. I have four-year-old twin nephews. They're like peas in a pod and totally different at the same time."

"Renee and I were fraternal twins, not identical, but I guess you get the idea."

The deputy's expression had softened. "I do, ma'am. I'll let the sheriff know, but he's away for a few days, so you won't hear anything until next week at the earliest. And this is an extra busy time of the year, too, with so many tourists coming into the area."

"I understand. Thank you for the help." Tessa felt as if she was escaping as she went out the door. Talking about Renee was hard and she didn't like showing emotion to strangers. Tears didn't help anything and she was half-afraid that if she started crying, she'd have trouble stopping.

She sat in her SUV for a few minutes, composing herself.

Finally, she took out her phone and began looking up shops that might carry the drafting tools she needed to work on her landscape designs. Over the past few months, she'd learned focusing on a task could help restore her equilibrium.

None of the stores in Elk Point looked promising, but there were more possibilities in Kalispell. It wasn't a long drive, so she headed for the larger community and quickly found what she needed, or at least workable alternatives.

Her brief stay on the Carson Double C had quickly made her accustomed to peace and quiet, so the more bustling atmosphere of the shopping area was jarring. She shook her head at the thought; it was nothing like Tucson, a far larger community. Adjusting had taken a day or two after her vacations to places like the Caribbean, and it wouldn't take long once she'd returned home from Montana.

WHEN JILLIAN ARRIVED at work that morning, she discovered the news of her supposed engagement to Andrew had already spread. She accepted the congratulations of the other wranglers with mixed emotions.

At the time, a fake engagement had seemed the best way to discourage Andrew's ex-wife. But now Jillian was less certain it had been the best solution, especially since only their close family could be told about the deception.

Trust wasn't an issue, just the realization that the more people who knew a secret, the easier it was for someone to accidentally slip and reveal the truth. Besides, it also meant fewer people would be required to lie for them.

Michael's ring shifted between her breasts and she sighed. He'd been gone for several years and she hadn't forgotten him, but the loss was more of a melancholy memory now, instead of the fierce, stabbing pain it had been for so long. One thing she was certain about, though, was that Michael would have approved of her using his ring to help protect Andrew and Derry.

"Thanks, everyone," she said to her team, who seemed genuinely pleased on her behalf. "But there's a three-night horseback tour group going out this morning, so we'd better get busy. Richard, you're going along as support on this one, right?"

"Yup."

The coveted assignment of going on overnight trips was rotated among the wranglers. Their duties were to look after the horses, including saddling and unsaddling them, ensure the animals were properly secured each evening, set up and break down camp and help guests with any riding issues. But a lot of time on a trip was just spent riding or enjoying the food and company. Now that Lee Sutter was in charge of the kitchen, the meals served on trips were particularly delicious. She didn't take a turn in the rotation herself; spending days away from the Carson Double C and her father's ranch was too much of a challenge.

Once the group left a couple of hours later, she had some breathing space. Since she knew Andy had the day off, she went over to the house he shared with his aunt and uncle.

It was Emma who came to the door. "Hi, Jillian. What's up?"

"I'm second-guessing myself. I keep wondering if I made things worse by announcing a fake engagement. What if Mallory finds out it isn't true?"

"How can she? Come in. I made fresh play dough, so Derry and Andrew are having fun. Reminds me of when I used to babysit Andy before Lee and I were married."

At the door of Derry's playroom, Jillian's doubts vanished as she watched father and son. Andy adored his little boy. They belonged together and she wanted to do whatever she could to help. While he might have nothing to fear from Mallory, it wasn't worth taking any risks.

"Hey, Derry," she said.

"Jilly," the three-year-old exclaimed, jumping up and running over to give her a hug. He was an enthusiastic bundle of energy, always excited and happy.

"What are you doing?" she asked as he dragged her to the small table, where Andrew was sitting on a child-sized chair, his long legs stretched out to one side.

"Makin' stuff."

"I see." Colorful bags of Emma's homemade play dough were on the table and Derry had pressed several lumps together and flattened them.

"Is that going to be a rainbow, Derry?"

"Uh-huh."

He returned to shaping the dough and Jillian kneeled on the floor to watch. Even at his young age, he showed artistic promise. Not so much with play dough, perhaps, but his drawings were unusually advanced for a child barely out of the toddler stage…at least in her opinion. She didn't know how many times she'd wondered how his mother could have turned her back on him. His sunny, easygoing personality had been evident, even as a newborn.

They'd spent a good deal of time together since he was six months old. After Mallory left, Jillian had taken care of Derry while Andrew and Clay renovated the second ranch house on the Carson Double C. Andy had been living at the ranch when he got married—it was Mallory who'd wanted a fancy apartment in the middle of Elk Point. Moving back to the Carson Double C had made sense.

Andrew's mother would have come to care for Derry, but Laura had been recovering from carpal tunnel surgery on her wrist. Then Laura's sister and brother-in-law had offered to retire in Elk Point and lend a hand. They were healthy, in their late forties and well able to look after a child. One thing had led to another until Lee was playing a huge role in making the adventure company an even bigger success.

"What are you thinking about?" Andrew asked.

"About those weeks when you were fixing up the house."

"You were a pal to watch Derry for me. I

wouldn't have been comfortable leaving him with anyone else in Elk Point."

She shook her head. "The hard part was letting Emma take over."

Their gazes met over Derry's head and Jillian saw the tension Andrew couldn't hide. How could she reassure him? They'd both seen things come out badly in their lives, though in his case, he'd gotten a wonderful child to raise. But life *didn't* always turn out badly and they were both due for a long run of good fortune.

He gestured to suggest they leave and she nodded.

"I'm going now, Derry. I'll see you later." She kissed his cheek and received another enthused hug.

Outside in the hallway, Andrew released a sigh. "I know everything should be fine, but worry keeps sneaking up on me."

"Have you talked to Sheriff Maitland to see if there's anything he can do?"

"Now that Mallory has made contact, I've called my attorney to see what he thinks about getting the sheriff involved. He feels we should hold off for a while, so it won't look as if I'm harassing her. I'm going to go with his judgment since I haven't been trusting my own lately."

Jillian put her hands on her hips. "Andy, you can't keep blaming yourself for what happened. We all make mistakes—you have to stop beating yourself up over this one. That said, your lawyer may be right about not giving the appearance of harassing her. He has the letter she left, doesn't he?"

ANDREW NODDED. THE brief note was burned into his brain.

I'm done with being married unless I find a guy with real dough. Keep the kid, I don't care about him. Mallory.

Jillian nudged him. "Okay, we've done everything possible for the moment. Let's drive up to Lake McDonald and have a picnic. It's a romantic setting and we'll take selfies of the two of us, the way engaged couples do. I'll put the ring on and wave my hand around as if I'm showing it off. We should have that kind of picture in case it's needed."

"Are you all right with using Michael's ring that way? I can get a different one."

"And let you go into deeper debt because

of your ex? No way. Anyway, Michael would support what we're doing. Come on, let's go. You should have a change of scenery."

Andrew didn't need more encouragement.

Some of his edginess began to unwind up at the park. They'd stopped for fruit, cheese and French bread at the market, and now sat at the lakeshore, eating and drinking sparkling apple cider.

The snowcapped mountains of the Continental Divide were reflected in the lake, and thick forests rimmed the water's edge. Swimming here was a unique experience because it could be so clear, you felt as if you were weightlessly suspended above the colorful rocks in the lake bottom.

"Too bad we didn't bring our swimsuits," he said, looking at the crystalline water.

Jillian was busy shooting pictures of their picnic with her phone, using the lake as a background. "I'm taking a long lunch to get pretty pictures that look romantic, not play hooky for the day."

"Clay wouldn't care. You already put too many hours into the job. You should let your wranglers assign horses to guests and handle more of the other work."

"That's what Clay keeps saying. But

whether I have the time or not, it doesn't matter. I've tried swimming here this early in the season and nearly froze. Besides, we came to get selfies with us both in the picture. Our phony engagement probably won't last long, but I don't want anyone to guess it isn't real in the meantime."

Andrew leaned forward. "More pictures are fine, but we already have a bunch from over the years, including ones with you and Derry. Besides, everyone has expected us to get married because we're such good friends, so nobody will be surprised."

"I suppose," Jillian said slowly. "I just don't want to take any chances."

He got up and posed with her as she took the sort of photos that someone would expect of two people planning to spend their life together. They tried to get one of them kissing, but started laughing so hard it was impossible to keep the phone steady.

This was like all the other times Jillian had rescued him over the years, including when he'd accepted a dare from one of her brothers to pole vault the creek in his church clothes. She'd told him not to do it, but at eight, having a six-year-old taunt his courage was more than he'd been able to accept. When he'd landed in the water, not really understanding how pole-vaulting actually worked, Jillian had pushed her brother in and followed herself.

With the three of them dripping wet and claiming they'd slipped accidentally, both sets of parents had thrown up their hands and declared they were impossible.

"What are you thinking about?" Jillian asked.

"The vacations and long weekends we spent in Elk Point. They were the best times of my childhood."

"Mine, too. We had other families rent the guesthouse, but none like the Carsons. Of course, now that I've moved in there, we aren't renting it to anyone. Mom was relieved to stop. It was hard work."

"I used to be jealous," Andrew admitted, "thinking you'd make friends with other kids and get into trouble with them. If you were getting in trouble, I wanted it to be with me."

Jillian chuckled. "As if I believe that. You aren't the jealous type."

"I suppose."

Yet now that Andrew thought about it, he remembered feeling a peculiar pang when Jillian had fallen in love with Michael Jamison.

A touch of envy, he supposed, because she'd found something that had eluded him.

And now they were both alone.

THE NEXT TWO weeks passed in a blur for Tessa. She read about the history of the area, studied the flora and fauna, and absorbed every bit of information possible from Clay.

He was the ultimate outdoor guide, able to easily handle any terrain, traverse the slickest stream bed with confidence and answer all questions thrown at him with an astonishing depth of knowledge. He even knew a significant amount about the adjacent states and Canadian province of Alberta.

And when Tessa went to sleep at night, images of wildlife and stunning vistas went through her head, rather than speculation about what had happened to her twin sister. It was a relief, yet lurking at the back of her mind was the question of why she hadn't heard from the sheriff's office about Renee's accident report. It was silly to wonder if they had something to hide—it was probably just buried under a mountain of paperwork—but her waking thoughts kept going there. She didn't think badgering them about it would help. Anyhow, the deputy had pointed out that they were especially busy in the tourist season.

The ranch was generally quiet in the early morning hours, but three weeks after her first official trip as a trainee guide, she came out of the bunkhouse to find a bustle of activity.

"Is something wrong?" she asked Jillian.

"There's a hiker missing," Jillian Mahoney explained. "A vacationing college student who didn't check in with his friends last night as expected. He's diabetic and alone except for his dog."

Tessa gulped, memories flooding through her of the time Renee had been reported missing. It was one of the worst feelings in the world for a family.

"His family must be frantic."

"Yeah. Clay and several of the guides are joining the search. Lee Sutter is driving everyone to the command center and the rest of us will hold down the fort, so to speak, making sure the booked excursions are covered and other business is handled."

"I'll get my backpack and see if they need me," Tessa said immediately.

Since Clay would be involved with a search-and-rescue operation, she probably wouldn't be going on a trip until he returned.

Except for a single two-hour afternoon hike up to Bull Moose Lake, he'd only let her go on excursions that he was leading, saying he didn't want to ask anyone else to take responsibility for a trainee. If he didn't allow her to help with the search, she could pitch in with the horses or handle other tasks and free somebody else to go. One thing she'd discovered on her short stay at the Carson Double C—there was always something that needed doing.

At the parking area, Tessa hurried toward a group of guides talking with Clay. Molly and several other dogs were with them.

"I want to help," she said. "Whatever you need me to do."

Clay gave her a swift, assessing glance. "Search-and-rescue volunteers usually require training from the county, but it should be all right if you team with me and Molly. I'll confirm it with the search coordinator. Everyone, grab one of the emergency supply bear bags for your backpacks. We leave in five minutes."

Tessa was glad that Clay trusted her abilities enough to let her participate. She checked the emergency supplies and found freeze-dried backpacker's food, along with a water filtration straw and other provisions. It duplicated some of the supplies already in her pack, but she put the bag in, anyway. Not knowing if they'd be out overnight, she'd also brought her tent and sleeping bag.

The normally talkative outdoor guides were silent on the drive. Even the dogs were quiet and watchful, sensing something important was happening.

The staging area for the search-and-rescue effort was crowded with both official and private vehicles. As they got out of the van, helicopters flew overhead, presumably to do an aerial sweep of the forest.

Clay suggested everyone stretch their legs while he went over to speak with the coordinator. As they waited, a volunteer came by and distributed fluorescent orange vests with *Elk County Search and Rescue* on the back, and the ECSR insignia on the front.

"The boss has an instinct for lost hikers," one of the guides named Belle Whitaker told Tessa as they donned their vests. "Clay has found more than the rest of us put together. It's uncanny. I don't know about this time, though. The missing kid just has one of those prepaid cell phones and the GPS isn't reliable on some of them. The last ping to a cell tower was in Elk Point."

"Then he didn't check in with a ranger station and let them know his itinerary?"

"Nope. One of the first rules of wilderness travel and he broke it. Probably along with several others." Belle's face was grim.

"That's cynical."

"Sorry, I've been on a few of these searches and it's awful when they turn out badly. I prepare myself for the worst because it's a real gut-cruncher when it happens."

Tessa didn't have any right to criticize Belle, especially since she'd never participated in a search-and-rescue operation, but she preferred being optimistic. It had to help, right? Belief was powerful. Maybe that was Clay's key to success—he didn't give up mentally.

Inevitably, Renee's memory rose in Tessa's mind, but she pushed it away.

A few minutes later Clay returned and told everyone where they were assigned on the search pattern. Apparently, the missing hiker, Aiden Stafford, had only told his friends that he was going to take a trail south of Elk Point. He hadn't returned as planned, or called his family, either. Each team received a detailed topographical map of their assigned area.

"You and I are taking the Ghost Ridge Trail," Clay told Tessa, his face unusually grim and unsmiling. "It's fairly steep in places, but you're sure-footed on rough terrain, so I volunteered us. Do you have any reservations about partnering with me?"

It seemed an odd question since she'd volunteered in the first place, but she shook her head. "I'm fine with that."

"All right. Everyone back in the van."

They climbed into the vehicle and Lee drove them to the various trailheads. She and Clay, along with Molly, were dropped off last.

Tessa got out and put on her backpack. Clay's expression remained taut as he spoke to his uncle at the driver's window.

She gazed at the high trees and undergrowth ahead of them. Even in the open desert, finding someone could be difficult, but the forest and thick understory would make things even harder, especially if the missing hiker had wandered from the trail for any distance.

"This way," Clay said as his uncle drove away.

Tessa read the sign at the trailhead.

Ghost Ridge.

Though she wasn't superstitious, it sounded foreboding. With an effort, she dismissed the thought as they pushed forward on the little-used path.

Getting a case of nerves wouldn't help the missing hiker or anyone else.

CHAPTER SEVEN

CLAY TOOK THE LEAD, trying hard not to explode at Tessa with a thousand questions.

Sheriff Spencer Maitland had frowned when he learned she was one of the volunteers from Carson Outdoor Adventures. "Are you aware that Tessa Alderman is Renee Claremont's twin sister?" he'd asked.

Renee Claremont?

Unexpectedly hearing the name had hit Clay with the force of a lightning strike. "No," he'd said harshly. "Tessa is a trainee guide at my company. Are you sure? She doesn't look like Ms. Claremont."

"Twins don't have to look alike. I spoke to Ms. Alderman in late September last year and thought she was satisfied, but when I got back from my conference recently and sorted through my backlog, I found a note saying she's here in Montana and wants to see the full accident report. That also means the witness statements."

Clay had groaned.

"I'm still deciding the best way to handle the request," Spencer had added. "It won't be easy for the family to hear the full story of what happened, which is why I'd hoped it wouldn't become an issue. It usually isn't, and after so many months, I'd figured the incident was closed."

They'd been interrupted at that point, which was just as well. The urgency of finding a lost hiker took precedence.

As for Tessa being Renee's twin?

There wasn't much resemblance between the two women. Still, Clay recalled thinking Tessa's smile seemed familiar and that could be the explanation. In a short period of time, Renee had taken practically every trip that Carson Outdoor Adventures offered, generally ones when he was the guide. So he'd seen a good deal of her the previous year. And after what had happened, her image was burned into his brain.

But Tessa had dark blond hair with natural sun highlights, deep blue eyes and peach-tinted skin. Her sister had been a brunette, with brown eyes and an olive-toned complexion. She'd bustled and moved quickly, reminding him of a robin in spring, while

Tessa walked with smooth, fluid grace, like warm honey pouring from a jar.

She was also an experienced backpacker, while her twin had known nothing about outdoor sports. Renee had struggled with even the basics of erecting a tent, though she had slowly improved. The two women were so different it was mind-boggling.

The temptation to send Tessa back to the ranch had almost won out, yet he didn't doubt her sincere wish to help a fellow hiker. Nor was he willing to turn away a qualified volunteer who could be part of the rescue effort. So despite his churning questions, he'd assured Spencer that she had the backcountry skills to join the search.

"Aiden!" he called a short distance up the trail, stopping to listen for any type of response. There was no way of knowing if the lost teenager could be miles into the wilderness area, or on the edge. They all feared the scenario where someone was close to the road, but was missed because rescuers assumed they were deeper in the forest.

At least Aiden had a dog with him—even if the kid was unconscious, his animal might respond by barking. The canine senses of smell and hearing were sharper than a human's, too, which was one of the advantages of bringing Molly. Lately he'd been leaving her at the ranch with Aunt Emma and Derry as a precaution, but it had seemed important to have her along as part of the search-and-rescue effort.

Clay called again. Nothing came back in return and even the normal sounds of the forest seemed muted.

"Is the missing hiker familiar with this area?" Tessa asked when they resumed walking.

"Not as far as I know. He's from Seattle and took the spring quarter off from college to travel with a few buddies. The sheriff's office is canvassing the area to see if anyone else remembers talking to him. The hope is that he told a shopkeeper or food server where he might be headed, so the search area can be narrowed. I'll get a message on my satellite phone if they learn anything."

The concern deepened in her face. "I was talking to Belle Whittaker and she said they weren't able to get any worthwhile GPS information from his prepaid cell."

"Nothing accurate enough to help. We have to do this the old-fashioned way."

Tessa nodded. "The modern way being

tracking smartphone GPS signals, or an actual GPS locator?"

"Among other things. GPS helps, but even with the best devices, accuracy can be affected by dense trees and mountains. People also turn them off, forget to charge their batteries before leaving, or don't bring a solar charger or backup battery. Then there's my favorite explanation they drop them in a creek."

"That almost sounds personal."

Clay's jaw tightened. He'd done search and rescue for missing people all over central Montana and down into Wyoming. It was an incredible sensation when you found someone alive and could help them, and soul-crushing when things didn't turn out well.

So, yeah, it *was* personal, and went right to the core of what he was doing with his life. Guiding was a way to share the wilderness and keep folks as safe as possible at the same time. But Renee Claremont had lost her life despite his best efforts to provide a safe whitewater experience.

Even knowing Renee had broken the safety rules he'd drummed into the group was little comfort.

An ache twinged in his left arm as images

of that awful day crowded into his brain. It was just remembered pain. His arm had gotten broken while he was trying to help Renee, and other parts of his body hadn't fared well, either. But there was no permanent damage.

"Clay?" Tessa prompted.

"Every case is personal," he said in a clipped tone. "That's how each member of the Elk County Search and Rescue group feels." It would be a challenge not to second-guess everything he said to Tessa. "GPS is still a great tool, even with its limitations. Sometimes we're able to track someone to their last known location and work from there. Just not this time."

Tessa didn't say anything else and Clay pushed forward.

He could tell someone had taken the Ghost Ridge route over the past week and watched carefully for any signs that they'd deviated from the established trail. The route was indistinct to begin with, and an inexperienced hiker could have lost their direction altogether.

Yet between calling Aiden's name and searching, a corner of his mind remained distracted.

Tessa had been in his thoughts far too much

since the day they'd met. His brain stubbornly kept recalling the weekend trip she had volunteered to go on and her faint silhouette inside the tent, backlit by a full moon, and then later by a small flashlight. It wasn't simply that she was beautiful—a woman's form was hardly a mystery to him—but something about Tessa was compelling.

Now he'd learned she was connected to Renee Claremont.

He was angry and frustrated and regretful at the same time. After all, *Tessa* was the one who'd lost her twin sister. The repercussions to his business and reputation couldn't compare to a death in the family.

Still, why was she here?

Behind him, Tessa cleared her throat. "Do you ever take groups on this route?"

Focus, he reminded himself.

"None to date. I would if someone wanted a private trip and requested Ghost Ridge specifically."

"But you've hiked it yourself?"

"A few times. I've been all over the area. There's over two million acres of protected wilderness in and around Glacier National Park, so it would be hard to know every sin-

gle inch of it. Do *you* know the entire Sonoran Desert?"

"No, of course I don't. It's a big place." She
sounded taken aback and he realized his tone
must have sounded as if she'd accused him
of something, simply by asking if he'd taken
a particular trail in the past.

They would have to discuss her reasons for
being in Montana, but now wasn't the time
or place to clear the air.

"Most of the trips I offer are rated as easy
to moderate in difficulty. This route is more
demanding," he said, trying to restrain his
voice. "But scenic."

"Very."

For a long while they didn't talk, just alter-
nated between calling for Aiden and listening for a response.

"Belle mentioned you have a talent for
finding lost hikers. Do you have a special
feeling about the Ghost Ridge Trail?" Tessa
asked.

"Hard to say," Clay said, though when the
sheriff had mentioned Ghost Ridge was in the
search area, he had gotten a flash of something, similar to what he'd experienced on
other search-and-rescue missions. It wasn't

scientific, but more often than not, his intuition turned out to be on target.

"Molly seems to understand we aren't on a pleasure hike."

He reached down and rubbed the golden retriever's neck. "She's very sensitive to moods."

TESSA THOUGHT MOLLY was fabulous. While alert to the woods around them, she didn't have the tense energy of dogs like wirehaired terriers or border collies. Her parents had adopted both breeds during Tessa's childhood and they were nice, but there was a lot to say for Molly's more peaceful nature.

They were deep in the woods now and Tessa touched the GPS unit attached to her belt. How strange to think that even here she was connected to the greater world through the small device.

Clay required guides to carry a satellite phone when leading a trip, and support staff to carry a high-end GPS tracker that could send and receive short text messages. They were provided by his company and each device was assigned to a specific employee. She kept hers fully charged and had quickly gotten in the habit of putting it on every morning, whether or not she expected to go anywhere.

"Have you been involved with a search-and-rescue mission before?" Clay asked when they stopped to eat a handful of nuts and dried fruit. He took a bowl from Molly's backpack and gave her a drink, along with a high-energy dog treat.

"Informally. I scout the desert around my grandparents' property when someone is missing. It seems logical for me to do it since I know the terrain so well."

"The first twenty-four hours are the most important. But, in this case, we don't know how long Aiden has been in trouble. He's been gone for three nights. That said, it's easier not to dwell on the worst possible outcome."

Tessa's muscles tightened. She recognized what Clay was saying—the chances of a positive outcome weren't necessarily good. "Then the search coordinator assumes Aiden is in trouble."

"He's alone, overdue and the family says his doctor advised him not to hike by himself because of his diabetes. So we have to assume he needs help unless we hear otherwise. With any luck he's just lost track of time because he made a new friend, or for another reason. I'd rather find him that way, than not at all or too late."

She gulped. "We'd better get moving again. I'm fine with a faster pace."

Clay shook his head. "Faster could mean we miss something. Conserve your energy as much as possible. This is a marathon, not a sprint."

"I understand. I've seen boot prints that look recent, probably since the rain we got three days ago. Also crushed grass and other growth on the path. Nothing to show someone left the trail, though, or came back this way."

Clay's hard expression softened. "You have good eyes. But not having return footprints isn't too unusual." He took out the map he'd already consulted several times and showed it to her. "See? This trail intersects with another, about twenty-six miles from the road. Our standard SAR procedure is to start by searching established routes and any nearby shelters. Then we look up and down waterways, and so on."

He tucked the map in his pack and started off without another word, Tessa following with Molly. A couple of hours later they ate again.

Tessa wanted to ask if something was bothering Clay beyond a missing hiker. He rarely looked at her and mostly spoke in clipped sentences, but maybe if she'd known him longer it wouldn't seem odd. They were trying to find someone in potential danger, so all other considerations might disappear while he was in a search mode.

By the middle of the afternoon they'd seen amazing views, tumbling mountain creeks, lush meadows, the most beautiful woodland imaginable and a profusion of birds and animals, but no missing hiker. The trail still showed signs of recent passage, however, and neither one of them suggested turning back. Eventually, they found a recent campsite.

Clay went over it carefully, but he found nothing to suggest the identity of the user.

"I hate finding trash, but seeing a used glucose test strip or lancet would have been promising. Just one person slept here, though," he murmured, brushing off his hands. "Single hikers are more rare than groups."

They continued and shortly before 5:00 p.m., Clay received a call on his satellite phone. His side of the conversation came in short bursts. "Yeah…I see…A single hiker was here since the last rainfall, camped one night and moved on, that's all we've seen…We're too far, miles from the trailhead…No, I don't want to be relieved…Right, I'll let you know if that's necessary."

He disconnected.

"Aiden is still missing and they don't have any other information on which route he might have taken," Clay explained. "We can't reach the trailhead before the light drops too low for safe travel. I'm staying, but a mile back I saw a clearing where a helicopter could pick you up."

"I don't want to be picked up."

"Give it serious consideration. Search and rescue isn't the same as recreational back-packing. It's emotionally exhausting. I've seen new volunteers suddenly lose energy and have trouble even walking."

Tessa lifted her chin. "I'm fine. Besides, I brought my tent and sleeping bag, knowing we might have to spend the night. Let's go—we can still cover more ground today. I'm sure we're on the right track." A sense of urgency was plucking her nerves, as if time could be running out for the missing teenager.

"I suspected you'd say that."

The temperature was falling and rays from the sun were growing long when Molly darted to a spot ahead of them and let out an excited bark. There were signs that someone had scrambled down the hill and they caught a glimpse of something in the underbrush at the bottom.

They quickly descended, but only found a discarded backpack. There was a sleeping bag, clothes, a camp light, and stove and food in a bear canister, but nothing to suggest the owner had any health issues.

"Why would someone leave this here?" Clay muttered. "You aren't supposed to cache supplies in these areas, but if they expected to retrieve the pack, they would have left it hidden closer to the trail. This wasn't even truly hidden."

"Aiden is diabetic and on a strenuous hike. What about hypoglycemia? Couldn't that make someone confused and disoriented? He could have come down here and tossed the pack away if he wasn't thinking straight."

"It's possible. Whoever it was, he or she went that way." Clay pointed in a direction that ran southeast of the Ghost Ridge Trail, or at least southeast of the portion they'd been hiking the last hour. "So we'll follow, since this is our best clue yet. It's late. If we don't find anything, I'll call the command center and suggest additional teams be assigned to this area tomorrow, along with more intense aerial searches."

They divided the contents between their own backpacks and Clay attached the empty pack to his own, knowing it would have to be retrieved later, regardless.

They continued on.

Twenty minutes later, Molly raced forward and disappeared down a slope. Clay didn't call her back, though she normally wasn't allowed to roam.

"Aiden?" Tessa yelled.

"H-here," croaked a tired voice.

He was near the bottom of the slope, one of his feet wedged between two large rocks. Molly had tucked herself next to his body and put her muzzle on his shoulder.

"G-gosh, I thought I was a goner," Aiden gasped when he saw them. "I couldn't get loose. I'm pretty sure my leg is broken, but the rest of me is okay."

Clay took the boy's pulse. "I'm Clay Carson and this is Tessa Alderman. We've been looking for you. I see you've been testing your blood sugar." He gestured to the discarded test strips and lancets nearby.

Aiden managed a smile. "When I'm hiking

I carry my glucose meter, insulin pens and glucose tablets in a hip pack. Also some protein concentrate. I checked an hour ago. My sugar level is okay. Not great, but okay. I've been rationing my glucose tabs and protein."

"Good for you." The warm approval in Clay's voice erased some of the anxiety in the teenager's face. "I'm a wilderness EMT and I'm going to examine you for any other injuries."

When Clay had finished checking Aiden's upper body, Tessa unzipped the sleeping bag they'd found in the abandoned backpack and tucked it around him. His fingers were moving in Molly's fur and he seemed to draw comfort from her presence.

"What happened, Aiden?" she asked.

"I had my dog on a leash, but when Skeeter saw a herd of deer, he broke free and chased after them. I yelled at him and followed, but he was just *gone*. And he hasn't come back. Skeeter is barely a year old, he doesn't know how to survive out here by himself." Misery grew in Aiden's eyes. "I have to find him. We take care of each other."

"One step at a time," Tessa said gently. "Right now we need to look after *you*." She glanced at Clay. "Do you need me to do something?"

"Yeah. Hold his leg to keep it from moving when I shift the rocks. Aiden, this is going to hurt."

"I figured." He sounded resigned.

She got into place and Clay dug around the base of a downslope boulder. His muscles bunched and flexed as he rolled it far enough away to apply the splint.

Molly whimpered and Tessa glanced at Aiden. His eyes were closed and he'd gone pale.

"I think your patient has passed out."

Clay finished applying the splint. "Will you check his pulse for me?"

Tessa scrambled over and put her fingers on Aiden's wrist. "It's fast, but strong. And his breathing is deep and regular."

"Good."

The teen's color began to improve and his eyes opened. He released a sigh when he saw her. "Thank God. I thought I'd dreamed you and was still alone."

"You can't get rid of us that easily," Tessa teased.

"You're going to be fine," Clay said. "I'll notify the command center that you're safe, and someone from there will get in contact with your family. It will be dark soon, so they'll probably wait until morning to send a helicopter—these woods are thick and finding a landing area is tricky. After we set up camp and get some food in you, we'll call your folks and let you talk to them directly."

"They must be totally freaked out."

"That's what parents do. It's part of the job description," Tessa told him.

She got a wry grin.

Clay stepped away with the satellite phone. Since Aiden was safe and in fair condition, Tessa doubted they'd try moving him to another site. And other than not being completely level, their location wasn't bad for camping. She couldn't spot any obvious game trails, no trees were directly above them and a water source wasn't too far away.

A minute later, Clay put the phone away.

"We're staying put for the night. A team will be helicoptered to the nearest possible landing site in the morning. They'll bring a basket stretcher for you, Aiden. I'm afraid you won't be hiking for a couple of months, at the minimum."

"It'll take longer than that for my mom and dad to stop yelling at me," Aiden said glumly.

"I'm the youngest and still get treated like a baby."

They didn't try setting up the tents. Mostly they made the patient as comfortable as possible, easing a Mylar emergency blanket beneath him to reflect his body heat. Then Clay warmed water for packets of freeze-dried chicken and dumplings, while Tessa collected the used lancets and glucose test strips into a container.

"I never thought something could taste so good," Aiden said as he ate the meal, propped up on the backpacks.

"Slow down and keep sipping fluids," Clay advised. "You haven't had much in your stomach for a while. We'll test your glucose again in a couple of hours and see how you're doing."

When the empty food packages and trash had been tucked into a bear bag and the remaining food supplies suspended properly in the air between two trees, Clay dialed Aiden's family on the satellite phone.

Tessa's heart ached as the teenager reassured his parents over and over, saying he was fine except for his leg, and that the break wasn't serious. He claimed it didn't even hurt much now that a splint was on.

"At least Aiden's mother and father have gotten good news," Clay said in low voice.

At least...?

It seemed an odd way of putting it and Tessa raised her eyebrows. He hadn't seemed himself all day and she didn't know what to make of the comment. On the other hand, since participating in a search-and-rescue mission had raised disturbing memories for her, she could be reading more into it than was warranted.

Her sister had been missing for several hours before they learned for certain she was gone. The waiting had been awful, partly because Tessa had known in her heart that Renee wouldn't be found alive, yet had still tried to encourage her mom and dad.

Did twins have a connection stronger than other siblings?

Maybe.

While working at a landscaping site the day of the accident, she'd suddenly felt something was terribly wrong; three hours later they'd been informed that Renee was missing. Before they could get on a flight to Montana, they'd received word that her body had been located. Tessa hadn't realized it was possible to hurt so much. And now, all of the questions and wondering wouldn't let go. It was just as difficult for her mother and father, but in a different way; the agony of losing a child was something she couldn't fully comprehend.

Tessa would have gone to Montana regardless, but her mother had collapsed upon hearing the news. It turned out to be a ministroke, luckily with no lasting damage, but they'd spent the next few days at the hospital, making arrangements by phone. Tessa had even slept in her mom's hospital room each night as reassurance.

Then her father had to identify Renee over a video conference with the coroner. The Tucson hospital had helped by setting up the video link, and everyone involved had been kind and supportive, but nothing could completely ease the burden of identifying your deceased child.

Tessa glanced at Clay. He was keeping an eye on Aiden, who seemed more tired after talking to his parents than before. Until then, determination must have kept him going.

The teenager had managed his blood sugar to the best of his limited resources and had pulled dry leaves over himself at night for insulation, reducing the chance of hypothermia.

He also proved to have a wry sense of humor and had them both laughing several times.

All the while Molly stayed close, an alert nursemaid and source of warm comfort.

Tessa slid into her sleeping bag, watching Clay as he retested Aiden's glucose level, along with taking his pulse and making sure his extremities were warm with adequate circulation.

She hadn't known Clay was an emergency medical technician, but it made sense. He'd urged her to consider taking a wilderness first-aid course if she hoped to continue being a guide, and more advanced certification would obviously be a plus.

The thought of guiding as a career held an appeal, but she also loved creating sustainable landscapes for people, and then going home to tend her own garden each evening. She had fruit trees and grew masses of vegetables, herbs and flowers through most of the year. It was a point of pride to share boxes of produce and fruit with her family and everyone at Alderman Pool Company. Friends teased and said she was a farmer at heart.

But Clay didn't spend many nights at home during his busy seasons. He led more groups than any of his employees, and the rest of the time he ran the company. It was a 24/7 commitment. So in his own way, he was just as much of a workaholic as he'd described his father.

She yawned and recalled Clay's warning to conserve her energy. It was easy to understand. Adrenaline and anticipation took a toll. And what about cases where rescues weren't successful? The weight of failure must land especially hard on a new volunteer, though she was sure it affected everyone in a search, no matter how much experience they possessed.

Was that how Clay had felt when Renee had been found?

Perhaps one day she'd be able to ask.

CLAY GLANCED AT his companions. They both appeared to be asleep, so he turned off the small camp light and settled down, knowing he needed to wake every hour to check on Aiden.

Emergency Services would have tried to find a safe landing spot if the teenager's condition had been critical. But he seemed to have adequate circulation in his feet and toes, despite the diabetes and his leg being broken and trapped. He'd also kept his head together enough to monitor his blood sugar and use his glucose and protein tablets properly. Because of it, nobody needed to risk their lives to pull him out. Landing a helicopter at night in the forest was rarely attempted—it was too difficult to spot snags and other hazards.

Clay put his head back and contemplated the space around the campsite, his respect rising even higher for the teenager. It must have been unnerving to lie here for two nights, unable to move and wondering if this small clearing would be the last thing he'd ever see. Even an outdoor expert would have found it challenging to stay calm.

While Clay didn't expect to have children of his own, a kid like Aiden would make a mother and father proud.

As for Tessa?

Clay frowned. She could make serious trouble for the company, but his brother and nephew were his most pressing concern.

If Tessa filed a lawsuit over her sister's death, Andrew would probably be named in the suit because he'd also been present on the whitewater raft as a representative of the company. And Mallory would undoubtedly use that in a custody battle, or in a bid for another large payoff.

The more Clay thought about it, the angrier he got.

Tessa probably could sue his company, whether or not she believed he'd been negligent, but she didn't have any right to interfere with his family's well-being. It would kill Andrew to lose his son, especially to the selfish mother who'd already put Derry's life in danger.

CHAPTER EIGHT

THE NEXT MORNING Tessa woke at dawn to find Clay in a lousy mood. He was pleasant to Aiden, but kept looking at her with a cold, narrow expression, barely saying anything beyond terse, one-syllable responses.

Well, fine.

A part of her was finding him more appealing than was comfortable, so maybe it was better to see this side of his nature. But why had he turned into a surly bear overnight? She hadn't messed up or held him back during the search.

A helicopter flew overhead once it was light enough to find and evaluate a landing site, but Aiden became agitated when he saw the rescue craft.

Brow furrowed, Clay did a blood-glucose test and examined him carefully to ensure nothing was going wrong.

"Are you okay?" Tessa asked Aiden.

"I can't stop thinking about Skeeter. *Skee-*

ter," Aiden yelled, as he'd done many times that morning and the evening before. They'd joined in, as well, trying to convince him to conserve his strength and let them do the calling.

"I'll search for Skeeter when you're safe," she promised.

"I'm safe now. He's a black Labrador with a red collar, and friendly to everyone. His leash was still on him when he disappeared into the brush." Aiden handed her a crumpled piece of red cloth. "He usually wears this, so it has his scent. I took it off when he got overheated the other day."

Clay gave her a warning glance as she accepted the bandana, then he clasped the teenager's shoulder. "I'm afraid dogs don't do well out here alone, Aiden. You mustn't get your hopes up. Besides, the pilot will want us to fly out with you. We can spread the word that there's a lost dog in this area and ask hikers to keep watch."

Tessa didn't care what the pilot wanted, she was going to look for the missing animal. She tucked the bandana in a pocket, though without having a dog trained to follow a scent, it wouldn't be useful.

The rescue team arrived an hour after the

helicopter had flown over. They wore broad smiles at seeing Aiden and gave him an honorary ball cap with the Elk County Search and Rescue insignia on the crown. One was a physician, Dr. Molvar. Four of the others wore the blue-and-white Star of Life on their jumpsuits to show they were emergency medical personnel, and the sixth member of the team introduced himself as a deputy sheriff.

Clay gave Dr. Molvar a rundown of what he'd done for Aiden, then the doctor performed his own examination.

"You're in good shape, Aiden. Since you don't have a concussion, I'm going to give you a shot for the pain before we put you in the stretcher," Dr. Molvar explained, reaching into his medical pack. "We'll fly directly to the hospital helipad."

"I don't need a shot. My leg hurts, but it isn't too bad."

"Do you have an allergy, or a history of addiction you're worried about?"

Aiden's eyes widened. "No allergies and Mom would kill me if I did drugs, and Dad would only help her."

A chuckle circled around the rescuers at the teenager's hyperbole. Tessa had heard enough about Aiden's parents to know they were concerned and loving. While they hadn't been thrilled about him taking time off from college, they seem to have understood that after all the restrictions of growing up with diabetes, he'd needed to get away and be independent for a while. To feel like everyone else his age.

"I still think you should have something for the pain," the doctor told him. "It has nothing to do with your diabetes, but we have to carry you over uneven terrain and it's going to be tough. We're already impressed with how you managed out here by yourself. You don't need to be an iron man."

"All right," Aiden agreed reluctantly.

The tense lines around his mouth eased as the medication took hold. Tessa suspected he'd been in more discomfort than he'd wanted to admit.

Because the helicopter was in the general direction where Skeeter had disappeared, she hiked with the others as they carried Aiden in the basket stretcher, carefully noting landmarks and features of the terrain. She had a compass and her GPS unit, but it was smart to be cautious.

Clay stayed behind to conceal the signs of

their presence at the impromptu campsite, then quickly caught up.

At the helicopter, the squad loaded the stretcher while Tessa and Clay sorted out Aiden's belongings and returned them to his backpack. Clay handed it to someone inside, then turned and signaled her forward. She shook her head.

He stomped toward her and Molly leaped out to follow. "You need to get on board, Tessa. The chances of Aiden's dog being found at this point are practically zero."

"I don't believe it's impossible, so I'm going to try, while you get back and take care of your business. Besides, you've been in such a lousy mood this morning, I'd rather take my chances with a grizzly bear."

"Oh, for pity's sake." He turned and made an upward spiraling signal with his hand and index finger. The waiting crewman shrugged and lowered Clay's backpack to the ground, then closed the door and the helicopter lifted off.

Great.

He was staying?

When the helicopter was some distance away and the noise had decreased, she crossed her arms. "Why don't you tell me what's bugging you today. Even more than yesterday, and you weren't that much of a picnic then, either."

"LET ME THINK, I guess it has something to do with you being Renee Claremont's twin sister and getting a job at Carson Outdoor Adventures in order to make trouble for my family," Clay exploded, unable to contain himself.

Tessa's eyes darkened and her chin rose. "Why would you assume something like that? What sort of person do you think I am?"

"Why else would you apply for a job with me?"

"Because I want to understand why my sister, who disliked being outdoors, died in a river fourteen hundred miles from her family. I want peace at night and to stop wondering if I failed her in some horrible way. I want my mother to stop crying in her office behind a closed door because she's grieving so hard and doesn't want us to know, and my father to smile and laugh the way he used to. I want the family to celebrate the holidays without feeling there's a huge, aching hole in the middle." Her voice rose with every sentence until she was practically screaming at him.

Clay's chest tightened at the pain in her face. "The solution isn't here, Tessa."

"It isn't at home, either. I thought if I could just be in her shoes for a while, I might figure out something. Or...I don't know. But staying in Tucson wasn't helping. When Renee died, it was as if half of me got ripped away. Wouldn't you want answers if our situations were reversed?"

Tessa swallowed hard, the anguish in her face impossible to doubt. Clay was close to Andrew and his sister—he would feel the same as Tessa.

"How did you find out, anyway?" she asked.

"Because you told the sheriff's office that you wanted to see the full accident report. Sheriff Maitland is the search coordinator. He told me who you really were when I gave him your name yesterday."

Tessa seemed to regain some of her composure, irritation overcoming the grief in her expression. "Who I really am? I'm *really* Tessa Alderman. Renee kept her ex-husband's name when she got divorced. I didn't hide it, I just didn't tell you about my sister. That isn't a crime, it's an omission at worst."

"An omission?" he repeated incredulously.

"Yes. And by the way, I never planned to ask for a job, I simply needed an explanation when you wanted to know if I was from that computer company. It was a spur-of-the-moment thing. Who would have guessed you'd turn around and hire a total stranger?"

"You still accepted the job. Fine, poke through my records. Observe the ranch all you like."

Tessa threw up her hands. "That isn't what I've been doing. I've never looked at anything that wasn't part of my responsibilities. I haven't snooped or pried and I've tried to earn my keep. But I quit. I'll leave as soon as we get back."

"No, I want you to stay."

Even as the words came out of his mouth, Clay wondered if he'd lost all of his reason. Yet, after a night of sleep and some belated reflection, he didn't think Tessa planned to cause damage to his family, a conclusion he would have reached sooner if he hadn't been so worried about Andrew and Derry. The thought of Mallory returning still didn't sit well with him. Either way, ordering Tessa off the property could look as if he had something to conceal, which he didn't.

"I can't remain at the ranch now," Tessa asserted.

"Yes, you can. You're a decent guide, or will be once you learn the trails and more about the area. The clients like and trust you. Your instincts are excellent and you relate to them well. The short hike you handled by yourself the other day was a big success."

She gave him a wry smile. "It must be killing you to say that."

"I'm just being honest. All I ask is that you're honest in return."

She narrowed her eyes. "At the risk of adding fuel to the fire, I *wasn't* dishonest. We can debate the rights and wrongs of harmless lies, but it wasn't even that. Haven't you ever kept something private for a good reason?"

In light of his brother's supposed engagement, the question hit uncomfortably close to home. Clay knew he'd have to evaluate the implications later, including Tessa's "omissions," but she hadn't said *yes* or *no* to remaining and it seemed important to get the matter settled.

"Everyone has things they keep private," he said. "Shall I assume you're going to continue working for Carson Outdoor Adventures?"

"I suppose. I'm homesick for the desert and

my family, but I don't think about Renee quite as much up here. Whether that's good or bad is hard to say."

"Maybe it means you're moving on, or at least moving forward. Being stuck in the past doesn't seem like a healthy way to live. Stay," Clay urged. "We can talk about your sister or whatever you need, and you can try to sort things out. It's the least I can do. As you said, I'd want answers in your place."

The churning emotions in her eyes were hard to read, and he suspected she wouldn't be able to explain them herself. He couldn't imagine how awful it would be to lose a sibling, much less a twin.

"I'll remain in the bunkhouse since it isn't displacing anyone," Tessa said finally. "And I want to help wherever possible. But I can't be an employee. It didn't sit well before, and would be worse now. I'll be a volunteer or intern, like the programs they have in some state and national parks."

"Private companies can't accept free labor."

"Then consider me paid through the value of trips, eating at the ranch barbecues and my lodging. I can be a private contractor, not an employee, with payment-in-kind."

Clay would need to speak with the payroll

company who took care of his paperwork to make sure he didn't break any rules, but Tessa's solution could work. Besides, as a regular employee, she might not be comfortable talking to him openly, and that's what he wanted.

"Right now we should be looking for Skeeter," Tessa added.

He sighed, worried about her despite his reservations. "You should prepare yourself, Tessa. The chances are poor for finding any trace of him."

"They're worse if we don't look at all. Maybe you can't understand, but I *need* to finish the search. Besides, I read about three Australian shepherds that got lost outside Elk Point and were found weeks later, miles and miles from where they started. Tired and hungry, but in okay condition. It could happen with Skeeter. Miracles happen every day if we're willing to see them. And sometimes they just need a little help."

Clay heaved a breath. He suspected Tessa was an optimist to her core, despite her grief and the struggle to understand what had happened to her sister.

He'd heard the story about the dogs being found and had thought it was a one-in-a-billion chance. Of course, the sooner they started searching, the better the odds were of success.

He went over to retrieve his backpack from where the helicopter crew had left it. "All right, let's get going. Give me that scarf that Skeeter was wearing so I can let Molly take a sniff."

Clay hated that Tessa's answering smile made him feel good. She confounded him. Last night he'd been ready to order her off the ranch, alarmed at the potential damage she could do to Andrew and Derry, yet now he was insisting she stay. He didn't think it was entirely due to her appeal as a woman, though that could be part of it.

For him, beauty was more than a pretty face. It was humor and wit, compassion and integrity. Intelligence was far more appealing to him than a woman's external appearance. Tessa was smart and her sense of humor was genuine, if dampened by grief. Her compassion also wasn't in doubt.

But he had to be careful because the situation with Andrew's ex-wife remained problematic and he didn't want to take any chances. As far as they knew, Mallory hadn't returned to the Carson Double C, but she'd gotten a job at a restaurant in Elk Point and was sharing an apartment with three other seasonal servers. The family often heard news about her from friends in town.

Because she was still around, presumably watching the situation, Andrew and Jillian had announced their supposed engagement in the newspaper. The phones had been ringing constantly with people congratulating them.

"Skeeter," Tessa called, breaking into Clay's less-than-comforting thoughts.

They headed toward the last place Aiden had seen his dog, calling and listening the way they'd called and listened for his owner the day before. Every few minutes Clay let Molly smell the oversize red bandana.

"She seems to understand," Tessa said as Molly darted back and forth, sniffing the ground and the air.

"She's trained to follow scents, though tracking isn't a skill she uses that often. But whatever else, we need to get on an established trail as soon as possible. It's one thing to leave the trail this much to save someone's life, another to risk a second accident or emergency."

TESSA UNDERSTOOD. CLAY was a fierce protector of the wilderness, and being off a defined trail for more than basic needs was contrary to his instincts…contrary to her own instincts, for that matter.

But Aiden loved and felt responsible for his canine friend, and losing Skeeter would haunt him for a long time. So to her, being off the trail was absolutely necessary.

It wasn't that she thought Clay didn't care about animals. He even provided a home for horses too old to work. They lazily grazed in the ranch pastures and had a snug stable to keep them comfortable in harsh weather. It spoke well of him. Still, she supposed a strong element of practicality was required for someone who challenged the great outdoors so often. Skeeter could be miles from where he'd first chased those deer, and in any direction. The odds of two people finding him on foot were small.

But she was just a visitor and didn't need to be practical or realistic. She wanted to be hopeful, because despite what had happened to Renee, things didn't always turn out for the worst.

Tessa glanced at Clay's set face, doubting he was completely over his anger with her. She was trying to be a good employee, though she didn't have much practice with the employee part; at Alderman Pool Company she ran the show in her own department. Being your own boss had its advantages. Nonetheless, she'd worked hard, helping out in the barn and doing other tasks without being asked.

He wouldn't even know about her connection to Renee if she hadn't gone to the sheriff's office. It seemed unlikely Sheriff Maitland would have remembered talking to her last fall, but with her request to see the full accident report fresh in his mind and her name included in a search-and-rescue mission? That was a different story. Subconsciously, she may have even wanted the truth to be revealed.

Secrets didn't sit well with her. So come what may, she was glad her full identity was known. She wouldn't have to keep guarding every word and Clay had invited her to talk about Renee. Not that this was a good time. He might deny it, but emotions were too raw for both of them.

"Is there something I should know since you're so worried about someone making trouble for your family?" she asked, deciding it was all right to tackle one part of the issue. "Is it because of that redheaded woman? Everyone was awfully uptight about her showing up. I'm guessing she's Derry's mother." The physical resemblance was easy to spot.

Concern filled Clay's eyes before it was masked. "Yes, but I don't want to get into it. We should focus on finding Skeeter."

"All right," Tessa said.

She understood how painful custody issues could get after watching friends go through a divorce. Anything that upset the balance would be a worry when it came to Andrew's custody of his son.

"Skeeter," Clay called.

They paused and listened, but heard nothing that sounded promising. Even Molly didn't react.

A light breeze was blowing through the trees and the vibrant green of late spring growth was muted by clouds gathering over the sun. As the light dropped, so did the temperature of the air.

"I hope you're prepared to get wet," Clay said as they resumed hiking. "We can get a fair amount of rain this time of year."

"Rain doesn't bother me, except that it might erase Skeeter's scent."

"Yeah." He held out the bandana to Molly again and she sniffed it carefully.

An unwelcome flutter went through Tessa's midriff as she watched. Clay had been turning her inside out from the day they'd met, but while she felt a decided physical attraction, she kept going back and forth on whether she liked him.

Clay Carson had fine qualities. At the same time, he could be difficult, uncommunicative about anything important and seemed driven to make his business a success. While she understood his angry response to her being Renee's sister, another part of her was offended that he'd assumed she meant to hurt his family. They'd been acquainted for a while— surely by now he'd realized she wasn't a vindictive person.

Still, it was nice that he had been concerned enough to urge her not to become emotionally invested over the missing Labrador retriever...not that it would do any good; these days she felt any loss keenly.

She was especially hopeful since Skeeter was young and energetic. A Labrador retriever wouldn't have Molly's thick coat of fur, but while it had been chilly at night, temperatures had only dropped into the upper thirties, so hypothermia was unlikely.

"Is Molly allowed to go on all the trails around here?" Tessa asked curiously.

"Some trails prohibit dogs. On a number of others, they have to be kept on a leash. Any dog in the wilderness needs to be trained to obey voice commands and not to chase wild-life."

"Molly is very obedient and I haven't seen her chase any wild animals, unless we include your nephew. Then it's fairly equal as to who is chasing whom."

Clay chuckled unexpectedly. "Yeah, Derry is a great kid."

"I've never met a child with such an easy-going nature," Tessa said. "It's wonderful to see how much Jillian and Derry already adore each other. He's getting a terrific new mother."

"We're pleased about the engagement."

"It's great that you have family on the ranch. As a kid I used to wish we could live out on my grandparents' property."

"So you could be around the horses more of the time?"

"Partly." Tessa stopped and called for Skee-ter before continuing. "But I also wanted to see Grandma and Grandpa every day. They live in a wonderful old adobe. It's a historic hacienda called the Agua Hermosa, and it's been in our family for generations. Grandma Lucia was born there and that's where Dad grew up with his sisters."

"I suppose it's too far out in the desert for your parents to easily commute into town and run their business."

"The commute isn't too bad, but my folks prefer being around more people. Dad said he always wanted his kids to..." Tessa cleared her throat. She had to stop getting emotional whenever something reminded her of Renee. "He wanted his children to have more childhood friends. Or the opportunity to have them, at least. Ironically, Renee was shy. She preferred curling up with a book, while I was more social. We were an odd pair for twins."

"But close."

"Yes. Except something seemed to change when she came up here. I've thought and thought, and I just can't think of what caused it."

Molly let out a whine, distracting Tessa from saying anything else. The golden retriever began sniffing around, going in a wide circle, then looked at them and let out a bark.

"Skeeter," Clay and Tessa yelled in unison. They didn't hear anything, but Molly's ears pitched forward and her body quivered with excitement.

Please be Skeeter, Tessa prayed.

Clay put Molly's leash on and urged her to follow the scent. They hiked for over a quarter of a mile and Tessa was starting to wonder if it was a futile detour when Molly strained against the leash and began barking.

A faint "rrfff" came in return and Tessa hurried with Clay around a downed tree, where they found a black dog, its flat, red nylon leash tangled in the branches, leaving him only a small amount of movement. His tail whipped back and forth at seeing them.

"Poor baby," she exclaimed, shucking her backpack and dropping to her knees by the trapped dog.

"Be careful," Clay warned, "he could panic and bite."

She was tempted to laugh. The look in Skeeter's eyes was apologetic, while also pleading for help. She rubbed his neck and ears and he pressed as close as possible to her; if he'd been a cat, she had no doubt he would have purred.

"Yeah, he's really panicked," she said in a dry tone.

"It was a possibility. You might want to be more careful."

Clay began untangling the leash from the dead branches. "We'll need it if he's able to walk," he explained when she suggested cutting the strap instead. "We don't want to lose him again. Fortunately he's had something to drink," he said, gesturing to the water seeping over rocks on the hillside where the tree had fallen. The mud below was crisscrossed with Skeeter's paw prints. Tessa was relieved; it would have been a nightmare to be that close and unable to relieve his thirst.

Once the Lab was freed, Tessa found herself flat on the ground with Skeeter's muddy paws on her shoulders, tail whipping back and forth in a wild frenzy as he licked her face.

She laughed and sat up, gently pushing him to one side.

"You have a friend for life," Clay said, crouching next to her. For the first time in two days he was genuinely smiling. Tessa couldn't help herself—she threw her arms around his neck and kissed him, feeling as exuberant as the Labrador retriever from gaining his freedom.

After a shocked moment, Clay deepened

the kiss and pulled her tight against his body. She was lost in sensation until a cold, canine nose pressed into her neck and she jerked away, breathing quickly.

"What was that about?" Clay muttered.

"I'm sorry," she gasped. "It's just… It's just that I haven't been this happy for a while. Finding Aiden, and now Skeeter… I got carried away."

"So you would have kissed Bigfoot if he'd been with you?"

Tessa lifted her shoulders and let them drop. "I wouldn't say *that*. I'm not a huge fan of facial hair. It tickles."

Her reply seemed to lighten the moment because Clay laughed. "I'm glad to hear you draw the line somewhere."

A whine for attention came from Skeeter and she rubbed his neck. "It's okay, baby. You're going to be fine. Let's get you something to eat, that'll help you feel better."

Clay nodded and took Molly's bowl from her doggy backpack. He soaked a handful of dog food with water before letting the black Lab eat the small amount. Skeeter whimpered and his eyes politely begged for more, but it was best to reintroduce food to his stomach slowly. Molly also got a treat, but she carried half of it over to Skeeter, who gobbled the piece down before they could stop him.

"Does he have any injuries?" Tessa asked after Clay had given the dog a quick exam. Though he was an EMT for humans, most of the principles probably applied to animal care, as well.

Her heart, as well as her mind, was still racing. She hadn't planned to kiss Clay and didn't have a clue of whether he'd objected or not…though his initial reaction suggested it hadn't been unwelcome. Then the usual shutters had come down in his face. Was it because he was remembering Renee?

Her stomach turned over; Renee's emails had talked about Clay as if they were planning a life together. It didn't fit with what Clay had said about his own vision for the future, but that didn't mean they hadn't been important to each other.

"No injuries that I can find," Clay said. "He probably got trapped soon after he took off, chasing the deer. We aren't far from where we found Aiden, just not close enough for Molly to have heard him barking, or she would have alerted us."

He took out his satellite phone and pressed a few buttons. "Hi, Spencer, it's Clay…Yeah,

I know we should have gone with the helicopter. But we have reassuring news for Aiden Stafford. Tell him that his dog has been found and seems to be all right…Oh, pleased to hear that. We'll try hiking out today, but with the weather turning, we may not make it before sunset…Don't worry, I'll call the ranch when we need a pickup at a trailhead, so you won't need to send anyone…No, possibly not Ghost Ridge. I have to consult the map first."

"How is Aiden doing?" Tessa asked when Clay disconnected.

"He's in good shape. His parents arrived from Seattle last night and were waiting for him at the hospital. An orthopedic specialist set his leg, surgery wasn't needed and he'll stay a day or two for observation. No complications are expected. Hearing about Skeeter should do wonders for his spirits."

"I'm glad he's doing well."

CLAY DIDN'T SEE a hint of "I told you so" in Tessa's face, something she might have felt justified in saying.

Finding the dog was unexpected, but plainly it hadn't been as improbable as he'd assumed. Or perhaps Tessa had an instinct for lost animals, the way he seemed to have one for lost hikers. Life had its mysteries and he was willing to give credit where credit was due; she'd refused to give up on Skeeter, and now they'd found him.

While her hair had been bound back in a French braid, it was loosening, gleaming with soft glints of gold in the low forest light. He desperately wanted to kiss her again, but it would be a mistake of colossal proportions.

Clay tore his attention from her and took out the topographical map to consult, along with his compass.

"We might have to spend another night out here," he said, trying to sound unaffected. "Skeeter may not be able to travel quickly and I want to give him time to get calories into his system before we start."

"That's okay. Will we return to the Ghost Ridge Trail?"

"I don't think so." Clay showed her the map and pointed to a spot. "We're located right about here, which is roughly an equal distance between two trails. If we head south and west, we'll meet up with this one, which is a shorter hike out to a trailhead than if we go by Ghost Ridge."

Her finger traced the line on the map. "The terrain looks less demanding, too, which would be better for Skeeter." Tessa bent and gave the black Lab a hug.

"I think you're already in love with that dog," Clay said in a dry voice. "Don't forget he belongs to Aiden."

"I know he isn't mine, I'm just reassuring Skeeter that he's all right. He seems less distressed. Do you think he could have more food?"

"It should be okay. He's obviously healthy and wasn't out here long enough to go into starvation mode."

Clay gave the dog another small meal, wishing he could explain to him that they weren't being stingy, just making sure he wouldn't get sick from having too much in his stomach at once. There was plenty of food for both Molly and Skeeter, even if they spent another night. In fact, Skeeter was doing so well, the two dogs were starting to romp around together.

Tessa laughed as she watched and desire hit Clay again. She was beautiful and filled with spirit. Despite everything he was intrigued by her, but the circumstances were even more complicated than when he'd thought she was a seasonal employee who didn't plan on staying permanently in Montana.

"We should get going," he said. "By crossing to the other trail, we might be able to reach the trailhead by late afternoon."

"Okay."

They put on their packs and set out with Molly and Skeeter, both on leashes. Skeeter looked perkier by the minute and gobbled down the high-calorie treats he received periodically. Molly accepted the treats, as well, but did the same as before, giving half to the other dog, who licked her face in appreciation.

When they were an hour away from the trailhead, Clay contacted the ranch and asked if someone was available to pick them up.

"They'll be waiting for us," Clay said when he disconnected the call.

Tessa was glad that somebody from the Carson Double C was coming for them—she wasn't sure she wanted to see the sheriff or one of his deputies right now.

Their pace didn't slow, even though it had begun raining steadily. Instead of becoming more fatigued, Skeeter seemed to understand he was getting close to the end of his adventure, and kept pulling on his leash. He was young and healthy and should recover quickly from his ordeal.

Lee Sutter was waiting at the trailhead in one of the smaller company vans. He wore a huge smile at seeing them and gave his nephew a hug.

"So this is the famous Skeeter." Lee gave the black Labrador a neck rub. Molly got her share of attention, too. "I spoke to Sheriff Maitland and told him we could keep Skeeter at the ranch until things were sorted out, but the Staffords are staying in a hotel that allows dogs. They'll probably feel better to have him with them. I have their number, so connecting won't be a problem."

"I want to drop by the ranch and take a shower first, but we'll bring Skeeter by the hospital after that," Clay explained. "Maybe Aiden can get a look at him through the window."

"I'm going, too," Tessa declared.

"I assumed you'd want to."

The ranch barbecue was in full swing upon their return, but Tessa didn't eat, as Lee urged. Instead she raced to the bunkhouse, dropped her clothes on the floor and jumped into the shower. She didn't linger, though the hot water felt wonderful after slogging through damp leaves, sodden meadows and dripping rain.

Tessa was the first to return to the parking area and Lee immediately brought her a plate of barbecued chicken kebabs and vegetables. "Get in the van where it's dry," he urged. "Or come over to the picnic area where there's cover."

"I'm fine in the van."

Lee reminded Tessa of her own father, who could seem gruff, but was really just a big teddy bear at heart.

"Where's Skeeter?" she asked.

"He's receiving some TLC from Jillian, and Molly is having a well-deserved dinner of our best chopped sirloin."

Tessa got into the passenger seat. The food tasted wonderful and she'd just finished when Clay arrived with Skeeter. His eyes widened when he saw her. "I thought you'd take longer. I ate before showering since I figured there would be plenty of time."

"Because you thought I'd be primping and putting on makeup?" She shook her head. "Have you ever seen me wear makeup?"

"Uh, no," he admitted, looking embarrassed. "But my sister used to take forever getting ready to go anywhere. As kids, Andrew and I always wanted to pull our hair out waiting for her."

"I don't have experience with big brothers, but I wouldn't be surprised if she did it just to annoy you."

"I wouldn't be, either," he muttered.

At the hospital they didn't need to ask which room Aiden might be in—a nurse wheeled him out as they approached the front entrance. Skeeter barked and strained on his leash, so eager that he was able to drag Clay forward a step. With an effort, they kept him from jumping onto the patient, though Tessa didn't think Aiden would have minded.

Tessa was instantly engulfed in hugs from Aiden's mother and father, who kept telling her how grateful they were to her and Clay for everything they'd done.

"You have a fine son," she said, embarrassed and pleased at the same time.

Being part of the rescue gave her a good feeling, as if a little piece of something missing had been restored to the universe.

"That's right. Aiden did a great job of keeping his head in a tough spot," Clay told them.

"We're proud. Except for him going off alone like that."

"Aw, Mom," Aiden muttered. Skeeter's forelegs were now across his lap and he gazed adoringly at his owner, his tongue lolling from the side of his mouth.

"Well, I wish everyone was that level-headed in an emergency situation," Clay interjected.

"Gosh, Tessa, thanks for finding Skeeter," Aiden said earnestly.

"It was a joint effort with Clay, and it was Molly who caught his scent and led us to him," she explained hastily.

Clay took Skeeter's bandana scarf from his pocket and gave it Aiden, who promptly put it around the Labrador retriever's neck.

Skeeter let out a happy yip. His world had righted itself very quickly with the reunion. The group chatted for another few minutes, but when Aiden began to look tired, Tessa nudged Clay and they said goodbye.

"Nice family," Clay murmured as he drove onto the road.

"Yeah. Aiden's sister and brother are flying in tomorrow, so they'll have a full load going back to Seattle."

"Especially with Aiden's leg in a cast and a year-old Labrador retriever along."

Tessa shrugged. "It's okay, they have an SUV where the cargo area can be converted into extra seating."

"How did you find all of this out?" Clay asked, looking puzzled. "We weren't there for very long."

"Just talking with his mom."

Warm satisfaction filled Tessa as they returned to the Carson Double C. She hadn't been able to do anything for her sister, but she'd helped save Aiden's life and been a part of finding his dog.

Even if she never found any answers about Renee, it was something positive she could remember and hold on to.

CHAPTER NINE

JILLIAN GLARED AT her pretend fiancé and chucked the jewelry box at him. "I told you *not* to buy a different ring."

"It's better this way. Try it on."

"No. Get your money back."

Andrew shook his head. "That isn't going to happen. I drove to Helena to shop at a jewelry store where nobody was likely to know me. What's wrong? You haven't even looked at the thing."

"I didn't want you to waste your money."

He gave her a mock wounded look. "Most fiancées wouldn't consider it a waste. Are you going to be the kind of wife that pinches pennies on everything? I don't care what you say, we're serving more than potato chips and hot dogs at our wedding reception."

"Give me a break." She glared at him again. They'd been having a nice time taking a scenic drive with Derry, and now Andrew was spoiling it.

The outing had started well. Spirits at work were high. Clay and Tessa's success at finding the hiker and then his dog had given everyone at Carson Outdoor Adventures a wonderful sense of accomplishment.

Skeeter had seemed little worse for wear. Thinking his owner would feel more reassured if he wasn't covered with dirt, Jillian had given him a quick warm-water wash and toweling. He'd loved every minute of the attention and a number of employees had come to give him some love, along with guests from the barbecue, who were excited that guides from the company had been involved in an actual rescue.

Earlier this morning Jillian had been reading an article about Aiden's rescue in the *Elk Point Morning Star* when Andrew had suggested they take Derry to the St. Ignatius Mission. They'd visited St. Ignatius before, but Andrew wanted his son to be familiar with the landmarks and history of Montana. She suspected it had something to do with his childhood, when his father's long work hours had kept the family from doing anything together until his health forced him to spend restful weekends and vacations in Elk Point.

"I don't understand," Jillian said to Andy,

trying to calm down. "Why would you buy another ring when I told you not to?"

He shrugged. "I didn't feel comfortable having you use the one from Michael. I realize the gems aren't as big as—"

"You think that matters to me?" she asked incredulously. How could he believe she cared about how large the diamond or other stones might be? "Don't be such a dolt."

He laughed. "That's the woman I know and love."

Jillian didn't think it was amusing. Any of it. And she didn't know why she was angry. Andrew was a great guy. Normally she enjoyed joking around with him, but maybe all the good wishes from friends were getting to her. Since only a few people knew the truth, she was having to pretend an excitement and anticipation she didn't feel. It brought back echoes of those first wonderful days after she and Michael had gotten engaged.

Problem was, she also kept remembering her life falling apart soon after.

And, while it was giving her father something to think about aside from recovering from his tumble from the fouling burn roof, her mother kept hinting that she and Andrew might genuinely fall in love if they just gave it a chance. Jillian was already tired of reminding her that they were best friends and nothing more. Not that a best friend wasn't one of the greatest things in the world; Andrew had supported her through all the skinned knees and broken hearts of her youth and early adulthood.

Jillian glanced over at Derry, who was napping on a blanket under a shade tree. He was lying there with complete abandon, lost in sleep, a chocolate smear on his cheek from the cake Jillian's mother had sent with them. She ascribed to the old adage that the way to a man's heart was through his stomach.

"Come on, take a look," Andy said, holding out the ring box. "It's an antique, found by a construction crew while doing restoration on an old Victorian house. I figured you'd appreciate the romance and history."

"Fine." Jillian grabbed the box. Inside she saw red gold shining against white velvet. Four rubies were set around a small diamond in a beautifully detailed setting. "Andy, it's…"

"Not a complete disaster?" he asked hopefully. "They buffed the gold so it's bright and shiny."

She lightly punched him in the shoulder.

"It's beautiful, but I'm still unhappy you spent the money."

"Sad. Our first fight as an engaged couple. At least now we can kiss and make up."

"Stop talking like that, especially around my mother. You're giving her ideas," Jillian scolded. "And how could you consult her about a picnic before asking me to go? I expect better of you."

"It wasn't like that. Not exactly. When I came over this morning and you weren't at the house, I asked about your plans for the day. I mentioned hoping we could take a drive, so your mom offered to put a picnic together. And what do you mean that I'm giving her ideas?"

"Mom wants grandkids. My brothers aren't obliging and she sees Derry as an instant grandchild."

A fond smile crossed Andrew's face. "Evelyn would be a terrific grandmother. Derry already sees her that way. I think my own mother is envious because she can't be up here as much as she'd prefer."

"That isn't the point. It'll be a huge letdown when Mom realizes nothing is going to happen." Jillian pursed her lips. "Maybe I can get Tyler to come for a visit. He'd be the perfect distraction."

"Your brother annoys the heck out of your mother."

"That's the point. He's an architect who abandoned a successful career to run a dive shop in the Channel Islands. If he's around, she'll forget about me and focus on *his* choices."

"That's why he won't come."

"Maybe. But I can be very convincing." Jillian fanned herself and fastened her hair into a ponytail for coolness. "Will the jewelry store give you the money back when this mess is over?"

They were sitting on the tailgate of Andrew's truck and he stretched out his legs. "I'm not returning it. Anyway, it wasn't that expensive. See if the size is right."

She slid the circlet onto her finger, hoping the spirit of the previous owner was pleased that the lost ring was being appreciated again. As rings went, it was one of the most beautiful pieces of jewelry that Jillian had ever seen. Andy's choice was unexpectedly perfect; it was just too bad he'd screwed up in other ways.

"What do you think?" he asked.

"It fits. All right, I'll wear the ring whenever I'm not working with the horses. You can give it to your aunt or mother after everything is settled."

"Or you can keep it as a thank-you."

Andy yawned and Jillian regretted giving him a hard time. He had circles beneath his eyes and lines around his mouth that hadn't been there before his ex-wife's return to Montana. For the most part, he was a happy guy, easygoing and fun to be around. The way Mallory had taken advantage of him had infuriated all of his friends, but everyone had their blind spots.

While it seemed almost certain Mallory couldn't win a court battle against Andrew, it was still a concern. There was no justice in having to fight this battle another time. If only his ex would go back to where she'd come from, everything could return to normal.

"Were you really, truly angry at me?" Andy asked after a minute. "It seemed like you might be."

She hunched one shoulder. "A little."

"But why? I didn't get a huge diamond or other stone, and you were upset before you even looked inside the box."

Jillian scrunched her nose. "I suppose because it finally seemed as if Michael's ring could be used to do some good. Lately I've wondered why I keep it with me if it makes me sad, and then suddenly there was a great reason."

Andrew sighed.

He hadn't thought about it that way, but Jillian was usually a few steps ahead of him when it came to figuring things out. Even now he didn't understand why he hadn't wanted his pretend fiancée wearing another man's ring. The idea had bothered him more and more until he'd gone shopping for a different one.

It had been an unexpected stab of male ego when it came to Jillian, because even as a teenager he'd never seen her in a romantic light.

Or maybe he'd chosen not to see her that way because romance came and went, but friendship lasted. It was a lesson he'd learned quickly in adolescence.

Not that Jillian wasn't pretty. She had long, dark brown hair with gold and red highlights, sparkling green eyes and a figure that could make a man feel glad to be alive, simply for the pleasure of looking at her. She also was intelligent and loving and had a great sense of humor. And her gift with animals was unrivalled, no matter what species.

"Andy?" Jillian prompted in the silence.

"It seemed better for you to wear a ring from me," he muttered, unwilling to admit his other thoughts. "Besides, I figured you were uncomfortable about using Michael's ring, which is why you keep forgetting to put it on."

"I'm not used to wearing jewelry, that's all."

Andrew wasn't convinced. "Having a different ring is just as well. Even though it's been a while, somebody could recognize the other one and start asking questions. I wouldn't want that getting back to Mallory."

"I suppose, but it isn't as if I flaunted my ring when I was engaged for real."

He suspected she was still annoyed. That was new, too. Over the years they'd argued, especially as kids, but everything had always blown over quickly. He was determined to keep his son, but he didn't want to lose his best friend, either.

"Let's stop talking about it," Andrew suggested. "I think it's making us both uptight."

"I wasn't uptight until you showed me

this." Jillian waved her left hand in the air and light flashed off the gold and gems. "Not that much, at least."

Ironically, he'd been pleased to find a ring that seemed to suit her, but maybe he should have explained ahead of time what he planned to do. After all, Jillian didn't like surprises.

He should have remembered that.

TESSA HADN'T EXPECTED to be particularly tired the day after their return with Skeeter, but when she woke up in the morning, she blinked at the time on her phone.

It wasn't morning any longer, it was afternoon.

Drat.

She yawned. Last night Clay had said she wouldn't be assigned to a trip for a couple of days. In a way, she was disappointed, yet she knew they both needed time to process the change in their relationship. Although *relationship* was a strong word to describe their uneasy connection. And now that she was a contractor rather than an employee, her position on the ranch was even more nebulous.

Kissing him hadn't helped, either.

Tessa turned over and put her arm under her neck, wondering what Clay was telling his brother about her, along with everyone else on the ranch. Carson Outdoor Adventures employees were fiercely loyal to both him and his brother. Depending on how he explained the situation, they might be hostile.

It was too bad. She'd enjoyed the camaraderie on the Carson Double C, but it was Clay's decision.

Tessa got dressed, then baked a batch of corn bread and made a pot of chili, unsure of what else to do with her day. It was different in Montana than back home, where she had her garden and friends and could always go out to see her grandparents at the Agua Hermosa.

She'd already finished preliminary landscape designs for the clients in Arizona and had sent them to her team, but maybe she could do something about the Carson Outdoor Adventures office. While the area was clean and neatly trimmed, there was nothing to make the place visually attractive. A number of half barrels and other planters were around, filled with dirt, but no flowers or plants were growing in them. Not even weeds. Those could be dealt with at the very least, perhaps with a mix of native grasses and flowers. She was sketching her ideas when a knock on the door broke her concentration.

It was Clay.

"Sorry to bother you," he said, "but a reporter from the *Elk Point Morning Star* wants an interview with the two of us. The *Morning Star* is our town newspaper."

Tessa tensed. "I don't want... That is, you aren't going to tell them about Renee or that she's my sister, are you?"

"I haven't told anyone yet. It's complicated."

"The newspaper doesn't have to know. Anyway, the story should be about you and Aiden. I shouldn't even be a part of it. You're an official volunteer with the Elk County Search and Rescue organization, I'm not."

Clay's expression turned curious. "You helped find Aiden and you're the reason we found Skeeter. I give credit where credit is due. Is there any reason you don't want your name out there? Because it's too late to keep under wraps. You aren't in the witness protection program or something like that, right?"

Tessa rolled her eyes. "Hardly. The thing is, I truly don't want to cause problems, and you never know how the media might interpret my being here. That is, if they care enough to connect the dots and that isn't…"

She stopped, unsure of what she was saying.

Renee's death had devastated her family, but it couldn't have been more than a sad event to most everyone in town, presuming they even remembered her.

At the same time, Clay's reaction suggested something different. Tessa didn't know how the situation could impact Andrew's custody of his son, but it was the only reason she could think of that might worry the Carsons. Well, unless Clay was concerned about a lawsuit, which her family had no intention of filing. There wasn't any basis for legal action. The sheriff had stated in no uncertain terms that the guides and equipment *weren't* at fault; the bit of information she'd found online had said the same thing.

It briefly crossed her mind that the sheriff might be trying to protect his friend, but she immediately dismissed the notion. Clay was so careful, it was difficult to imagine him being negligent in any way.

He was looking at her inquisitively. "You seem a million miles away."

"Sorry, my mind was drifting. I couldn't

get to sleep last night, then I slept late for the first time in forever. I'm normally up before dawn, since that's the coolest time to work or ride outside. I don't think I'm fully awake yet. Did you say something else?"

"No, but having you duck the interview is more likely to rouse curiosity than appease it. We aren't talking dozens of paparazzi with their cameras in your face—it's Ruby Jenkins, who runs a travel agency when she isn't writing human interest pieces for the newspaper. Very low-key."

"I suppose that would be... *Drat!*" Tessa exclaimed when a burning smell caught her attention. She spun and rushed to the bunkhouse kitchen. Luckily, it was just the chili boiling over and scorching on the burner. She turned off the stove and gave the contents a stir.

"I thought the building was on fire from the way you reacted, but that smells good," Clay said from behind her. "Beneath the smoke."

"It's white bean chili with chicken and Hatch green chiles. I was homesick for the flavors of home, so I ordered a batch of roasted peppers while I was working in the office. They come packed in dry ice, but this is the first chance I've had to use any.

You're welcome to a bowl. It only scorched on the outside of the pot. I took a shortcut with canned beans, which would appall my mother. She believes in making everything from scratch."

"I WOULDN'T MIND a taste." Clay's stomach let out a loud rumble, making Tessa laugh.

She gave him a generous serving, accompanied by a square of corn bread and a warning that he might find the mixture spicy. "The warning is because the food I've encountered in Montana is tame compared to what I'm accustomed to eating," she said.

"Dishes on trips and for the ranch barbecue need to be mild to accommodate a wide range of taste preferences," Clay explained. "You can add spice, not take it away. That's why we provide crushed red pepper for guests who are more adventurous in their culinary preferences."

He ate a spoonful. Tessa was right about the chili being fiery, but it was delicious, full of diced chicken breast, garlic and green chiles. The contrast with the sweet, fresh corn bread seemed to heighten the flavor. She served herself and sat at the table across from him.

"I didn't know you could cook," he said.

A sad expression crossed her face. "I suppose Renee told you her sister was terrible in the kitchen, but I'm not bad. It's just that she was a gourmet, which made my efforts pale in comparison to hers."

"Using specially ordered frozen green peppers seems fancy enough to me. But to be honest, I don't remember Renee talking about her life in Arizona." As soon as the words came out of his mouth, Clay wanted to call them back. Renee Claremont's family probably hoped she'd spoken fondly of them before her death. "That is, I don't recall what she may have said," he added awkwardly.

"I see." Tessa rubbed her upper arms as if chilled.

Clay leaned forward. "What is it that you think I know about your sister?"

"Nothing."

He raised an eyebrow and Tessa shrugged. "Renee explained that you were involved, so it's possible you have some insight into what she was thinking during those last few months. Her emails to us were filled with stories about you and the things you were doing together."

Clay stared. Renee Claremont had been a

nice woman, but the idea of a relationship with her had never entered his mind.

"Tessa, there was nothing like that between us. She was a client. We didn't interact more than I do with any other guest. Less, in a way, because it was difficult to draw her into a conversation. I sometimes wondered if I annoyed her."

Tessa stirred the contents of her bowl and ate a bite. "You were the guide on almost every trip she took."

"That isn't unusual. If clients prefer a certain guide, they often try to schedule trips based on who might be leading it or make a special request, but there was nothing going on with Renee. I have a personal rule about that sort of thing."

"You weren't happy about Patrick Frazier flirting with me. I wondered if it was because…" She stopped and seemed to shake herself. "I guess not, and that explains why you didn't come to the memorial service."

Clay drew a harsh breath. He could imagine how the Aldermans must have felt to think Renee's boyfriend couldn't be bothered to attend her memorial service. If he hadn't still been under medical orders not to travel, he would have gone out of respect for the family.

But how could he explain he'd been injured, without revealing too much about what had happened that day? Then there was the damage it had done to his business and reputation. Tessa and her parents didn't need to know about that, either—it wasn't their problem.

Some of his anger and frustration ebbed away.

Secrets weren't necessarily about hurting someone. *He* was keeping secrets from Tessa because the truth would cause unnecessary pain. Spencer Maitland was concerned for the same reason, which was why he was dragging his feet about showing her the full accident report. The other clients on the raft had been furious with Renee Claremont when giving their statements—they'd told the unvarnished truth, describing her behavior in bitter, outraged terms, his brother among them.

The effects of that nightmare day were still reverberating down through the months. When would it stop?

"I'm sorry I couldn't come to the service," Clay said carefully. "And I'm sorry I couldn't save her. I tried."

"I know." Tessa swept a tear from her cheek and made a disgusted sound. "I really hate crying. It doesn't accomplish anything."

"You could blame the spice in the chili."

She managed a weak smile and ate another bite. "This is mild compared to what I grew up eating. Dad says that my mother cooks like the grocery store in Hades had a closeout sale on their hottest products. Lately she's talked about experimenting with a pepper called the Trinidad scorpion. They're insanely hot, but Dad told her that he draws the line at anything named after a poisonous arachnid."

"The name says it all," Clay murmured with an obliging grin. If the situation had been different, he might have enjoyed meeting Tessa's family. They sounded like interesting people. "It would be great if you'd share your chili recipe with Uncle Lee. This would be a good option for guests who don't eat beef, though he couldn't make it this spicy."

"I threw it together without measuring anything, but there are dozens of recipes for white bean chili. He can find them on the internet. Some of them call for oregano, but I usually don't put it in. And there are milder green chilies available that he can use."

"I'll talk to him." Clay's humor vanished as he thought about her twin's claim that they'd been dating. "Um, why would your sister tell you that she was involved with me when she wasn't?"

"I don't know." Tessa got up to put the lid on the pot. "I'll reread the emails she sent us, but we all thought that's what she was saying. Just add it to the list of mysteries that may never be solved when it comes to Renee."

"Is it possible she was jealous because you'd gotten serious with someone? What if she wanted her family to think she had somebody, too? You mentioned she'd been divorced. Maybe she was feeling competitive or left behind."

Tessa shook her head. "I don't see how. There hasn't been anyone special for me in a while. If ever." She made a face. "My boyfriends seem destined to swiftly become friends and nothing more. I must be doing something wrong, or else the guys back home don't see me that way. Renee, on the other hand, met a well-off art collector when she was in graduate school. They were a glam couple while it lasted. He was a nice guy, they just weren't right together."

Clay thought the men in Arizona had to be complete idiots if they didn't recognize Tessa as an utterly desirable woman. It wasn't just Tessa's face and figure—the way she moved and the silky timbre of her voice, often filled with humor, had been threatening his peace of mind since the day they'd met.

The impulsive kiss she'd given him after finding Skeeter had only thrown fuel on the fire.

Much as he disliked admitting it to himself, he'd even tried to discover whether Tessa was in a serious relationship. It was the real reason he'd asked if her sister could have been trying to compete with her.

"Maybe you just haven't met the right man," he said. "Or you haven't been ready for more and they sense it."

Tessa gave him a funny look. "That's what my dad says."

"Oh, great, I'm in the mental head space of someone much older than me. How reassuring."

"My father is generally considered to be very wise."

"But I'm not fiftysomething. I don't want to be wise, I want to be mad, bad and dangerous to know. At least that's what I used to say when I was fourteen," he clarified, realizing that it wasn't the best goal for a wilderness guide, particularly a guide connected to her sister's death.

A smile tugged at Tessa's mouth, so apparently she wasn't bothered. It was nice that she didn't look for reasons to take offense.

"So you wanted to be like Lord Byron," she said.

"A poet who died young a few hundred years ago? That's worse. Is that phrase really about Byron? When I was fourteen I thought it meant being a wild and crazy guy—one who was lots of fun and didn't intend to settle down."

"A close friend of Byron's described him that way, possibly because he seemed incapable of returning love. But the phrase has been used since then by other people."

"A close friend of Byron's, as in…?"

She turned around, the corners of her mouth twitching. "A *very* close friend."

"You mean a woman who had reason to understand how bad and dangerous he was to know?"

"Look it up if you want the details," Tessa interjected, still seeming amused, rather than prudishly offended.

The brief repartee seemed to have eased some of her tension, and increased his own.

He didn't flirt with employees, though the exchange could barely be considered flirting. Of course, Tessa wasn't an employee any longer—she was a contractor. He'd already called the payroll company he used to tell them about the change. Being a contractor gave her more autonomy; he wasn't sure about himself.

Tessa didn't say anything else and Clay glanced at the large pad of art paper lying to one side of the table. It was open and he saw a pencil sketch of the company office, except in the drawing there were landscaping features that didn't currently exist.

"This looks interesting," he murmured.

"Just some ideas I had," she said, seeming flustered as she grabbed the pad. "It's an occupational hazard of being a landscape architect. For me, at least. I see a place and think about doing this or that or the other thing as an enhancement."

"Do you mentally rearrange rocks and trees when you're in the backcountry? Perhaps reroute a river or move a lake or two?"

Tessa shook her head. "Definitely not. That's one of the reasons I find it restful. Nature does a far better job of making a place beautiful than humans. We just get in the way. But when we put in roads and parking lots and buildings, we can't always let nature take over."

"Well, you're welcome to do whatever you want on the ranch. I have a company account at the hardware store. They've got a section with yard stuff. Get what you need."

YARD STUFF?

Tessa bit her lip to keep from grinning. It was safe to assume that Clay wasn't a gardening aficionado. She glanced out the window and saw the blue rise of mountains beyond the horses grazing in the rolling foothill pastures; he probably didn't feel the need for landscaping with such a stunning backyard.

Still, ideas kept popping in her brain, ways to make the office look more like a rustic cabin fitting into the sweeping landscape than a modern log building. First impressions were important. Right now it was entirely plain and basic around the different ranch structures—no trees or bushes or anything else to make them look inviting. Her thoughts involved a whole lot more than just putting plants in a few half barrels, though even that could help make the place more welcoming.

"I'll take a look at what's available," she murmured. She didn't even know why she was interested in making Clay's business look more appealing, other than her instinctive desire to create a pleasant setting. That, and because working in an environment outside of the desert would be a professional challenge.

Then she returned her gaze to Clay and knew it had nothing to do with professional challenges.

He was too interesting. Too compelling. And somehow, learning that he'd never been romantically involved with Renee had transformed the situation to something freer...and more risky. He was too controlled and emotionally distant to be the easiest man to know, which may have been another reason Renee had found him attractive.

"Let's go to the hardware store together," Clay suggested. "After the interview with the newspaper."

Tessa gave him a long, considering look. He'd claimed that ducking the interview might make the reporter curious. On the other hand, he could probably find a reasonable way to explain her absence, one that wouldn't raise questions. But did she want to take the chance?

"All right," she said reluctantly.

"Good. We're supposed to meet Ruby at her travel agency at four o'clock."

Exasperation filled Tessa. "You agreed before talking to me? That was presumptuous, though I suppose it's good publicity for your company. Raises your profile and that sort of thing."

"My company profile has nothing to do with it," Clay said, sounding annoyed. "The director of Elk County Search and Rescue called and asked if we'd do the interview, so I'd go whether you agreed or not. ECSR is a volunteer organization that supports the sheriff's department. Donations go up when there's a successful rescue."

"You should have told me that part in the first place. Of course, I'll do it."

His eyes narrowed. "You just love giving me a hard time."

She shrugged. "*Love* is such a strong word. *Enjoy* is a better description."

"Fine. It's close to four, so we should leave now."

Tessa was amused as they drove into Elk Point.

She couldn't recall the last time she'd sparred with anyone the way she had sparred with Clay. She'd forgotten how much fun it could be. As a matter of fact, lately she'd forgotten how to have fun.

CHAPTER TEN

"THEY CAN'T SERIOUSLY think people will buy lawns in pots," Clay said at the hardware store following the interview. "Lawn that already needs to be mowed, no less. That grass must be eighteen inches long at the very least."

They were in the outdoor garden section, checking out the native grasses they had available. One of the employees was close enough to hear Clay's remark and looked offended.

"They're supposed to be long—they're ornamental," Tessa said firmly. "And they have a very nice selection here. Much larger than I expected."

"It's still just grass. We've got grass all over Montana, why would anyone buy it in a pot?"

She pushed the cart forward a foot. Native grasses and plants were popular in landscaping, but Clay must be one of those people who needed to be shown how attractive they could look, rather than being able to conceptualize it. And even then he might not be convinced.

"You don't want people digging plants in wilderness areas, do you?" she asked.

"Of course not."

"Then be grateful they sell this in pots. The challenge is when nonnative plants are sold or brought in and they start taking over. You mentioned growing up in ranching country. Isn't that a problem for ranchers?"

Clay's face turned thoughtful. "Sure, they want to eradicate invasive growth that isn't good for cattle."

"Well, it's the same in most places, for various reasons. Scotch broom is a gigantic headache where I'm from. It crowds out native plants, offers little forage to wildlife or stock, and is a fire hazard. And don't get me started on the kudzu vine."

"You seem to know a lot about the subject," said the gardening employee who'd appeared offended by Clay's comments.

Tessa smiled at her. "I'm a landscape architect in Arizona. It comes with the territory."

"Cool. We have someone who knows stacks about Montana plants if you want to talk to her."

"We're just looking at the moment, but I'd love to come back when I have more time."

"Okay. Let me know if you need anything."

"That was diplomatic," Clay said when they were alone.

"What happened to *your* diplomacy? Or are you only polite to your outdoor adventure clients and newspaper reporters?"

He frowned. "I wasn't rude."

"You ridiculed what they were selling."

"Oh. You're right, sorry. I was just surprised. I've seen the grass they're selling at the side of roads."

Tessa put the cart back into the rack. "Surprised or not, it wasn't your finest moment. Let's go back to the ranch. I'll think about what they have here and consider the best options."

CLAY WAS EMBARRASSED. Tessa was right, he hadn't been courteous.

He wanted to be on good relations with the merchants in town and hadn't intended to offend anyone. It was a reminder to be more careful about what he said, in case he was overheard. Even a joking comment could be taken the wrong way.

At the Carson Double C, the ranch barbecue was in full swing, so he waited until it was over before getting the family together, along with Jillian, to explain about Tessa.

"Tessa is Renee Claremont's twin?" Andrew looked thunderstruck. "How is that possible? I wouldn't have even guessed they were sisters."

"Their smiles are similar," Clay found himself saying.

The five of them had been meeting every few days to discuss the situation with Mallory, so his revelations about Tessa had come out of the blue. He'd considered keeping it to himself, only to decide they deserved to be told.

"What does Tessa want?" Uncle Lee asked gravely.

"She's probably trying to find a basis to sue the company," Andrew muttered, gazing into the playroom, where his son was fitting large plastic puzzles pieces together. Molly was lying nearby, looking back and forth worriedly, picking up on their emotions.

"I can't believe she'd be that devious," Jillian protested. "The horses like Tessa, and they're better judges of character than most people. They know when someone is untrustworthy. Coal Dust is particularly fond of her and he doesn't warm up to very many people."

"Horses don't need to consider the same things we do," Andrew reminded her.

They exchanged a glance and Clay thought he detected tension between them, which was odd because they usually got along. But then, the situation had to be wearing on their nerves. Jillian couldn't have expected the fake engagement to last more than a few days or a week at most. Who could have guessed that Mallory would hang around Elk Point this long?

"Tessa says that her sister didn't enjoy outdoor sports or travel or doing anything that might be risky. She wants to understand why Renee came up to Montana and started behaving so much out-of-character," Clay said quietly. "I don't believe Tessa intends any harm, so I'm letting her stay at the ranch. But she'll be a contractor from now on, rather than a Carson Outdoor Adventures employee."

His brother's face was dubious. "Are you sure that's a good idea? What about the mistakes she made while working in the office? They would have been expensive if they hadn't been caught. Maybe that was her plan."

"I refuse to be paranoid. Anyway, I'm convinced the mistakes weren't intentional. And how would it look if I asked her to leave?" Clay countered. "There's nothing to hide, but it might appear that way."

"I agree," Aunt Emma said and Uncle Lee nodded.

Clay hated putting his family in a difficult position, but this was new territory for him. A nagging sense of guilt and failure had haunted him since Renee Claremont's death. Intellectually, he knew he'd done everything possible to rescue her, yet it was hard to convince the part of himself that still felt responsible. Most of the time he was able to push the feeling away. After all, he couldn't second-guess every decision he made when out with a group of guests. But now that he was aware of Tessa's connection to the tragedy, she would be a constant reminder.

"No one else needs to know about Tessa. It's best if we keep this between us," he said. "I'll work with her on any trips, so you won't have to interact with her more than absolutely necessary. Is there anything else we should discuss?"

"Uh, yeah. I talked to my mom earlier," Jillian said. "She's starting to get calls, asking when the engagement party will be. I think there are expectations because of the big bash my folks threw when Michael and I got engaged. They know we can't do much until Dad is better, but they're still curious."

Aunt Emma gave her hand a squeeze. "This must be bringing up painful memories. We'll start planning an event. Everybody will understand if we have it at the Carson Double C. The end of the month might be a good time. It'll be fun."

"That's right," Andrew agreed, looking more cheerful. "But Mom and Dad usually spend July here, so what about an Independence Day barn dance with desserts and homemade ice cream? We'll decorate with red, white and blue bunting and balloons. We can announce it as an engagement bash, and if Mallory is gone by then, just say we decided to go ahead with our plans and have a great party. Is that okay with you, Clay? We've talked about having a big Fourth of July event here at the ranch. This could get us to do it."

Clay saw conflicting emotions on Jillian's face, but if having an engagement party was necessary to convince Andrew's ex that Derry was going to have a new mother, then they needed to have a party.

"Sounds good," he said. "What do you think, Uncle Lee? We can hire extra people to make desserts in the kitchen, or else order from a bakery."

Uncle Lee snorted. "No one is using a bakery if *I* have any say in the matter. I can arrange everything in-house. No need to hire temporary staff. The kitchen crew will be delighted to have a few extra hours."

"And I'll do my part," Aunt Emma asserted.

"Dad won't be able to help, but my mom will want to be involved," Jillian added. "She loves this kind of thing."

Clay nodded. "Then we have a plan. Look, I'm going over to the office. Whatever you decide is fine, just let me know what I'm supposed to do."

Andrew caught up with him at the office porch. "Clay, I'm still concerned about Tessa being here," he said in a low tone. "Isn't it odd that she came up here from Arizona? It's been months since the accident."

"With mostly winter between then and now, it may have been her first good opportunity. Regardless, I might have done the same thing in her shoes." Clay unlocked the door and gestured his brother inside, then closed it behind them to ensure their privacy. "Tessa and her family are grieving. You haven't seen her face when she talks about Renee. Don't forget, she's the one who lost her sister."

"And I almost lost my brother because Renee Claremont was reckless," Andrew returned in a raised voice. "Tell Tessa whatever she wants to know and get her out of here."

"I don't know what to tell her, and I don't want to ask her to leave. But it isn't because of what she might think, or because of how it would look," Clay admitted. "I'm having trouble dealing with what happened myself. Maybe talking together will help us both sort things out."

"You can talk to me."

"If it wasn't for Tessa, I probably wouldn't be saying anything about it in the first place," Clay said tersely.

Andrew winced. "Yeah, getting you to talk about your feelings isn't impossible, just next to impossible. But I still don't like you being on backcountry trips with her."

Clay ran his fingers through his hair, searching for the right words. "What Renee did isn't her sister's fault. Tessa is knowledge-able about wilderness safety and has been very helpful. A few days ago I even let her take a group out alone. Just for a two-hour hike, but the guests raved when they got back and great comments have been posted to our social-media pages. People are really excited when they go the extra mile to write a letter or post something electronically."

"Yeah. You know, life was a whole lot simpler when we were kids."

Andrew dropped onto the office couch, his face drawn. The past few years had been hard on him between the mess with Mallory and the need to raise a child on his own. The accident with Renee Claremont had taken its toll, as well—Clay hadn't even realized how much before seeing the anger in his brother's face. And now Andrew was afraid, however unlikely, that he could lose custody of Derry, or at the very least, face an ugly, expensive court battle.

Some coffee remained in the pot, so Clay filled a cup and stuck it in the microwave.

"We just thought times were simpler when we were younger," he said over his shoulder. "But they weren't. We didn't understand how serious Dad's heart condition might be, or how sick Grandpa Bartholomew was with his chemo treatments and how close we came to losing him. There were other scares, too, like when Great-Aunt Eloise had a burst appendix. Mom and Dad protected us, just like you try to protect Derry."

"I know."

The microwave dinged and he removed the cup.

"You'll never sleep tonight, drinking coffee this late," Andrew told him.

Clay took a swig of the strong, black brew. Having started out as high-quality beans, the flavor wasn't bad, even reheated. "Doesn't matter. Anyway, it's probably decaf. That's what Oliver usually makes in the afternoon."

"It was a good move to put him in here in place of Tessa. He's excellent at managing the office."

"Yeah. By the way, Tessa has figured out the relationship between Derry and Mallory."

His brother groaned.

"It's going to be fine. She isn't the kind of person who would do or say anything to hurt the situation. Now go talk to Jillian. I suspect she's unhappy with you. Tell her you're sorry."

"Why are you assuming I did something wrong?"

Clay lifted an eyebrow.

Andrew sighed and got up. "You're right.

I'll apologize again. Who would have guessed that a trip to a jewelry shop would put me in the doghouse?"

"I'm not even going to speculate on what that's supposed to mean. I'll see you tomorrow."

TESSA HAD PROMPTLY gone back to the hardware store after returning to the ranch with Clay.

She'd been amazed by the store's broad selection of native grasses and had filled the back of her SUV. She wanted to get the planters sorted out when he wasn't around, but had overlooked the fact that he was almost always around unless he was with a group, and then she was with him.

Her hope was to surprise Clay with how natural the planters would look with the grasses, softening the lines of the building. It might be the only way he could see their value.

Now, she watched from the front window of the bunkhouse after seeing Clay and his brother disappear in the direction of the office. A short time later Andrew reappeared and went back into his house.

Tessa waited a while longer, then finally

went out to her SUV and drove it around to the public parking area closest to the office. She had a feeling it would be difficult to surprise Clay, no matter how hard she tried.

Though the ranch probably had gardening implements, she'd purchased a selection of hand tools. As soon as she moved the planters to where she wanted them, she began spading up the contents, removing dead root systems and adding organic compost. Much as she loved being up in the mountains, exploring meadows and woodland trails and hearing the bright rush of water in creeks and streams, there was a soothing normality to the task.

She was so focused that when the office door opened, she jumped and put a hand to her throat.

"What are you doing?" Clay asked.

"Preparing the dirt, though this isn't dirt exactly, it's really old potting mix. You can't just stick plants in and expect them to grow well. You said it would be all right for me to do what I wanted out here."

"I didn't think you'd start this evening. Where did those bags come from?" He pointed to the compost containers.

"The hardware store in Elk Point. I went back. You're right, they have quite a bit of yard...*stuff.*" Tessa had trouble keeping her face straight. "The mixture in these planters is drained of nutrients and the compost will help fix that. I thought about replacing the contents entirely, but I think this will be okay for now."

She dug her gloved hands into the rich compost and threw another load into the planter.

"It's great that you want to dress the place up, but do me a favor and don't make things too—" Clay stopped and Tessa cocked her head.

"Too cute or flowery?" she teased. "In town they have lovely baskets hanging from hooks on the old-style streetlights. They're filled with trailing flowers. Don't you want to fit in with all that charm and atmosphere?"

"That kind of thing looks good in Elk Point, but I'm not sure it's the right image for an outdoor adventure company."

Tessa grinned. "Believe it or not, I agree. I might add something a little fun out here, but will you trust me not to make everything too colorful and fussy? Because I assume that's what you're concerned about."

Clay sat on the railing. "Since I gave you free rein, I don't have much say in the matter."

"I don't agree. You probably wouldn't allow me to dig up the front, for example."

Tessa tried to keep a hopeful note from her tone. She kept envisioning a water feature that looked as if the cabin had been built over it, with water cascading over large rocks and spilling into a small pond or trickling creek, with native trees and bushes on the other side. She often incorporated water into her landscape designs in Arizona, usually supported by a rain collection and storage system, but this would be on a grander scale than most of her previous projects.

"That depends. How long would it have to be dug up?" Clay asked warily. "We're going into a really busy season. It would be challenging to have the area looking like a construction zone for an extended period."

It was a good point. She'd prefer doing the work herself, which could take weeks or longer, and there were also the potential issues of permits and water rights. The tantalizing images in her mind began to be replaced by more practical options that would be swifter to implement.

"A few days at most," Tessa said. "I need to consider what would work best."

"I guess that's okay. It's getting dark. Are you done?"

"For now. Have a good night." Tessa tucked the gardening tools in her vehicle, then gathered the old root tangles and empty compost bags and walked them over to the discreetly concealed dumpsters and recycling bins.

Clay was gone when she returned and she breathed easier.

Tomorrow she'd come out at first light to deal with the plants in her SUV. With any luck she'd be able to get everything into the planters before he saw them. She was looking forward to seeing the display herself; the native grasses were different in Montana than in Arizona, but they were just as beautiful.

It was probably too much to hope he'd be impressed, but it was nice to think about the possibility. And ridiculous. On the other hand, it could be a step toward proving to everyone that she wasn't here to cause trouble.

AT DAWN THE next morning, Tessa went the long way around the outer buildings to avoid disturbing anyone in the ranch houses. She unloaded the pots from her SUV and swiftly got everything into the various planters she'd prepared.

Finally, she watered everything.

She was pleased with her efforts. It wasn't a true landscaping job, but it was gratifying to see what could be done economically with a few plants.

She stepped back and evaluated the office with a critical eye. Soft ornamental grasses in the half-barrel planters now highlighted the steps up to the office porch. The open area under the porch was obscured by the old box planters she'd found and filled, as well, helping to visually anchor the building. The gardening expert at the store had assured her that some of the grasses turned rich colors in autumn, which would add variety. A single pot of flowering native plants sat on the rustic table between two chairs, balancing the deliberate asymmetry of the design. She would have to find the right fanciful touch to put her mark on the place, but that shouldn't be too hard.

Tessa collected the empty containers and set them in the cargo area of her SUV. The hardware store had said they'd be used again by their local grower if she returned them, so she'd take care of it when she had other errands to run in Elk Point.

"I'm impressed," said Andrew Carson as she tucked the coiled hose under the porch.

"Oh, hi."

From the way his gaze avoided hers, Tessa guessed that his brother had told him about her relationship to Renee. She understood, even though she wished it hadn't been necessary. Her friends in Tucson had finally moved past the awkwardness that seemed to follow a death; now she saw the same awkwardness in Andrew Carson.

She decided to be frank. "Andrew, I realize Clay must have told you about my sister, but there isn't any need to say something about it. In fact, I'd prefer it if you don't."

He seemed to marginally relax. "That's nice of you. I'm lousy at finding the right words."

"Join the club. So you're okay with what I've done out here?"

"Sure. I've told Clay a skirting is needed on the base of the porch, but this works even better."

"I hope he agrees. He wasn't enthusiastic about the idea of ornamental grasses, but they're more natural than other options. These are all native species, so they won't be invasive."

Andrew smiled wryly. "Other than knowing invasive species can be an issue, I know nothing about gardens. Brown thumbs must run in the family because my mom and dad can barely keep a lawn alive, and Clay is just as bad."

"That's okay. Without people like you, I wouldn't have a career," she teased. "I don't know if your brother mentioned it, but back home I'm a landscape architect. Um, I'd better move my SUV to the private lot before guests start arriving."

Feeling as if she was escaping, Tessa drove to the parking area reserved for employees. Despite what she'd said to Andrew, and his reply, she sensed an underlying uneasiness. She regretted it. To date she'd had little to do with anyone in the family besides Clay, but had enjoyed being in a place where her emotional baggage wasn't known.

Of course, the problem with trying to get away from it all was that you take yourself with you. So while Clay and his family hadn't known of her connection to Renee until the sheriff had spilled the beans, *she'd* known. The hardest part now would be convincing everyone she didn't have undesirable motives for coming to Montana; she could see how it might look under the circumstances.

She showered and French-braided her wet hair. There wasn't much tidying needed in her small room or the rest of the bunkhouse, but not knowing when the other occupants would be arriving, she gave the kitchen a good clean, along with the communal social space.

Someone knocked on the door and she found Clay on the doorstep. "Yes?"

"I was wrong, the grass stuff you planted looks great," he said with an embarrassed expression. "And, uh, I know I told you to take the day off, but I've had guests calling about the overnight trip that leaves this afternoon. They've asked if the 'dog heroine' can go along. You're a celebrity."

Heat rose in her face. "I'm not a heroine."

He held up a newspaper. On the bottom half of the front page were two pictures—one of Aiden and Skeeter, the second of her taken in Ruby Jenkins's real estate office. The title of the article was Montana Newcomer Rescues Lost Dog. The caption under her photo read "Dog Heroine, Tessa Alderman of Corson Outdoor Adventures."

Tessa wrinkled her nose. There was nothing

heroic about her; she'd just been in the right place at the right moment, which was exactly what she'd told Ruby Jenkins. "How many times do I have to say it wasn't just me?"

"You're the one who insisted on looking for Skeeter. Credit where credit is due," Clay reminded her. "It's a nice article. Ruby is a dog lover, which is why she wanted to do a second story. The first one had gone to print before we got back with Skeeter."

"But it was Molly who was responsible more than anything," Tessa protested. "We never would have found Skeeter without her ability to follow scents. The name of the story should be 'Golden Retriever Has Golden Nose' or something along those lines."

Clay cocked his head. "Molly gets her share of accolades. Is there a reason you don't want to be given credit? You've done a good job of trying to avoid it. I can't help wondering if it has something to do with your sister."

"Are you talking about survivor guilt?" Tessa shrugged. "Don't people often feel guilty when they're alive and someone they love isn't?"

A bleak look crossed Clay's face and there was a flash of pain in his dark eyes. "Not just someone you love. You can feel that way about somebody you barely knew."

Suddenly tired, Tessa leaned against the door frame. "I didn't mean you, Clay."

"I know, but I *do* feel guilty. I was in charge, I should have been able to save her. Somehow. I've gone over that day a thousand times in my head, trying to think if there was anything I could have done differently."

The admission was startling. Not because he felt that way, but because he'd said it out loud. "Well, stop it," she ordered. "You aren't a superhero."

He looked startled. "I'm not claiming to be, but you said you were angry about what happened. It's logical to think you're angry at me."

Tessa shifted restlessly. "Maybe in the beginning, but I never wanted to heap guilt on your head, especially for something that wasn't your fault. As stupidly illogical as it sounds, I'm mostly angry at Renee for coming up here in the first place. She loved studying in a library, not whitewater rafting. And if she had to come, why didn't she ask me to go with her?"

Clay shook his head. "She wasn't your responsibility. You're an outgoing woman who loves to try new things. Renee seemed far more introverted, so even if she wasn't competing with you romantically, maybe she felt the need to prove something you didn't even know about."

Was he right? Tessa felt a renewed stab of sorrow. She'd never felt the need to compete with her sister, especially since they were so different, but when they were kids, Renee had often tried to turn things into a contest between them.

"Renee was more successful professionally," Tessa said slowly. "I was working for our parents, while she'd gotten a promotion to associate professor at a private college. A publisher wanted a second book from her because the first one had sold so well. She was really going places."

"But were you happier?"

Tessa swallowed. "Maybe. I don't know. How do you measure happiness? I enjoy my life and what I do. It has purpose. I have stress and concerns about the future like most people, but I was happy, and I thought Renee was happy, too. She talked all the time about what she was doing and her plans. It could be hard to get a word in edgewise."

Molly nosed her way around Clay's leg.

Tessa crouched and gave her a hug, needing the contact with a warm, loving creature. She didn't know why, but she wished more than anything that she could just sit for an hour with Clay's arms around her.

She gave another hug to Molly and straightened. "Come in, I want to show you a selfie that Renee sent us a few weeks before the accident."

Tessa got the phone from her room and accessed the photo of Renee that she kept on her SUV's sun visor.

CLAY GAZED AT the picture of Tessa's sister, memories crowding forward.

"This is how Renee seemed the day of the accident. A little nervous, but determined. I've had hundreds of conversations with guests saying they want to challenge themselves. That's one of the reasons people take these trips. Renee and I spoke before we left and I didn't see any hint that she had doubts about going on the raft."

He returned the phone to Tessa and their fingers brushed, sending a warm pulse to his gut—partly from desire, and partly something more. The *something more* bothered him the most. He had too many responsibilities to consider a relationship, and Tessa was out of bounds, regardless. She was temporary, complicated and had too many reasons not to have confidence in him, despite what she'd said about her sister's accident.

And yet he couldn't stop thinking about her.

"I shouldn't be here," he said, needing to get out of the bunkhouse. "I'll ask someone else to go along as support on the trip today. The guests will understand."

"No, I'd prefer doing it. Tell me about the hike."

He measured the certainty in her eyes. "It's an easy one. About three hours of gentle walking this afternoon, and back tomorrow by the middle of the day, with pack animals leaving ahead of us, carrying supplies and belongings. This is one of the few overnight trips where children as young as eight are allowed, so it isn't strenuous. Daypacks are usual for snacks and beverages and I carry the usual safety items, such as bear spray and a first-aid kit."

"I'll get my gear ready. Do you want me to go with the wrangler and pack animals, or hike with the group?"

"Hike with the group. Bring your gear to

the staging area at noon. Because of being on the search-and-rescue effort this week, I planned to have someone else lead the outing, then changed my mind. This is one of my favorite trips because we introduce younger kids to the idea of backpacking without it being too difficult for them. I'll see you later."

Clay dropped the newspaper on a side table and hurried out.

Before Tessa's arrival, he'd never gone into the women's bunkhouse when it was occupied unless repairs were needed. She kept upending his best intentions. He *had* to remember to call from now on. And when necessary, arrange to meet at a neutral location, like the staging barn or the office.

It would have been smarter to send Tessa with one of the wranglers to deliver supplies and set up camp, but he'd foolishly turned down the option. Self-preservation should have sent him running for the hills the minute she'd kissed him. It wasn't the kiss itself—he'd kissed his share of women—it was the way he hadn't wanted it to stop that worried him.

Forever wasn't a word Clay used in connection with women, yet Tessa kept sending his thoughts there.

When he got to the yard shared by the ranch houses, he unlocked the gate to let Molly inside. She seemed to miss spending more time with him and he regretted the need to leave her with Aunt Emma and Derry. Still, she understood her role as his nephew's protector.

The ranch house seemed unnaturally quiet when Clay went inside and he looked around, seeing it in a different way than ever before. He'd done little with the place—even the furnishings were minimal. His mother teased whenever she came for a visit, saying it had less comfort and personality than a motel room. She was right, but he spent so little time at the house, what was the point of dressing it up?

Tessa, on the other hand, had added little touches to her temporary home that made it warm and inviting, like a plant on the table and a richly colored blanket on the couch with a Southwest-style pattern.

For a brief instant he wondered what her house in Tucson might look like, then banished the thought.

It would be best to stop thinking about her so much…yet he had a dismal conviction that not thinking about Tessa would be impossible.

CHAPTER ELEVEN

IN THE MIDDLE of the afternoon, Jillian took a break, climbing to the loft of the barn above the horses. The ring Andrew had given her swung on the chain around her neck, a constant reminder.

Even in the low light, the rosy shade of the gold glinted and she clenched her teeth. Andy had tried to talk to her last night, probably about the ring again, but there had been too many people around for a private conversation.

He was her friend, and real friends could do and say dumb things without ending friendships, so she needed to get over being miffed and forgive him.

Problem was, she wasn't entirely sure of why she was annoyed. True, it seemed wasteful and meant that Michael's ring wasn't being put to a good use. But, in a way, it had been a relief to finally leave the diamond solitaire in her jewelry box, like a door gently closing on the past.

So why did the new ring bother her?

Jillian settled down and leaned against a bale of hay. The loft was quiet because all of the horses were either out grazing in a pasture, or on trips. Yet almost immediately, her phone buzzed in her pocket and she sighed; there went her few minutes of peace. She pulled it out and looked at the display before answering.

"Yes, Mom. Is Dad all right?"

"He's fine. The doctor says he's doing extremely well, though he won't be able to dance at the party. So please stop asking that every time I call, it makes me nervous."

Mittens had followed Jillian up the steps and jumped onto her thighs. The cat settled down and began purring.

"You didn't see him go sailing off the barn roof. My heart still stops when I remember. What do you need, Mom? I'll be home in a few hours."

"I was hoping you'd ask Andrew and Derry to dinner. I just put a large pot roast in the oven and I'm making a pan of apple dumplings. It's their favorite and if they don't come, we'll have leftovers coming out of our ears."

Jillian rested her head on a post. "Mom—"

"I'm not trying to push the two of you together," her mother said quickly. "But we often have Andrew and Derry to dinner. How would it look if they stop coming to see us when everyone believes we're going to be related?"

Jillian ground her teeth, unable to say what she wanted in case one of the wranglers was downstairs and could overhear. Besides, her mother was right.

"Emma may already have a meal planned."

"I'll call to invite her and Lee, too. There's plenty of food and we can talk about the party. It isn't that long from now. I want to fix my peanut-butter-cup brownies and several other desserts, but Lee will have his own ideas and I don't want to step on his toes. Speak to Andrew when he gets back. It would make your father feel better to have company."

Guilt thumped in Jillian. Dad loved being around people and getting involved in community activities. His convalescence had been hard on him. "All right, I'll talk to Andrew. *Bye*, Mom."

She disconnected and looked down. Mittens was flexing her paws, looking extremely satisfied with herself.

"What do you think?" she whispered, rubbing behind the feline's ears.

A trilling purr sounded.

"Yeah, I know. It isn't your problem."

She waited another few minutes, then put Mittens on the floor and went down the steps.

Because of Mallory's comments about him being away from home overnight, Andrew was only leading day trips, though he preferred doing the longer ones. He was an easygoing guy, except where his son's well-being was concerned. Jillian was just as determined to protect Derry. She'd even marry Andy for real if it came to that.

For real?

Her stomach swooped and then settled. There wasn't any need to think about marriage as an option. Andrew had never come close to suggesting a marriage of convenience. His ex-wife didn't have staying power. Once she realized she couldn't profit out of the situation, she would go back to wherever she'd come from.

Still, was marrying Andy such a terrible idea? There were worse foundations for marriage than friendship.

Jillian went out to one of the pastures, trying to shake the thought from her head. In order to cover needs at both ranches, she'd moved a number of the weaned fillies and colts from her father's spread to the Carson Double C, along with a creep feeder. Clay didn't mind and everyone benefited. Guests enjoyed watching her work with them and the weanlings played and grazed with the elder horses, who not only helped to socialize the youngsters, but seemed enlivened by their youthful antics.

Nearly two hours later she saw a group coming around one of the hills. Andrew was so tall and well-built it was easy to spot him, laughing and talking among the others. He was great with guests—even better than Clay, whose intensity could get in the way of his relating to people. Not that she'd ever say that to him. He wasn't just her employer, he was almost as good a friend as Andy.

She finished with the last filly. Training at this age was primarily a series of activities such as lifting and inspecting their feet so they learned balance and were accustomed to being handled. Also grooming and leading them around by a soft halter, and making sure they didn't develop bad habits such as biting or striking out with their hooves.

Mahoney Horse Ranch was known for both

the weanlings and the fully trained young horses they sold. They had a long waiting list. Her dad had considered expanding when the Carson Double C came up for sale, then decided it was best to keep the operation within a more manageable size. But he felt better about having Clay next door, rather than someone he didn't know. Good neighbors were important, whether you lived in town or out in the country.

Jillian walked toward the barbecue area. The trips didn't all conclude at the same time, so there were a variety of entertainments that guests could enjoy when they were waiting for the meal. Options included volleyball, horseshoe, croquet and cornhole, where players pitched sixteen-ounce bags of dried corn at a board with a hole. A modified version of cornhole was available for young children, with smaller bags.

Andy was demonstrating the horseshoe toss. He was an expert and the watchers cheered as he threw three ringers in a row.

Jillian clapped, as well, and he looked over at her with a grin. "Hey, everyone, this is the fiancée I've been telling you about."

"I want to see your ring," a gray-haired woman exclaimed. Jillian obliged by lifting it on the chain for her to see. "How sweet and romantic," the guest murmured wistfully. "Andrew mentioned it was an antique, but he didn't say if it was a family heirloom."

Jillian met Andrew's gaze over the woman's head. He looked wary and she shrugged. It felt strange that he was telling clients about their supposed engagement, but he was probably just practicing for when he was around people who knew them both. Neither of them had much talent at putting up a false front.

"No, not an heirloom." She slipped the ring from the chain and put it on her finger. "But Andy knows I appreciate Victorian jewelry. I'm the head horse wrangler here at Carson Outdoor Adventures and I worry about damaging the setting, so I try not to wear it when I'm working."

Andrew put his arm around her shoulders, obviously doing his best to look the part of a pleased and proud fiancé. "She told me my choice wasn't a complete disaster."

Jillian narrowed her eyes as she looked up at him. "Don't put words in my mouth. You said that as a question, and I told you it was beautiful."

His warm blue-gray eyes twinkled at her. "Ah, now I remember. I'm never going to win a fight once we're married," he told the group. "She remembers everything too well."

A round of chuckles sounded.

"Oh, my, a disagreement. I want a picture of you kissing and making up," the gray-haired woman said, holding up her phone.

Andy bent and kissed Jillian before she could think of an excuse to duck out of the embrace. She expected both of them to start laughing, the way they'd laughed at Lake McDonald while trying to get a picture, but it was different this time.

Tingles spread through her and she leaned into him, her senses suffused with the scents of the grasses and evergreens he'd been hiking through, and the faint tang of his after-shave. Without thinking, she slid her arms around Andy's waist and felt the hard muscles of his back beneath her fingers.

When she finally collected enough of her wits to wonder what she was doing, Jillian stepped back and broke the contact.

She summoned a smile and looked at the guest who'd wanted a photo. "I hope you got a good one."

"I did, and I'm totally envious. Enjoy being young and in love—youth is gone so quickly."

"Now, Karen, we're more in love than

ever," her husband reminded her. "And I'm a great kisser. Leastways, that's what you've always told me."

"True," Karen agreed. "But remember what we were like at their age? Young love is special."

"So is a marriage that has lasted fifty years. That's right, folks," her husband said, looking proud, "we're celebrating our golden anniversary next week. My wife was the prettiest June bride who ever lived and still is. We honeymooned in Glacier National Park at the Lake McDonald Lodge. We're going luxury this time in a deluxe suite. I've always wanted my Karen to have the best."

Jillian was glad when the chorus of good wishes drew attention away from her and Andy. She didn't dare focus on him until the guests had drifted away to begin playing horseshoes.

"Sorry," he whispered and she shrugged, not wanting to show how much the kiss had affected her. He seemed so *un*affected that she wanted to douse him with a hose or something equally chilling.

Her reaction was probably just because she'd allowed the thought of marrying him to cross her mind. The congratulations they kept receiving from friends weren't helping, either. Everyone claimed they'd been expecting an announcement like this for years.

"Mom has invited you and Derry to dinner," she said, determined to be nonchalant. "She's calling Emma to invite them, too, in order to discuss the party. Pot roast and apple dumplings are on the menu."

"Uncle Lee doesn't like to be away from the ranch barbecue Friday through Sunday, in case he's needed by the kitchen staff, but Derry and I would love to come. Your mom's apple dumplings are the best."

"Talk to Emma first. I don't want to inconvenience her if she already had plans."

"I'll do it now." Andy turned toward the ranch houses and she sighed, knowing she had to go with him to keep up appearances.

The business of being fake engaged was a whole lot more complicated than she could ever have expected it to be.

THAT EVENING CLAY sat and watched Tessa telling stories to the three children on the overnight trip. She had a sense of whimsy tempered by practicality, and it crossed his mind that she'd be a wonderful mother. Tessa was different from the women he knew socially. The idea of settling down with her was starting to sound less like a loss of freedom, and more like an adventure. Not that she'd shown any romantic interest in his direction; her kiss had been one of exuberance, not desire.

Besides, how could they get around the past?

She knew he hadn't been dating Renee, but he was still intimately connected to her sister's death. And as if that wasn't enough of a problem, they weren't a good combination. She was emotionally engaged, while he struggled with showing his deepest feelings. She lived in Tucson and her career was geared to a hot desert environment. She had parents, grandparents and other family tied to the Southwest. And her face when she talked about the desert was filled with a yearning love, as if her inner being was fused with the place.

Clay didn't care for deserts; he preferred rivers and grasslands and wet meadows over dry heat, but he understood being in love with a place. As much as he appreciated his hometown, he still remembered the first time he'd seen the vastness of snowy peaks rising above Lake McDonald, and the thick forests marching up the mountains to meet the descending rivers of glacial ice. He'd envisioned it as a great battle between two imposing forces.

He shifted restlessly and put another small stick of wood in the fire. This was one of the few areas used by Carson Outdoor Adventures where he was willing to allow a campfire, but he kept it to a minimum.

They'd roasted marshmallows over the flickering flames, and once it got dark, the kids had wanted to tell scary ghost stories. The parents had shaken their heads, so instead, Tessa had begun telling them about the various animals they'd seen earlier in the day, making up comic tales and mixing in a few Native American legends. In her stories, wolves and bears were friends and heroic figures, rather than being villainous, fearful creatures.

She had a gift with kids. They listened intently, but so did the adults, who were leaning toward her to be sure they didn't miss a word.

"But aren't wolves bad?" asked the eight-year-old named Penny. "Mom and Dad aren't scared of them, but I am. Red Riding Hood and her grandma got eaten by a wolf."

"That's just a kiddy fairytale," her brother scoffed.

"Fairy tales mean different things to different people," Tessa said gently. "When I was your age, my dad told me that Red Riding Hood really isn't about a wolf, it's about learning to make the right choices, and understanding that if we make bad choices, we hurt ourselves and other people, too."

She looked up and Clay caught her gaze for a long second. He couldn't be sure she was talking about Renee, but it seemed possible. Renee had made choices, one of which Tessa didn't even know about, and they had affected everyone around her. The impact of those choices was still reverberating, months after her death. The irony was that Renee *had* been successfully facing her fear and dislike for the wild. She'd just made a terrible mistake the day of the rafting trip.

Penny made a face. "You mean like leaving the door open when it's cold outside, so everybody gets cold."

"And the power bill goes up," one of the adults said in an ironic tone. Wry laughter came from the other adults.

"That's right. Stories can help us learn," Tessa told the children. "My favorite stories are about being strong and brave and car-ing, because that's the kind of person I want to be."

"You 'n' Clay rescued Skeeter, even when you never saw him before." Penny yawned widely. "That was brave."

"The nice thing about our hearts is that they're big enough to care about people and animals we've never seen," Tessa said. "You care about Skeeter and you haven't met him. Isn't that right?"

"Uh-huh. I'm awful glad he isn't lost anymore."

Smiles wreathed the parents' faces and Clay knew he was also wearing a pleased grin. Tessa had a talent for making everything fit. He probably wouldn't have done nearly as well. Maybe it was his way of putting up barriers, though he wouldn't have seen it that way if it hadn't been for Tessa. She was making him take a long, hard look at himself.

"This has been wonderful, but it's time for bed," Penny's mother declared after another few minutes.

Though the children made a token protest, soon all of the guests were tucked in their tents, which had been set up a good distance from the fire ring.

JD, the wrangler who'd brought the pack animals, was already asleep. His morning responsibilities to pack up the gear wouldn't begin until after the group had departed, but JD was rarely averse to getting extra sack time.

Tessa remained by the fire, sketching in the small art pad she'd brought in her daypack. Clay moved to sit next to her and watch her work. The faint, flickering light imbued the drawing with a mysterious quality and it would have been easy to believe it was coming alive. That was something else that was special about Tessa—she was stirring his long dormant imagination, making him envision possibilities beyond the moment.

"You're very artistic," he said softly.

"More determined than artistic," she murmured. "My favorite professor in college believed that despite the increasing use of computer-aided design programs and 3D technology, landscape architects need to be competent at sketching. Some of the students disagreed, but Professor Watt felt that working solely with a computer limits creativity. I took art classes to get better, because my initial efforts on assignments were pretty sad."

"But right now you're drawing kids and animals, not plants and trees."

"The principles are the same. I want to give a picture to each of the children as a souvenir."

"We send group photos to everyone by email, but this is something kids might relate to better."

Tessa nodded, adding several details to her last sketch.

She hadn't asked Clay for copies of the group pictures with Renee, and her twin had never forwarded any to the family. Renee's email account still existed—it was with a free service—but the tricky part was figuring out the password. So far Tessa hadn't been successful. Her account at the college wasn't active, but they'd told her Renee had rarely used it.

"What are you pondering so seriously?" Clay murmured.

"Just this and that."

"Really?" He gave her a long look and she shrugged.

"All right, I was thinking about how to get into Renee's personal email account. Maybe I haven't tried hard enough, or I've been worried about what I'd see. If feels like prying, but she's gone, and it would tell me who she'd been communicating with outside of the family, if anyone. She didn't have a large circle of friends. Practically everybody at the memorial service was there to support the rest of us or because they'd worked with her at the college or taken one of her classes."

Clay brushed some of the dust from his jeans. "If it would help, I can forward the emails we sent to her from the company office, and any she sent to us."

"That would be nice. I looked at the company pictures because you asked me to sort them, but I didn't make any copies of the ones with Renee."

"Why not?" he asked, sounding surprised.

"It didn't seem proper since they didn't belong to me. And I never looked at any of the paperwork on her trips. Nothing like that. Please believe me, I had no intention of prying. We aren't trying to find someone to blame, we just want to understand."

"I believe you." Clay was silent again for a long moment. "You said some of Renee's students came to the service. That means they'd liked and respected her as their professor."

He was right and it made Tessa feel better. "I hadn't thought of it that way."

The flames in the fire ring brightened for a moment and Tessa saw the light reflect off a pair of wild eyes at the edge of the clearing. Then they abruptly disappeared, as if aware of being observed.

"About her email account, will the provider help?" Clay asked after another minute.

"Unlikely. I'm the executrix of her estate, but privacy rules are fairly strict. In any case, I'm afraid to ask for fear they'll lock the account or delete it. I may have gotten too complicated with my guesses. The password could be as simple as our birthday. Sorry for being preoccupied."

"Don't apologize. I can't imagine how it feels to lose a twin. I told you we could talk about Renee if it would help."

Tessa glanced skyward, memories rushing through her. There was no moon, and the stars were like thousands of tiny diamonds strewn against black velvet. Weaving through the middle was the Milky Way, as distinct as she'd ever seen it.

"Even a night sky can remind me of how different we were," she murmured slowly. "I remember the first time our youth group visited an observatory. Renee and one of the other kids refused to go back. They said that so much emptiness made them feel small and insignificant and they didn't like it."

"What about you?"

Tessa gazed upward again, vividly recalling her rush of excitement and awe. "I felt connected to something grand and amazing, as if I was on the same journey with Galileo and the Egyptians and Mayans and everyone else who's ever looked at a night sky and marveled at the vastness, or ever *will* look at it. And I was certain that somehow we were all touching across time and space. It wasn't about being small, it was about being part of something that was immeasurably large and mysterious. The desert is like that for me, too."

Clay didn't say anything for so long, Tessa wondered if he was trying not to laugh, then he released a long sigh. "I've never been able to express it, but that's basically how I feel out here. Especially when I'm alone and can just let the energy of the mountains run through me. It's as if all the layers in time are overlapping."

"Exactly."

The last flickering flames died in the

fire ring, leaving only a few glowing coals. Tessa closed her sketchpad, unable to see well enough to continue. She wasn't even startled when Clay put an arm around her shoulders and pulled her close to him; exactly the way she'd longed to have him hold her earlier in the day.

She rested her head on his shoulder.

The contact wasn't provocative with all the layers of clothing she wore. Pleasant days and cold nights seemed to be the norm this time of year, so she'd donned a heavy jacket before the meal. Clay was accustomed to the cooler, moister weather and was only wearing a lined shirt, allowing hints of his warmth to filter through to her cheek…and every part of her body.

"How often do you go into the wild alone?" she asked after a minute of gazing at the embers in the fire ring.

"Not as much as I'd prefer. None at all during the summer, but I have more opportunities the rest of the year. I also enjoy going to Yellowstone during the winter. That's an experience like no other, with the buffalo sweeping their heads back and forth to brush snow aside, searching for food, and the otters romping in the snow. Every now and then

I spot a wolf pack, either up here or there. They're exhilarating to watch."

Tessa thought about the storms she'd heard about across the northern states with subzero temperatures, howling wind and snow. She shivered. "So you're mostly out here by yourself when there's ice and snow?"

"More or less. Weather isn't completely predictable, especially at high altitudes, which is why I require tents for everyone."

"The primary reason I use my tent in Arizona is to make sure critters don't crawl in with me at night."

"I remember. Scorpions."

"I'm not crazy about waking up with rattlesnakes or large spiders, either," Tessa said in a dry tone. "Have you ever been in one of the really big storms, the kind that drops several feet of snow in a day or two?"

"Sure, it's exciting."

She shook her head in disbelief. "Don't you stay in your tent until the worst has blown over?"

"It depends on the wind-chill factor. But I don't deliberately go into the wild when a bad storm is expected."

"I understand why you don't want to get

married. A wife would probably be bothered about that kind of…um, *alone* time."

"I suppose that would depend on the wife."

Tessa frowned. It almost sounded as if he was asking a question, which was absurd. He'd been very clear on how he viewed marriage. "I think most people would be concerned when their partners take risks," she said cautiously. "Would you want a wife that didn't care? Presuming you wanted one, of course, which I know you don't."

"I suppose not. So, to not so subtly change the subject, what would you be doing back home right now?"

"Probably deciding which seeds to start for my fall garden," Tessa said, preferring the more neutral topic. "It's too hot for tomatoes during the summer unless you use shade cloth, so I grow them as fall and spring crops. But there are other veggies that do well in the heat."

"Then on top of everything else, you're a vegetable gardener."

"It's satisfying to grow your own food." She was quiet for a minute, enjoying Clay's closeness, and at the same time wondering if it was fair to draw comfort from him; she wasn't the only one who'd been affected by

Renee's accident. "I also have a number of fruit trees. My house is relatively small, but the lot is large. I could probably live off what I'm able to grow."

"I planted cherry and apple trees in the backyard when I first bought the ranch. They didn't do anything."

Tessa let out a small laugh. "Andrew mentioned he belonged to a family with brown thumbs."

"They definitely aren't green. And neither are the trees I planted. Your parents must be taking care of everything while you're gone."

"They go over and check, but they don't need to do much aside from picking the fruit. I installed a drip system when I bought the house and the ground around the trees is heavily mulched to limit evaporation. The rest of the yard requires even less maintenance. Mom says the temps have been hotter than normal down there, but our monsoon season should start soon and refill my water storage tanks. I harvest so much rainwater throughout the year, I rarely need to use any from the municipal system."

Tessa felt Clay shift and looked up to see him gazing down at her, though it was too dark to read his expression. "Monsoon season? I thought Tucson was in the middle of a desert. How can you have monsoons?"

"It *is* a desert, but I'm not talking monsoons like they have in some parts of the world. We get about half our rain during the monsoon season, which usually starts in June and goes into September. It cools down a little and there can be dramatic storms, with lightning and hail and flash flooding down the washes and low areas from sudden downpours. It's really something to see."

"Sounds different from here."

Tessa yawned. "Yup. It can frost in the winter, but snow is a rare event. And even when it does snow, it's usually just a dusting."

"So it's safe to assume you aren't a fan of major winter weather."

"I go skiing several times a year near Flagstaff, but for the most part, I prefer being warm." She looked up at him again. "You can't be that curious about my life in Arizona."

"Why not? It must be interesting if you enjoy it."

"That may be the nicest compliment you've paid me." She pursed her lips. "Or possibly the only compliment. No, I just remembered, you like the grass 'stuff' I put in the planters in front of your office."

A low chuckle rumbled from Clay. "You'd better go to bed. You're so sleepy, you're getting loopy."

He was right, but was she loopy enough to give him another kiss? Tessa curled her arm around his neck and pulled his head toward her.

"Are you sure this is what you want?" he whispered.

"As a rule, I fall asleep like a lamp switching off, so you don't need to worry that I'm going to take advantage of you. I'll be lucky to find my tent tonight."

"Then maybe I should wake you up enough to both find your tent and get into your sleeping bag."

"There's a thought."

A sudden childish giggle from one of the tents was more chilling than a splash of ice water.

Tessa hastily dropped her arm and stood. With no moonlight and barely any embers left in the fire ring, the most anyone could have seen was two dark figures, sitting close together. With the thick forest as a background, they might not have even been discernable.

But their behavior wasn't something that either of them wanted a guest to speculate about.

"Shall I make sure the coals are doused properly, or do you want to do it?" she asked.

"I'll take care of what's needed. Good night."

"'Night."

CLAY FOCUSED ON his task, rather than watch Tessa walk to her tent using her small flashlight. She was a terrible influence on his best intentions. "No romance on the trail" was a good personal rule, and had never been an issue before now. Women sometimes tried to flirt, but if they got together with someone, it wasn't with him.

Maybe Tessa's vulnerability was the reason he was having so much trouble drawing the line. Now that the barriers had come down, she was astoundingly open, talking about Renee and her childhood and everything else. In his experience, people like that could be easily hurt, and Tessa had already been hurt enough by her sister's death. He'd never been that open with anyone, even with his brother.

But Tessa… She seemed willing to bare her heart, and it implied a trust that he wasn't sure he deserved.

CHAPTER TWELVE

OVER THE NEXT few days Tessa tried to forget that evening by the campfire. It had just been the magic of the moment under thousands of stars.

She doubted Clay had feelings for her; and if he did, he'd never admit it, even to himself.

Grace and Nadia arrived, moving into the bunkhouse with a good deal of noise and energy. The two postgraduate students were pleasant, but they were decompressing from a year of intense study. Suddenly the TV was on or they were playing music and had friends coming and going at all hours.

Tessa hoped things would settle down once they started guiding groups. In the meantime, to find some peace and quiet, she'd gone hiking or looked for something else to keep her occupied around the ranch. She'd give them another couple of days and if things didn't improve by then, ask them to abide by a few basic courtesies.

"You're here even more than usual," Jillian said as they cleaned the horse stalls together. "I'm guessing it has something to do with your new bunkmates. You should tell Clay if there's a problem."

Tessa shrugged. She didn't want to complain. Clay could have asked her to leave after learning everything and she was reluctant to put demands on him.

Neither one of them had brought up their near kiss on the trip. The next morning they'd chatted politely and the guests had said nothing about their guides getting cozy— no winks or double entendres, either—so that part seemed to be all right. But she still wasn't sure how Clay felt about it, although he'd probably prefer the subject was never raised.

"It's okay," she told Jillian.

"Okay? You slept in the barn's loft last night."

"My new bunkmates were having what they called an impromptu high school reunion with a whole lot of booze flowing. I gave up around eleven and came over here with my sleeping bag. Four of the barn cats snuggled up to me and purred all night. It was the best slumber party I've ever attended. I may sleep up there for the rest of the summer."

"The loft is one of my favorite places, too, but I'm sorry you had to retreat to the barn, just to get some rest."

"That's okay. It must be nice to feel that carefree. Anyhow, I'm sure it'll resolve in a few days. They must know Clay expects them to be at their best while guiding trips."

"You can use my place until things improve," Jillian suggested. "There's more than one bedroom. It's a guesthouse my folks used to rent out to people on vacation. I won't even be there. I've been staying at the main house to help while my dad is recovering from his fall."

"You can't want a complete stranger in your home."

"The horses trust you, so I trust you, too," Jillian said simply.

"Thanks, I'll think about it."

Tessa didn't intend to impose on Jillian, but the offer was another one of those kind gestures that made her emotional, like when Ginny had offered to stay in Montana in order to go on the first trip that Tessa guided. She'd exchanged email addresses with Ginny and they'd been writing back and forth ever since.

The couple was having a wonderful time in Grand Teton National Park and Yellowstone, and planned to see the Bighorn Mountains and Devils Tower in Wyoming before leaving for Alaska.

I thought I would miss my garden more, Ginny had recently written, *but we're seeing so many of the things we dreamed about, I rarely have time to think about anything else.*

When Tessa returned home she was going to invite them to visit her in Tucson. Sharing her hometown and the desert with Ginny and her husband would be a treat.

Tessa finished spreading fresh straw in the last horse stall and then went over to the business office to tend the various planters. Once the roots were well established, they might not need much attention. A little rain seemed to fall throughout Montana's summer months and it might be enough to support the native grasses, even in planters.

Clay stepped from the office as she was coiling the hose.

"Have you decided what other landscaping you want to do out here?" he asked.

"A water feature would be nice, but I have

to research what would work best. What do you need me to do today?"

"Actually, I wondered if you'd like to go riding together," he said. "To relax."

Her jaw dropped. "I didn't think you ever relaxed."

"No matter what you seem to believe, I'm not a workaholic like my father. Look at me." He gestured to his jeans and long-sleeved tan work shirt. "No buttoned-down suit. No tie. I only sit behind a desk for a few hours each week. I spend over half of each summer leading a group, not doing paperwork."

Tessa wasn't convinced. "It wouldn't be the end of the world to admit you take after your father a little. Surely he's a decent person."

Clay's eyes widened. "Dad is terrific, he just came close to working himself into an early grave. It took a stern warning from the doctor to force him to take more time for family and himself."

"More time for family?" Tessa pursed her lips. "That's an interesting way to put it. Did you resent him for making his job more important than everything else? Because you're turning into a version of him whether you like it or not."

CLAY WASN'T SURPRISED by the frank comment; it seemed characteristic of Tessa.

"I'm not turning into a version of my father," he said firmly. "For one, I don't think he ever backpacked in his life. And I didn't intend to imply his job was more important to him than we were. He just thought he had to work extra hard to take care of us."

Yet even before the words left his mouth, Clay knew what Tessa was driving at. As a kid he would have preferred seeing his father more, rather than have the huge house and expensive bicycles and other niceties. Being one of the "rich" kids in a small town hadn't been a picnic, either.

But the truth was, lately Clay had begun to understand his father a whole lot better. Now *he* was worried about what would happen to Andrew and Derry if Carson Outdoor Adventures suffered another major setback like the one following Renee Claremont's accident. The outdoor adventure business had been more enjoyable before he started feeling as if the weight of the world would land on him if it didn't do well.

"There are more ways than one of being like someone," Tessa murmured.

"Let's drop it. What about that ride?" he

asked. "I thought we'd lead one of the four-night horseback trips later next week, so we should test our saddle legs, so to speak. I haven't gone riding for a while and I don't think you have, either."

"Aren't Grace and Nadia doing most of the overnight horseback trips this summer?"

Clay tensed. "Not any longer. They were still intoxicated when they got to the staging area this morning and they smelled like a brewery, so I told them to look for employment elsewhere. Did you get any sleep? I warned them about the noise around midnight. It got quieter, but clearly the party kept going."

"It was fine after I took my sleeping bag to the loft in the horse barn."

"That explains this." Clay reached over and plucked a piece of straw from her hair. "I apologize for them. They did such a good job the last couple of seasons, this was the last thing I expected."

"I take it they're moving out of the bunkhouse."

"After they sober up. How about the horseback ride? You can take Coal Dust, I know he's your favorite, and I'll grab food from the kitchen."

"I'd enjoy it, but I'm surprised you aren't leading one of the groups today in Grace's or Nadia's place."

Clay shrugged. "Maybe I control things too much. I asked Jacqueline and Alfredo to take over. They're two of my most popular guides and they always appreciate getting an extra trip."

"In that case, I'd love to go."

"Great. I'll meet you in an hour."

TESSA QUICKLY DISCOVERED that Coal Dust had one of the smoothest gaits of any horse she'd ever ridden. He was a sweetheart. She'd never ridden an Appaloosa before, but could understand why they were a favorite breed with Clay's company.

She and Clay rode east from the barn and then up a little-used trail into the hills, quickly leaving behind any signs of human habitation, without even a scrap of trash left by another hiker or rider.

"It's different here than in Arizona," she mused after a couple of hours passed in companionable silence. "We don't always remove human debris in the desert."

Clay looked shocked. "Why not?"

"Oh, I'm not talking about plastic bags,

aluminum cans and designer water bottles—I collect those. I mean historic items left by the early settlers, or artifacts from the Hohokam people or other Native American groups."

"That kind of trash is interesting."

"Yeah, it's tough to resist the temptation to poke further. A few years ago I found a leather trunk buried in the sand. It was partially uncovered after a violent summer storm. But I notified a museum about it and kept my hands off."

Clay frowned thoughtfully. "I recall a high school history teacher talking about 'historic trash' on the Oregon Trail. People got desperate and had to discard extraneous belongings from their wagons, just to survive. Then some of the immigrants still didn't make it."

Tessa remembered learning the same thing in school. "My teacher called the treasures left behind 'broken dreams.' It's sad to think about the mementos that were abandoned, things like teapots and wedding dresses and clocks. Sometimes family bibles or other bits and pieces."

"Broken dreams—that's a good way of describing it. But lightening the load from the start might have saved more lives," Clay said matter-of-factly. "Bringing items unnecessary for survival put them all at risk."

Tessa shook her head. "Things that feed the soul and inspire us are important. Don't you think the hope captured in a child's drawing or a grandmother's handmade quilt, for instance, could give someone the strength to go on?"

They'd reached a narrow spot on the trail and Clay rode ahead of her. Of all the men she'd seen riding horses over the years, he looked the best. His personal mount was a gorgeous blood bay stallion, strongly built like his owner, although Firestorm seemed to be slightly more mellow.

"I don't deny you make a good case," he said. "But I still think practicality should have won out. I also think this is something we'll never agree upon."

Tessa regarded him. Clay was sexy and determined. He was protective of his family and even laughed at some of the same things she did. But he saw life in a different way, keeping his emotions locked tight most of the time.

Or was that entirely fair?

He didn't reveal much to her, but why should he? She was practically a stranger.

Still, she would have liked to have met him years ago, before the serious businessman had taken over.

"I suppose not," she said slowly. "Um, speaking of things we probably don't agree on…about that night at the campfire. I'm sorry I got carried away. Again."

"You didn't see me fighting you off, did you?"

Tessa laughed. "No, but I still apologize."

"There were two of us there, and I put my arm around you first. To be frank, I'm honored you trust me. It can't be easy, all things considered."

He meant Renee.

Tessa hadn't followed up on her request to the sheriff's office, partly because she had faith in Clay's integrity. Yet that didn't stop the sense that something was still missing from the story. But she wasn't sure where trust figured as far as a kiss went, although she did know that her feelings for him were becoming confused.

A while later they rode into view of another beautiful mountain lake, even smaller than the one where the two-hour Carson Outdoor Adventures hike turned around. "This is gorgeous," she said. "Which trips come up here?"

"None, I'm not that generous. This is one of the places I keep to myself. We're on public land, but few people know that it's here." Clay dismounted and stood gazing at the lake. The water was crystal clear and reflected the surrounding evergreens and white-capped mountain peaks in the distance.

Tessa got off Coal Dust and gave his nose a rub. He nudged her chest and nickered. "You know I brought apples, don't you?" she whispered. His head tossed and she laughed. She opened the saddlebag, where she'd tucked several apples, and fed one to him, then gave another to Firestorm.

Clay set up a sliding hitch to allow the horses to graze next to a stream trickling into the lake. They immediately dropped their heads to the lush grass.

Tessa sat down and let the peace sink into her.

Perhaps it was the quiet serenity, but she suddenly realized what had been nagging her about Renee's accident. Last fall, the sheriff had given her Clay's name as the raft captain, then had said the guides and equipment weren't responsible. At the time she'd heard it more as a general thing. Guides, plural, as in the guides at the company. But maybe Clay *hadn't* been the only guide on the raft.

A shiver crept across her shoulders, though it couldn't make any difference. Even if more than one professional guide had been on the whitewater rafting trip, it didn't mean that either of them was responsible or negligent.

Clay sat next to her with the insulated bags he'd unhooked from his saddle. "You got quiet all at once."

"Did I?"

She forced a smile, unwilling to say anything about Renee or the accident. It could wait for another day and it would be better to read the accident report before asking any questions. She'd been patient with the sheriff's office, but maybe it was time to call or visit again and ask the status of her request.

"I was wondering if you camp up here in winter," she added.

"Now and then, when I want to get away."

"It must be nice to have all of this amazing wilderness in your backyard. Have you considered leasing any acreage as grazing land?" Tessa made a broad gesture, encompassing the lake and grassland they'd ridden from. "Presuming it's available for leasing."

"I don't have cattle to graze."

"Yes, but wouldn't a lease give you more say in who can come up here?"

He shrugged. "I'm not sure, and since I'm clearly not a cattle rancher, a lease application would probably be denied. Besides, assuming visitors don't do any damage, I wouldn't want to prevent them from using public land. It's great that so much has been set aside for preservation in the area."

Tessa opened the bag that Clay had given her and found an enormous sandwich on a sourdough baguette. The thinly sliced turkey and cheese filling was at least two inches thick.

"Seriously?" she asked. "This thing must weigh two pounds."

"Would you rather have roast beef?" Clay offered her the sandwich from his bag. "Uncle Lee mentioned he's never seen you eat beef at the barbecue, but I'm happy to switch."

"This one is fine, but I can't possibly get all of it down. My stomach would pop."

"Uncle Lee says you've lost weight since coming to Montana and he's concerned. Please don't think he's been eyeing you inappropriately or anything. Aunt Emma is the one who pointed it out to him," Clay said hastily.

Tessa laughed. "I didn't think he was. Lee Sutter is a true gentleman. But I haven't lost weight—I'm just hiking more than usual, so I've trimmed down and built extra muscle."

"Are you sure that's all? You didn't need to do any, uh, trimming down when you got here. That is, you looked fine then, and you're fine now." Clay appeared embarrassed, as if he'd committed a faux pas by referencing her weight.

Or was it a compliment?

It was hard to tell. She hadn't been kidding when she talked about how her romances kept turning into friendships. It could be discouraging, though Clay and her father were both right. She'd never been ready for a real relationship. Of course, that presumed the men she'd dated had been interested in something long-term, as well.

In many cases they *had* wanted to settle down. A good many of her male pals were now happily married and she'd also become friends with their wives. She was "Aunt Tess" to a number of children and had been a bridesmaid on several occasions. At one wedding, she'd even stood in as "best man" when

Hector's brother couldn't get back from Antarctica where he was doing climate studies.

Ironically, now that she was feeling ready for more, she was attracted to a man who'd openly declared he wasn't interested in marriage or having a family. If Clay had his druthers, he'd probably live in a remote wilderness log cabin, surviving on his wits and he-man skills.

"Tessa?" Clay prompted with a wary expression.

"You can assure your aunt and uncle that I'm fine." Tessa was touched that his family was concerned on her behalf. Despite the complicated situation, they'd been kind to her. "I do a fair amount of digging and lifting while on a landscaping job or in my garden, but nothing to compete with the amount of activity here. I'll miss it when I go back home in September."

They ate for a while in silence, then Clay cleared his throat. "I've been meaning to ask how your parents are doing."

Tessa scrunched her nose. "They're okay. We talk often and face calls are a big help, it's just that they're accustomed to me being there practically every day. Mom even brings breakfast burritos to work and we eat together in the morning. But it isn't as if they don't have any-one else. Every Sunday the family—grandpar-ents and aunts and uncles and cousins—gathers out at the Agua Hermosa. Some of them work for Alderman Pools and we're all involved in each other's lives."

"But your parents, in particular, are still grieving for your sister."

She nodded. "Yes. I think it's extra hard because Renee pulled away a bit before her accident. She said she needed to concentrate on her new position at the college, which was understandable, but then she left for Montana and now they're torn, wondering if it would have made a difference if they'd pushed harder. And *I* wonder if I should have en-couraged them to…" Tessa stopped and made a frustrated sound. "Sorry, sometimes the circles inside my head are exhausting. I go around and around and never come up with an answer, just more questions."

"I'm sure we've all done that at one time or another."

"Yeah, but now I also feel bad about Nadia and Grace. Maybe if I'd said something when they first arrived, they wouldn't have had that party last night and gotten fired."

She put the sandwich down on the insulated bag, her stomach full. How much did Lee Sutter think she could eat?

Clay shook his head. "Grace and Nadia are adults. If they can't restrain themselves without a housemother to enforce good behavior, they aren't right for the job. When someone is leading a group, whether it's for two hours or a week, they have to be reliable. What they did is their own responsibility. It has nothing to do with you."

Tessa contemplated her peaceful surroundings and tried to put a brake on her churning thoughts. She supposed feeling guilty about Renee could lead to a sense of guilt about all sorts of other things. "You mentioned Nadia and Grace had done a good job last summer and the year before that, right?"

"Yes, but they were living with their parents and I only assigned them to day trips. I'm not happy about firing them, but I couldn't take the chance of sending them out with clients after they showed such poor judgment."

CLAY LEANED AGAINST a rock and stretched out his legs. He wasn't surprised Tessa felt bad for the guides he'd fired. She cared about people, enough to be concerned about the fate of two annoying bunkhouse roommates she barely knew.

His own disappointment had practical elements. He would have to look for more guides, or use a tighter rotation of the ones already on the payroll. A tight rotation was chancy, because an illness, injury or family emergency could throw everything off. Andrew was leading a fair number of the day hikes already, and Clay could count on Tessa to do others as long as she was in Montana, but that still left a coverage issue.

"Are you going to hire more guides?" Tessa asked, as if she'd read his mind.

"Thinking about it. There are fine ones available, it's mostly a logistical question of locating them and doing full background checks. It would be a whole lot easier if Oliver hadn't broken his ankle."

Tessa made a face. "I'm sorry he got hurt, but I'm glad not to be still stuck in the office. Of course, you probably would have fired *me* by now for messing up. Especially over the coffee fiasco."

"Ah. About that…" Clay contemplated the laces on his hiking boots. "Oliver recently found the supply sheet Andrew filled out, with the note about how much coffee we needed. What he wrote was pretty vague. Why didn't you explain how the mix-up occurred? You couldn't have thought I'd be angry at my own brother."

"Because it was still my fault. I should have double-checked instead of making assumptions. Anyhow, Andrew is your family and I'm temporary. Why make waves for him?"

Clay was afraid Tessa's soft heart would get her in serious trouble someday. But at least Andrew had stopped worrying about her being on the ranch once he'd seen the note and understood how the mistake occurred. It was also a reminder that they needed to be more careful when someone new came to work for them. Like most companies, Carson Outdoor Adventures had a shorthand language that could be easily misinterpreted.

"I think you should finish your sandwich," Clay said, ignoring the question, which was rhetorical and attached to a thought that was becoming difficult to contemplate—Tessa being temporary. He enjoyed her company too much.

"I've eaten as much as my tummy can hold. Do you want the rest?"

"Sure."

She handed him the sandwich. While he

was eating it, several elk came to the water's edge across the lake. He saw Tessa's attention was on the animals, her face filled with appreciation.

"How fast do an elk's antlers grow?" she asked after he'd finished the sandwich.

"About an inch a day. A set of antlers can weigh forty pounds by the time they stop growing each year and lose their velvet."

"That's a whole bunch of antler to strut around with."

He grinned. "Yeah, I'm grateful humans don't have them."

Tessa put her head back and regarded him. "I don't think antlers would become you. And imagine the challenge of making a cowboy hat to fit."

"True." They were in shade now, so Clay removed his worn hat and set it to one side. He didn't wear a cowboy hat for show or to create an atmosphere for guests—they were simply the best hats he'd found for hiking or riding.

"What were you like as a kid?" Tessa asked.

"According to the girls I knew back then, an incorrigible flirt. Even in grammar school."

He loved her quick smile. "Incorrigible,

huh? And I wasn't sure you even knew *how* to flirt."

"I have my moments. But I decided early on that it wasn't the tone I wanted to set on my outdoor adventure trips."

Tessa yawned and stretched, the fabric of her shirt pulling taut against her breasts. Clay averted his gaze; it didn't help.

He was too aware of her.

It would be best if she found her answers sooner rather than later, and going on a rafting trip might help. He wasn't blind. Despite what she'd said about believing he wasn't responsible, she wanted to see him in charge of a whitewater raft, to be assured that nothing had been amiss.

"Uh, Tessa, there was a cancellation for the raft trip on Monday, if you want to go. It's the half-day excursion."

She straightened. "I'd love to come along. Will you be the captain?"

"Yes. It's a pleasant outing, quiet most of the way, with just a few miles of rapids. It isn't on the same river," he said flatly, seeing the question in Tessa's eyes.

He was torn. While a part of him longed to explain exactly what happened the day her sister drowned, he also wondered if it was self-serving. He wanted Tessa to think well of him, but telling her the unpleasant details would throw a bad light on her twin.

What difference would Tessa's good opinion make once she returned home? And yet the thought of her returning to Arizona disturbed him more and more. She pulled him out of himself, stirring parts of his nature that he'd buried or forgotten.

Tessa was even reminding him of the intense, almost mystical connection he'd felt to the northern Montana wilderness.

CHAPTER THIRTEEN

WATER SPLASHED IN Tessa's face as the raft rushed through the turbulent rapids.

"Left forward, four strokes," Clay called from his position in the stern of the raft.

The instructions were simple and easy to follow for the less-experienced rafters on board. Tessa had captained whitewater rafts in the past and was impressed by Clay's calm control.

"All back, three strokes," he called.

Excited squeals rose from the others as they entered a narrower channel of the river. Clay read the currents with an uncanny accuracy, calling out commands and using his longer paddle to help maneuver and steer. After another mile, they exited the rapids into a more calmly moving section of the river.

Tessa had ridden rapids with a much higher degree of difficulty, but none since Renee's accident, and her heart had pounded through the miles of whitewater. She glanced back and locked gazes for an instant with Clay. It hadn't been a difficult run, so the strain around his mouth suggested he might also be remembering the accident.

She looked forward again and flexed her fingers in the rigging gloves he provided for the rowers. They all wore life jackets and helmets, and he'd meticulously gone over the various guidelines for safety. Nothing was wrong. Nothing even *close* to going wrong had happened, yet she was sick to her stomach.

Enough was enough. As much as she'd enjoyed rafting, she might avoid it in the future.

At the landing site down the river they were met by one of the van drivers from Carson Outdoor Adventures. Another crew was there in a truck to collect the helmets, life jackets and other gear, and to transport the raft. All the work of rafting, except for paddling on the river, was handled by Clay or his employees.

Back at the ranch, Tessa made a beeline for the bunkhouse, only to hear Clay call her name. She stopped reluctantly and turned around. The barbecue wouldn't start for another hour and a half and she wasn't hungry, regardless.

"Are you all right?" Clay asked.

"I'm fine. I just didn't…I didn't expect the trip to bother me this way," she admitted. "I never went rafting with Renee, but I guess it's one of the 'firsts' after losing someone, like the first Thanksgiving and Christmas. Firsts aren't easy. Our birthday was the worst. I'm not going to celebrate birthdays any longer. I don't think they'll ever get better."

He lifted a hand as if to touch her, then let it drop. "What can I do to help?"

She was grateful he didn't offer platitudes or tell her not to feel bad. Some people did that out of the best of intentions.

"I'm just going to take a long shower and…" Tessa's voice trailed because she didn't have any idea of what would help.

"How about a ride?" Clay suggested. "You're welcome to take Coal Dust."

Tessa wanted to throw her arms around his neck and hug him, but it wasn't the right place for that kind of display. "Yeah, I'd like that. But I can't go alone. Except for our ride the other day, I don't know the horse trails around here."

His smile washed over her. "Then get your shower and I'll meet you—"

"In an hour," she said, finishing for him.

Tessa rushed to the bunkhouse. She didn't

want to think about why Clay had known the right thing to make her feel better, or why it meant so much to her.

Maybe it meant a lot, simply because he'd cared enough to suggest something.

LATER THAT EVENING Andrew knocked on the Mahoneys' front door.

Evelyn Mahoney answered, holding out her arms to Derry. "Come in, Andrew, it's lovely to see you again so soon."

"Auntie Eve." Derry lunged from his father's arms into hers with his usual enthusiasm.

She laughed and hugged him close.

Andrew spotted the grandmotherly light in her eyes. He understood what Jillian was worried about, but he wasn't quite as concerned. Derry could benefit from another grandmother and Evelyn was terrific. Besides, he and Derry would always be in this area and friendly with the Mahoneys.

"It was nice of you to ask us to dinner again," he said, though he wondered if he should have accepted the invitation. Clay and Tessa had gone on a rafting trip together that afternoon and he'd hoped to talk to his brother about it afterward. But then Clay had left almost immediately for a horseback ride. *With Tessa*.

Andrew wasn't sure what it meant. She was a good person and she loved the outdoors, but he didn't know what would happen if his brother developed feelings for her.

"We always enjoy having you and Derry," Evelyn said. "Besides, I hoped to talk more about the party."

"Mom, you know it's just pretend," Jillian protested as she came into the living room and accepted a hug from Derry.

This was one of her official days off from Carson Outdoor Adventures, not that she took many of them during the summer. She went back and forth between the Carson Double C and the Mahoney Horse Ranch, setting her own hours and doing whatever was needed at both facilities.

"Pretend engagement, real party," Evelyn said firmly. "We're going to have fun. The doctor told us today that your dad will have the cast off his leg by then, though he won't be able to dance yet. Roger, don't forget what Dr. Tanaka said today, *no dancing*," she told her husband.

He returned her smile. "That'll be hard. We met at a barn dance."

"I remember. You were doing a do-si-do with Donna Greyson."

The two shared a private smile. Like Andrew's parents, they were a devoted couple. He admired them, but was embarrassed that even though he had grown up with great examples of marriage to follow, he'd made such terrible decisions with Mallory.

How could he have seen anything in her when he had a woman like Jillian, right in front of him?

The thought brought Andrew up short.

Jillian was remarkable.

She was beautiful, sensitive, talented and absolutely the most wonderful woman in the world. But was there any chance she cared about him in the same way?

Care?

Andrew kicked himself. Even now he was being cautious about his emotions. He didn't just "care" about Jillian as a friend or a woman—he loved and adored her. How could he have been blind all this time?

"What's wrong? Your face reminds me of someone who just got run over by a team of horses," Jillian whispered in his ear.

"Uh, well, I'm thinking, that's all."

She grinned. "Be careful, thinking is uncharted territory for you."

"Very funny. Obviously you still haven't forgiven me for getting the ring. Though I really don't understand why it was such a terrible crime. And it isn't like you to stay upset."

She held her left hand in the air and light glinted from the rubies and diamond in the setting. "I'm upset because you didn't talk to me before you went shopping, even after I said no."

"It wasn't all your decision. I'm not one of your wranglers or one of your dad's employees," Andrew reminded her.

Jillian blinked. "I didn't mean it that way."

He knew she hadn't, but he thought there was an underlying message in her objections, most likely because she didn't want things to change between them. He'd worried about the same thing, too. Over the years their friendship had been a constant, something they could both count on.

If he told her how he felt, she'd probably claim he was being swept away by the moment. But he was sure his feelings were real. It certainly explained his odd emotions when she'd gotten engaged to someone else and his reaction to seeing her put on his ring…and the way he'd felt when they had kissed.

On top of that came another thought—why would Jillian fall in love with *him*? He'd shown poor judgment by dating Mallory in the first place. His son was an unexpected gift from the disaster, but his ex-wife was a problem, and could continue to be one for the rest of Derry's childhood.

Then he remembered what Jillian had told him a few weeks ago. *You can't keep blaming yourself for what happened… We all make mistakes—you have to stop beating yourself up.*

Perhaps it was time to let go of the guilt and self-blame. A lot of people married badly; it didn't make him a man she couldn't or shouldn't love.

Andrew focused on the elder Mahoneys, who were talking to Derry with the fond attention of grandparents. Roger Mahoney sat in a narrow companion wheelchair, his broken leg propped on a soft ottoman—using crutches hadn't been practical with his broken ribs and arm.

"How are you tonight, sir?" Andrew asked, going over to sit on the couch next to the wheelchair. He ruffled his son's hair.

"Better every day. I'm no spring chicken any longer, so it was a relief to have the doctor say my bones are fusing well. But getting good news didn't stop the itching." Roger picked up a pencil and was easing it under the edge of the plaster on his leg, when his wife reached over and took it from him.

"You aren't supposed to be sticking things inside the cast," she scolded. "Do what Dr. Tanaka said—tap over the area where it's itchy, or we can try blowing air underneath the plaster with a hair dryer."

Andrew remembered the one time he'd worn a cast. The desire to scratch had been the most frustrating part of the experience, even more difficult to take than the break itself. The severe pain hadn't lasted long, but the itching had seemed to last forever.

"You've been lucky, Dad," Jillian told him.

"Lucky how?" Roger grumbled, determinedly slapping the plaster. From his expression, it wasn't helping the underlying itchiness.

"Because we've mostly had cool days. Imagine how much worse it would be in hot weather."

Roger smiled at her. "That's my daughter, trying to see the bright side of things,"

Andrew agreed, reminded of the evening he'd learned about Mallory showing up at the Carson Outdoor Adventures office. Jillian had said his ex might not have returned for negative reasons. That was one of Jillian's amazing qualities—even after losing her fiancé in a senseless crime, she wasn't a pessimist. She had her downhearted moments, the same as everyone, but they didn't last.

The meal was delicious, with Evelyn talking about the desserts she was going to bake for the upcoming Fourth of July party. Aunt Emma and Uncle Lee hadn't been able to come for the pot roast and apple dumplings the other evening, but the two couples were conferring over the phone. His mom was getting involved, as well, planning to make vast amounts of her strawberry shortbread cake—always a favorite—and lemon chiffon trifle. Uncle Lee was complaining that they weren't leaving anything for him to do except make the ice cream.

After eating, they sat on the deck playing a game with Derry. Game nights with their hosts had been a tradition when Andrew and his family were renting the guesthouse. Andrew had never missed one of the old-fashioned get-togethers, though when Clay had gotten old enough, he'd usually gone off on his own, exploring.

"What's on your mind?" Jillian asked when they were doing the dishes later. "You've had a weird expression all evening."

"Just this and that."

JILLIAN SHOOK HER HEAD. She knew Andy better than practically anyone and could tell he wasn't acting like himself.

"Did Mallory do something?" she asked.

"No. Although it bothers me that she's still hanging around. I keep expecting to get a letter from her lawyer, with a list of demands. It's strange that she hasn't taken action."

"I don't think a custody agreement can be changed easily. Isn't she the one who proposed the original arrangement?"

"Yeah, money in exchange for full custody. She probably knows it wouldn't look good in family court."

Jillian dried the pan that Andy had rinsed, lost in thought. She didn't doubt that his ex was someone who skated on the edge of the law. Was it possible she'd skated *over* the edge once or twice?

"What about a background check?" Jillian

asked after putting the pan in the cupboard. "It might be interesting."

Andrew sighed. "My lawyer did one during the divorce negotiations. Found speeding tickets and other traffic violations, nothing more. Well, she was named as a person of interest in a pyramid scheme investigation before moving to Elk Point, but there was no arrest warrant. It wasn't anything we could use."

"Maybe she's *more* than a person of interest now."

Andrew handed her the lasagna dish he'd washed. "That's possible. And there's no telling what she's been up to since the divorce. Getting all that money out of me could have made her cocky and careless."

Jillian put the casserole dish in the cupboard and tossed the damp dish towels into the hamper. "Exactly. I don't relish the idea of getting Derry's mother into trouble, but it's in his best interests for him to be kept away from her. We thought Mallory would leave if she believed we were engaged, but she's still here. So let's do something about it."

"I'll ask for another background check," Andrew said as he rinsed the sink. "I can do an online search myself, but it's best to go through the proper channels."

"Right." Jillian took her phone from her pocket. "In the meantime, let's get some selfies with the new ring. I didn't want to take chances, so I've deleted the pictures I took that showed the other one."

"Sure."

Andy's smile spoke volumes, she just didn't know exactly what those volumes were all about. He put his arm around her waist and pulled her snugly against his chest.

"Go ahead and take those photos," he whispered in her ear, and a slow, delicious quiver crept through her body.

Something had changed, and she liked it.

ON THE MORNING of the extended horseback trip, Tessa called her father's cell phone. His face popped up on her screen.

"Good morning, Tessa-bear."

The old nickname made her smile. "Hey, Dad. You're cheerful this morning."

"You know how you keep saying I should stop drinking espresso all day?"

She nodded. "Yes, along with the doctor and Mom."

"I finally did it a few days ago. Admittedly, I had the temper of a wet polecat while getting used to no caffeine, but I finally succeeded."

"That's wonderful. What led to such a momentous decision?"

"Your mom donated my espresso makers to an animal-rescue thrift shop. Both the espresso maker at home, and the one from work."

Tessa chuckled. "Direct action, leading to direct change. That's her motto."

"Well, she expects me to be around for another forty or so years. It's only right that I cooperate, seeing as she's already put so much time into improving me."

"I think it was a team effort. Are the clients happy with the landscape designs I've been doing?"

Her father's head bobbed on the small phone screen. "Yes, though they'd rather have you here, overseeing everything. How much longer are you staying in Montana?"

"As I told you, I don't feel right leaving before the end of the season. Clay took a chance hiring me as a trainee guide."

"Hmm. Would I approve of this Carson fellow?"

It was an unexpected question. "Um, yeah, I think so. He can be hard to figure out sometimes, but he's a great guy. Responsible and hardworking. I know that Mom blames him for the accident, but that really isn't fair."

"Sweetheart, she doesn't blame Mr. Carson, and neither do I. We wish we knew why Renee went up there, but that wasn't his fault. It's just that he's so close to what happened. You said they weren't dating. Are you sure?"

"Yes." Tessa shifted uncomfortably and cleared her throat. "I finally got into Renee's email account the other day and found a string of messages. She wanted to get back with Neil."

"What?"

"She wanted to reconcile. He didn't."

"Our poor baby. She was too good for him," Chuck Alderman said roundly. "What did he say?"

"Just that he couldn't return to spending his life with someone who refused to take any risks, along with a few other things. Basically, it was the same old stuff from their divorce."

Her father's face saddened. "They were a poor mix."

"Maybe coming to Montana was her way of proving she could change," Tessa said slowly. "His email before she left for Montana said if she'd been a little more like her sister, they might have been able to work things out. You know, Clay has asked a couple of times if Renee could have been trying to compete with me in some way or another. Now I wonder if it's true."

Her guilt had intensified upon reading the email message from her former brother-in-law. Yet it had also confused her. Neil wasn't a bad guy, so why would he say something hurtful? The divorce had been amicable. And the money Neil had given Renee beyond the community property division suggested he'd cared enough about her to provide financial security.

"Tessa-bear, you aren't responsible for any of this," Chuck said gently. "From the very beginning Renee was a shy baby, while you were endlessly curious about the world and everything in it. Just two very different personalities. When Renee became passionate about Renaissance art, we hoped the academic world would be the right place for her. And she really seemed to blossom there."

"I remember. Look, I called to tell you I'm going on a four-night horseback trip. We leave this morning. I've sent the codes on the GPS tracker I carry. Also Clay's satellite phone number, but please don't use it except in an absolute emergency."

"We understand. Oh, and that horse in the picture? What a beautiful animal. I hope he's the one you're riding on the trip."

She grinned, feeling more relaxed. "Yes, I am. Coal Dust is wonderful. I absolutely adore him."

"Then I'll see if Mr. Carson is willing to sell one of his horses. Your grandparents would be happy to keep Coal Dust at the Agua Hermosa."

Tessa wished she could hug him—a virtual hug just wasn't the same as an old-fashioned bear hug. "Dad, I adore you, but I'm not seven years old any longer and you can't buy me everything I admire. I'll hate leaving Coal Dust behind, but he's better off in Montana."

Her father looked disappointed. "But I want you to be happy."

And I want you to come home.

The unspoken words hung in the air, as clearly as if he'd said them aloud.

A sigh welled from Tessa. "I *am* happy. I just want to find a few more answers. Look, I love you both, and we'll talk again when I get back from the trip. Right now I need to pack the rest of my gear, I don't want to be late."

"All right. Be sa—" Chuck stopped. "Just have a good time. We love you."

Be safe.

It was what her father had started to say, and she appreciated him holding his tongue. They'd worried more about her since Renee's accident, but at least they hadn't fought her going to Montana. Partly because they wanted answers, too.

Tessa ended the call and packed the remainder of her gear into a duffel. She put some basic items in her daypack, unsure whether she'd wear it, or put everything in Coal Dust's saddlebags. The last thing she grabbed was the GPS tracker. She should get a similar device for her solitary rides in the desert.

The bottom of Tessa's stomach dropped at the thought.

As much as she missed home and her parents, leaving Clay was going to hurt terribly. For the first time in her life she was falling in love, and it was with a man who was totally wrong for her.

CLAY WAS WORKING in the staging area, but his mind was elsewhere. He was sure something was bothering Tessa more than usual. Ever since the rafting trip she'd been quiet and withdrawn. The silent horseback ride they'd taken afterward had eased some of the pain in her face, but she wasn't talking to him nearly as much.

The irony of missing those intimate discussions didn't escape him—after all, he was a guy who'd never enjoyed heart-to-hearts.

The guests loved her, so she must be talking with them, at the very least. She'd taken three groups on half-day hikes this week, and even though they had encountered a black bear the previous afternoon, she'd kept everybody from overreacting.

Tessa is wonderful, one of the men had exclaimed to Clay during the ranch barbecue. *She had bear spray ready, but she knew it was only bluffing. She had us wave our arms over our heads and stomp and yell. That huge bear left and didn't even look back.*

Clay hadn't gotten an opportunity to compliment Tessa, because while she'd eaten a small meal with her group at the barbecue, she had quickly left. He'd wanted to follow her and ask what was wrong, but had decided it might be best to give her some space.

It was better that way.

Then this morning, while heading to the

staging area, he'd spotted a delicate metal sculpture framed by the grasses that Tessa had put in the planters around the office. It was a winged fairy, blowing on a dandelion head as the seeds trailed away. The whimsy would delight people who enjoyed that sort of thing, yet was subtle enough that more practical guests could ignore its presence. It was such a great choice, he'd have to say something.

"Good morning. What can I do?" Tessa asked from behind him.

Clay turned and measured her expression. He'd thought she was resolving some of her torn feelings over Renee's death, but at the moment she looked more troubled than he'd ever seen her. He didn't know if he should keep getting deeper involved, yet his chest ached at the pain in her eyes.

"The wranglers pack everyone's gear," he explained, unsure of what to do or say. "They'll also fetch and stow the food from the kitchen. One of them will take the pack animals up to the first camping site, using a more direct trail. So right now we're mostly waiting for everyone to arrive."

"I saw Grace and Nadia here yesterday morning. Are they on the payroll again?"

Clay shook his head. "No, but they apologized, and sent an apology to you, as well. They seemed too embarrassed to ask if I'd reconsider their employment." He sat on the edge of one of the tables. "By the way, your group couldn't stop raving about how you handled that bear."

"Oh." Tessa blinked as if she'd forgotten about the encounter. "It was just a young, curious male. He was easily discouraged, but everybody felt as if they'd conquered Mount Everest when he ambled away with an aw-shucks look in his eyes."

"Bear encounters are rare and each one is different. From what I've heard, you dealt with the situation exceptionally well."

"Thank you."

Silence fell until Clay cleared his throat. "You must have gone out early this morning to put up that fairy-and-dandelion thing."

Tessa smiled faintly. "It's a woodland sprite. The surface is artificially aged, but the patina will continue to develop over time so it'll blend in even more. I got it from a local sculptor. She's quite talented."

"I'm usually not in to that sort of thing, but I like it. Let me know the cost and I'll reimburse you."

Tessa shook her head. "It's a gift. I was going to the sheriff's office yesterday morning and got sidetracked."

Clay's nerves went on alert. "The sheriff's office?"

The unhappiness in Tessa's eyes seemed to deepen. "To ask about the accident report again. I've realized more than one guide was on Renee's rafting trip, but Sheriff Maitland was very clear when I talked to him after the accident that your company and the equipment weren't at fault. So I don't understand why he's dragging his feet about letting me see the report."

Clay felt as if a war was being waged inside his head.

Spencer Maitland didn't want Tessa or her family to be hurt unnecessarily, and his own feelings aside, Clay had agreed until this moment. But if it was making things harder for Tessa and raising more doubts, then she and her family would have to know the whole story. And he could explain it more gently than a cold official document.

"This isn't the right place to talk about it, but we might get some time on the trip," Clay said. "If not, when we get back to the ranch. Reports like that are upsetting for families to read, which is why Spencer has been reluctant to show it to you. He's had experience with this kind of thing. So at least let me tell you what's in it first."

Tessa nodded and some of the distress seemed to ease from her face. "All right."

Clay hoped he was making the right decision. Ultimately, the sheriff probably couldn't prevent the Alderman family from seeing the accident report, but most people didn't push to know the unpleasant details. Spencer just hadn't realized how determined Tessa would be.

Neither of them had.

CHAPTER FOURTEEN

Jillian laughed as she and Andy squirted each other with hoses. She'd offered to help wash down the staging area with him and things were getting out of hand.

"It's good that Clay can't see us now," she said, hitting Andy with another stream of water and dodging the retaliatory spray.

"Because he'd think we were too immature to work for him?" Andy grinned. "My brother is too serious. What's life without a little play? It's okay to be silly sometimes—that's one of the things fatherhood has taught me."

Jillian swept a drip from her chin and giggled, unable to remember the last time she'd carried on like this. She'd avoided some of the deluge, but was still wet in a number of places, including her shirt.

Andy seemed to have noticed, too.

She took a deliberately deep breath and his eyes glazed. It was immensely satisfying. The past few days had been fun. Something had changed the night they'd taken pictures of them with her new ring. They hadn't talked about it, but she liked what was happening.

The funny thing was, they'd always been committed to each other as friends. There was nobody she trusted the way she trusted Andrew. She just wished he'd stop kicking himself so much because of Mallory, though he seemed to be improving when it came to self-blame. He'd even joked about the predicament with his ex-wife a couple of times lately, which was major progress.

The concern about Mallory remained, but the longer she waited to take any action, the more they wondered if she had something to hide. Maybe she hoped to simply scare them into paying her to go away, or was watching to see if the engagement was real, or to find another weakness. But Andrew was an amazing dad and the Sutters provided a platinum-standard level of childcare. Paying Mallory again would be like paying a blackmail demand when nobody had anything to hide.

He'd be better off going to family court and presenting all the evidence against his ex-wife. If Mallory was even willing to go that far, which seemed doubtful.

"Have you talked to your lawyer?" Jillian asked after they'd rolled the hoses and brought them back to the storage room by the picnic area.

"Yes. Gordon had already started an intensive background check. Some of the online databases aren't always complete, so it can take a long time to be sure. He's also checking variations of Mallory's name, including nicknames and alternate dates of birth. He did that before, but now he's widening the search."

She nodded. "Seems like you both have it covered. That's good. I feel bad, because if she's had a true change of heart, this has to be hard on her. But you can't take chances with Derry's safety."

"Do you have plans for dinner?" Andrew asked. "I thought we could go to the Taste of Sicily café. I already talked to Aunt Emma to let her know I was asking you."

Jillian cocked her head. "Not pizza, then? We usually go out for pizza and have to talk them into making it half-cheese for Derry's sake. I don't get what's so complicated about half-cheese. We don't ask for a discount."

"I guess when you're the only pizza parlor in town, you don't appreciate special orders. But I meant just the two of us going.

You know, like a date. Would you rather have pizza?"

Just the two of them sounded nice.

"I'd rather go to the Taste of Sicily. I've been craving scampi. We don't risk preparing seafood at home because Dad is so allergic to it. Even a trace amount can make him sick."

"Then I suppose crab puffs and shrimp cocktails are no-no's on the hors d'oeuvres list for our wedding reception."

"I suppose." Jillian pressed her lips together, fighting a smile. Having Andrew joke around about their mythical wedding no longer annoyed her. Instead she felt a sense of longing. She'd come a long way since she had first announced their fake engagement, though it had mostly started bothering her when her mom suggested they might fall in love for real.

Strangely enough, Jillian knew the pretense of being engaged had forced her to move forward. Or maybe it was Andy who'd done that. One thing was sure—she no longer felt as if she was living in some kind of limbo. She still didn't know what the future held, but it was exciting to think about the possibilities.

Especially if one of those possibilities was Andrew Carson.

THE COUPLES WHO'D booked the horseback riding trip wanted to explore independently after reaching the campsite on the second day. Clay went over the safety guidelines another time, handed out cans of bear spray and recommended two well-marked trails. Each couple was also loaned a GPS tracker.

A number of outdoor adventure companies offered periods of independent hiking as part of their packages. Clay had resisted incorporating a similar feature for a long time, but even Aunt Emma had declared he was overprotecting his clients. So, on the second and third day of this particular trip, there was a shorter horseback ride in the morning, with a longer period at the campsite in the afternoon to allow for solitary exploration.

The two wranglers were unsaddling the horses and would set up the tents when they were done, so Clay looked at Tessa with a question in his face.

She nodded and he gestured to a trail he hadn't shown the clients, headed in the opposite direction from everyone else. If they were going to talk about Renee's accident, they needed complete privacy, away from both guests and employees.

They hiked silently until they reached a

vantage point over a narrow ravine with a rushing creek at the bottom. Ferns and bushes concealed most of the current, but the sound of flowing water rose, along with the chirping of birds. In the distance, the ravine widened and the water spread out in a marshy, verdant meadow.

"A friend of my parents had me install a large water feature near her home-office window," Tessa murmured as they sat on a fallen log. "The doctor recommended reducing her stress to help resolve her high blood pressure and she thought the sound of moving water outside her house would help."

"Did it?"

"I like to think so. When it's cool enough, Patricia opens the windows and sees birds and dragonflies flitting around. And *my* stress was reduced when she agreed to use a system to collect rainwater. It seems strange to be in Montana, where so much water is available."

"There are excellent arguments for conservation here, too."

Tessa shrugged, then a smile peeked out. "You could benefit from a system on the ranch, especially with the amount of water needed for the horses and scrubbing down the picnic area every evening."

He wanted to suggest she stay and oversee the installation of a rainwater collection system, but he couldn't think why she'd agree to do such a big project so far from her home. Besides, once she had the answers about Renee, she might simply leave. How many times had Tessa made it clear that her heart was in Arizona and the desert?

"I'll think about it," Clay said. He took his canteen from his belt and turned it over in his hands, difficult memories flooding his mind.

TESSA WAITED, REALIZING Clay was trying to find a way to explain what had happened the day of Renee's accident. It couldn't be easy for him.

He finally sighed. "You know I don't allow beer or other alcohol on any of the company's rafting trips, right?"

She nodded, surprised. The rule was clearly stated on the website and he'd made it clear at the start of the rafting trip earlier in the week. It made sense. Alcohol was responsible for a lot of accidents on the water. The liability release was very specific on the topic, as well.

"Folks can drink in the evening if we're

taking them on an overnight trip," he continued, "but not on the river. It isn't worth the risk."

His grim tone made Tessa shiver. "I agree."

"We've always provided beverages—juice, soda and water—to drink while rafting, but some of our guests have preferred bringing their own reusable bottles. The challenge was that I couldn't be certain of what was *inside* those bottles. So this year I instituted a new rule that no personal containers would be allowed until we were in camp."

A prickle of warning ran across Tessa's shoulders. "I saw it in the release, but didn't know the provision was new."

Clay looked at her with a bleak expression in his eyes. "I had to do it because of Renee. She brought orange and lime juice in her canteen, heavily spiked with vodka. In fact, it was mostly vodka, with just enough juice to mask some of the alcohol odor. She didn't touch it until a half hour before we reached the rapids, then she gulped most of the contents. We know it was vodka because the canteen was recovered later and the remaining contents analyzed."

"You mean Renee was drunk."

Clay nodded. "The coroner did a test after

she was found. Her alcohol level was extremely high. During the whitewater run, Renee started declaring how brave she was and that nobody could say she wasn't willing to do something new. Then she suddenly threw off her helmet and life jacket and stood up, rocking back and forth. The raft started to flip and almost everyone on board was thrown in the rapids."

Tessa began to feel sick.

"Who else was hurt?"

"Aside from minor scrapes and bruises, none of the guests besides Renee, and the coroner thought she might have survived if she'd still been wearing her protective gear. The water was fast, but barely an intermediate level. Her injuries indicated she was knocked unconscious prior to drowning."

"You said none of the guests were hurt—what about you and the other guide?"

Clay was silent for a long moment. "Andrew was the other guide that day. He was okay. I had a few injuries. I tried to help Renee, but she was panicking and broke free. A person in that state can be remarkably strong and not realize someone is trying to help them."

"How badly were you hurt?"

"Bad enough."

"How bad?" Tessa asked insistently.

"I... Well, a broken arm, some lacerations and internal bleeding. I was trying to protect her and got swept into rocks a couple of times."

Tessa crossed her arms over her stomach and pressed hard, trying to quell her nausea. Cold beads of perspiration broke out on her face. "So Renee came close to killing everyone, including you."

"She didn't intend to hurt anybody," Clay said gently. "She was scared and used alcohol for false courage. It was the catalyst for her other behavior. I think she was trying to prove something to herself and it went too far. I'm not even sure she intended to drink, but brought it just in case she started to lose control."

"Trying to prove she wasn't afraid to take risks," Tessa muttered, recalling what her former brother-in-law had said in one of his emails to Renee.

Something cool and damp pressed to Tessa's forehead and she stared at Clay. "What?"

"You're awfully pale," he murmured. He poured more water onto the bandana and dabbed her cheeks and throat. "You know, I probably didn't spot the family resemblance because you're so fundamentally different from Renee. Even now it's hard to see how she could be your sister."

"And it's a wonder your family can stand the sight of me," Tessa whispered.

Clay shook his head. "Would you blame me if the situation was reversed?"

"No, but the situation *isn't* reversed. I can imagine what those witnesses said about her."

"They were angry and used language they probably regretted later, while I keep wondering how I misread what was going on that day on the raft."

Tessa let out a humorless laugh and a hint of color returned to her face. "You can't read minds and Renee was an expert at keeping emotions to herself. Anyhow, I told you before, you aren't to blame."

"Neither are you," Clay said firmly. "Okay. We both have to accept that this was Renee's doing, however unintentional. Spencer and I didn't want your family to know the unpleasant details, but not telling you was clearly a mistake. Your family needed answers about why it happened, so knowing *what* happened might have helped. At the least it may have enabled you to move forward."

Tessa's fingers were curled so tightly they hurt and she tried to straighten them. "Is it possible Renee was trying to kill herself? I haven't wanted to admit it, but that's what I've been afraid of since it happened."

"*No.* Spencer asked the same question, but I think your sister just wanted to confront her fears. We all do that at times. She never struck me as irrational. I still don't understand why she claimed we were dating, but maybe it was connected to her pride."

Tessa's eyes burned and she blinked rapidly, but the tears still fell. "I managed to get into her email account a few days ago. Before she came to Montana, she was trying to reconcile with her ex-husband. Neil said that while he still loved her, he couldn't be with someone who wouldn't take risks…who had no adventure in her heart. He also said that if she'd been a little more like me, they might have been able to make their marriage work."

Clay said something beneath his breath. "That was a cruel thing to say."

Tessa stared into his angry eyes. "It sounds as if she was trying to show she *could* be more like me with the backpacking and rafting, but I swear, as much as I enjoy outdoor sports, I've never been reckless or put other people in danger. And I barely know Neil. Why would he compare us?"

Clay dripped more water on the bandana and pressed it to Tessa's wrists and the insides of her elbows. He was so gentle her throat ached.

"We don't know what was going on in either of their minds," he said. "But it would have been kinder if he'd honestly explained there weren't any conditions under which they could reunite. Instead, it sounds like he tried to put all the blame on her."

"Renee was under a huge amount of stress at the time," Tessa recalled, the tightness inside of her beginning to unwind. "She'd been promoted to associate professor and the college was urging her to get her second book ready for publication. They saw her as their rising star, which was good, but it also meant expectations were high."

"So her ex-husband wrote those things to her when he likely didn't know she was more vulnerable than usual and doing her best to cope."

Tessa smiled sadly. "Yes. Neil shouldn't have mentioned me, but while I'd love to blame him for everything, the accident was still Renee's doing. She chose to sneak alcohol onto the raft, even though she knew it wasn't safe and against the rules. She acted rashly, and if she'd lived, I'm sure there would have been consequences."

For a few minutes Tessa concentrated on breathing and collecting her composure.

"Do you think Renee believed I was involved with Neil?" she asked finally.

"Nobody could suspect you of being underhanded."

Tessa gave him a wry look. "Oh, yeah? You thought I'd gotten the job at Carson Outdoor Adventures to make trouble for your family."

"Very briefly, and mostly because I was worried about my brother and nephew. Custody issues are tricky."

"Surely Andrew isn't in danger of losing his son. He's too good of a father," Tessa said.

Now that she knew Andrew had been the other guide on the rafting trip with Renee, she understood how Clay and his brother would worry about the accident being used in a custody battle—even an implied failure in reliability might sway a judge.

"It's unlikely, but when it comes to Derry's safety, we're all sensitive. When Mallory walked out on the marriage, she also abandoned Derry. Left him alone in their apartment. Andrew was at work, so a six-month-old baby went without food or care for over eight hours."

"That's awful. Is that why you're keeping Molly with Derry and Emma most of the time?"

"Yeah. I miss having Molly on hikes, but Derry comes first and she would never let a stranger approach him."

CLAY KISSED TESSA'S FOREHEAD, wishing there was more he could do. At least her skin was no longer as cold. Perhaps he should have delayed the discussion until after their return to the ranch, but putting it off again could have been worse. And if Tessa read the accident report now she'd be prepared for its blunt, official tone. The coroner's statement alone was enough to haunt Renee's family.

"I'm sorry for what she put everyone through," Tessa said. "I must have made it worse by showing up here."

"Don't apologize. It was a tragedy we all wish could have been prevented. For her sake, and for you and your family. As for you being in Montana?" Clay brushed the bandana down the curve of her cheek. "I'm glad you came."

Tessa's eyelids flickered. She lifted the braid from the back of her neck and fanned herself with her other hand. The expression in her eyes remained sad, but she was no longer pale.

"I'm still unhappy with Neil. *And* my sister," she said. "But I'll get past it. Did Renee ever get comfortable with being in the wild?"

"I wish I could give you an unqualified yes. While she was able to carry her own backpack, she was still struggling with some aspects of hiking and camping. But she was getting better and I think she was enjoying herself more."

Tessa didn't say anything else for a long while, then she frowned. "Clay, you said you had to change the liability release because of Renee. Did somebody sue you?"

"No, but my insurance company wanted everything spelled out in the body of the release, even though it already stated that clients agreed to abide by the company rules." He rocked forward. "Do you want me to have someone ride up here to take over the trip? They could get here quickly, and then we could go back early, or do whatever you want."

It was an offer he couldn't have imagined

making a month ago, but Tessa had become more important to him than anything else in the world.

"I'm fine," she whispered. "Maybe it's for the best that I didn't know all of this before I accessed Renee's email. Now the pieces are starting to fit. You see, she forwarded all of the Carson Outdoor Adventures group pictures to Neil, not to us. She was trying to show him that she could change."

"Did he ever reply?"

"If he did, she deleted the messages. My mom and dad will have to know what happened. It will be hard for them to hear, but Renee was an adult and responsible for her choices. I think they'll be able to accept that. It's what they always taught us. I just wish she'd confided in me about Neil."

Clay gestured to the satellite phone on his belt. "Do you want to call your parents? I can step away and give you privacy."

"I already told Dad about Renee hoping to reconcile with her ex-husband. I'll let them digest that piece of news for a while. When we get back I can do a video-conference call with them both and explain what happened. We need a little time to deal with all of this.

I'm sure we'll have more than one long call over the next few weeks."

"Then you're staying for a while."

Tessa met his gaze. "If you'll have me, but I don't want to cost you any time, or cause any problems."

"You've been a valuable addition to Carson Outdoor Adventures. But I wouldn't care, I'd still want you to stay."

Clay looked down and saw he had laced their fingers together.

He'd never been overly demonstrative, but with Tessa it seemed instinctive. He wanted to hold her, not just out of desire, but for comfort and the simple pleasure of touching.

Their lives were still far apart, but he wasn't going to run from what he felt; something important was happening between them and they both knew it. He wasn't sure where it would lead, but he would be a fool not to give it a chance.

"Could we walk for a while?" Tessa asked.

"Sure."

They stood and continued along the trail, Clay keeping a close watch to make sure she was steady on her feet. Yet he also trusted her instincts. She'd done an amazing job with both Aiden's and Skeeter's rescues, staying energized with her positive attitude. Clay didn't doubt that her optimism had buoyed Aiden when he was still worried about his lost dog.

Of course, Clay had come to the conclusion that there was little Tessa couldn't do.

I've got it bad, he acknowledged. So much in love he could hardly see straight.

And maybe, for the first time in his life, he also had something completely right.

CHAPTER FIFTEEN

TESSA SAT CROSS-LEGGED on the bunkroom couch, laptop on her knees, trying to assess the expressions on her parents' faces.

She'd contacted them using a video-conferencing application and the discussion had been going on for almost an hour with alternating tears and smiles. They wanted to remember the wonderful things about Renee, not just how she'd died.

After returning from the three-night horse-back trip, Tessa had found a large manila envelope waiting for her. When she'd opened it, she found a note from Sheriff Maitland, along with a copy of Renee's accident report.

Clay contacted me yesterday and asked that you be given a copy. I'm sorry if the delay made things worse, but please know it was with the best of intentions. Nobody wanted your family to experience more pain than it already has. I never met Renee Claremont, but if she was your sister, I think she must have been a special person, who simply made a mistake she didn't have time to set right. S. Maitland

"Mom, Dad, do you want to see the accident report?" she asked.

Chuck shook his head. "We've learned what we needed to know. I've been afraid Renee killed herself, and that somehow we missed the signs."

It was what they'd all feared, but hadn't wanted to acknowledge to each other.

"I think Renee was simply trying to figure out how to live more fully," Tessa said slowly. "She just made a bad choice that day."

Her mother wiped the tears from her cheeks and squared her shoulders. "Tell Mr. Carson we're sorry he was injured, but we appreciate him trying to save her."

"You'd really like Clay. He's a good man."

Melanie leaned closer to the computer camera. "And you're in love with him."

Tessa sighed. "Is it that obvious?"

Melanie sniffed and smiled. "Yes. Is he in love with you?"

"We haven't talked about it, but I think he

feels the same. He has trouble opening up, and that's a challenge in any relationship. It's complicated even more because my entire life is in the Southwest, and his entire life is here in Montana."

Tessa saw her mother and father give each other a long look.

"I don't believe a woman should always be the one to give up her career and home," her mom said finally, "but I have to point out that if you're in love with Clay Carson, then your entire life *isn't* in Arizona."

"I hate to agree on this particular issue, but your mother is right," Chuck added. "As usual."

Tessa struggled to hold on to her composure, knowing how difficult it must have been for them to say something like that—in essence, that they would understand if she decided to stay in Montana.

"I've been researching Elk Point," Melanie said, looking thoughtful. "It sounds like a pleasant town. I doubt they need a pool construction company, but I also couldn't find a single business that installs systems to harvest rainwater."

"And thanks to Tessa, we know quite a bit about the subject," Chuck added. "A company that operates just a few months out of the year would be a nice change for folks within ten or so years of retirement. A few months in Montana, the rest in Arizona. That could work. Not that we'd let you interfere too much with our daily lives, Tessa. We need time for ourselves."

"Now, Chuck, we could babysit once in a while," Melanie interjected. "That would be all right. And maybe have a Sunday dinner now and then."

Tessa started laughing. "Promise you won't decide anything unless I have a ring on my finger," she said.

Her mother blew a kiss into the screen. "Promise. We're leaving in a couple of days to drive up there. Maybe see a few sights along the way. We wanted it to be a surprise, but after all this, I thought you should know."

"If you get here by Independence Day, there's going to be a huge barn dance at Carson Double C," Tessa explained. "It's an engagement party for Clay's brother. Kind of a town shindig. I'm sure you'd be welcome."

Chuck rubbed his hands together. "A barn dance? That sounds great. I'll make hotel reservations. We can always sightsee on the way home."

"I don't know if we should go to the party, dear," Melanie said. "It might be awkward for the Carsons."

He nodded. "True. Well, we don't have to decide now."

They talked another few minutes before saying good-night. Then Tessa sat for a long time, absorbing the calming atmosphere of the ranch. Her parents' generosity in affirming whatever choice she made was incredible, but a life with Clay in Montana was still a huge step.

Even if her parents started a business and lived in Elk Point part of the year—which was a big *if*—the rest of her family still lived in the Southwest. She loved the desert and would have to learn a lot in order to practice her profession in Montana. And winters in the north would be radically different. Supposedly Elk Point wasn't snowed in for months at a time, but there was plenty of snow at the higher elevations. It would be hard watching Clay take groups out in freezing weather, and even harder to watch him go out by himself.

Then she thought about his gentleness while telling her about Renee's accident. The concern in his eyes that he hadn't tried to conceal, the anger on her sister's behalf at how Neil had responded to his ex-wife's overtures. The way Clay had offered to have someone take over the trip, so he could be there in whatever way she needed. And there had been other moments when he'd revealed something deep within his soul.

Clay wasn't sentimental and he had trouble opening his heart, but he would do anything for the people he loved.

Couples had started out with a whole lot less going for them.

ANDREW FINISHED TALKING to his lawyer and couldn't resist pumping his fist in triumph as he ended the call. Mallory was gone, or soon would be. And she wasn't likely to return.

He went to the playroom and gave his son a grateful hug. Despite the stress Mallory had caused, he couldn't regret having known her. Because without his ex-wife, he wouldn't have Derry.

"Is Daddy happy?" Derry asked, hugging him back.

"Daddy is very happy."

Derry let out an exaggerated sigh. "I don't like when you be sad."

"I know. I'm sorry I've been acting funny lately."

"Not funny. *Sad.*"

Andrew laughed and hugged him again. Derry understood more nuances than many children his age, but "acting funny" was a concept that might take longer.

"Okay," he said. "I'm going out to talk to Jillian."

Derry instantly stood up. "I wanna go."

"Not right now. Daddy and Jillian need to have a grownup talk," he told his son. "But I'm sure she'll come to see you soon."

"Goody. I love Jilly *this much*!" His son opened his arms as wide as he could get them, his small fingers stretching out.

Andrew smiled broadly. "So do I. Now give Daddy a kiss and I'll see you later."

His son's kiss was noisy and accompanied by another hug.

Andrew winked at his aunt as he left the house and gave her a thumbs-up. She'd known he was calling the lawyer, so she'd guess that he'd gotten positive news.

Jillian was in the pasture, working with her weaned fillies and colts. He climbed the fence and walked out to her.

"You seem pleased," she called.

"More than pleased." He pulled her into his arms for a long kiss, his pulse surging with hope and pleasure.

JILLIAN HAD SEEN the embrace coming and she reveled in the moment; it was the first time they'd kissed without someone watching or as a show for their fake engagement.

Finally, Andrew lifted his head a few inches, keeping her tightly held against his chest.

"Mallory is no longer a problem," he said. "It turns out that she married me without getting a divorce from two prior husbands, so she's committed bigamy twice. She's also done time for fraud and blackmail. All under various names. There are several warrants out for her arrest."

"Then we don't have to worry about her any longer."

"Not until Derry starts asking about his biological mother, then I'll have to do some careful explaining. But maybe he'll be so happy about his new mommy, he won't get curious for a while."

"New mommy? Who would that be?" Jillian teased. They hadn't talked about the future, but she was certain where they both wanted it to lead.

"The woman I've been in love with forever and didn't know it. The woman who doesn't hesitate to tell me what she thinks and when I've messed up. Who backs me up, even when I do something stupid, and then helps me fix my mistake. A woman who's so beautiful she takes my breath away."

"Oh. That's a relief. For a minute I thought you were talking about me."

Andrew laughed and the rumbling sensation against her made Jillian shiver with anticipation. "You know who I'm talking about."

"Yeah." She kissed the tip of his nose. "I'm in love with you, too. Surprised the heck out of me."

He tipped her chin upward to gaze intently into her sparkling green eyes. "I know how much you cared for Michael and dreamed of a life with him. He was a terrific guy and he would have become a great friend of mine, as well. But we can have our own dreams. Just as big. Just as wonderful."

"No argument here. And at least I won't have to teach *you* how to ride a horse or split a piece of firewood."

Andy stared for an instant, then laughed.

"That's right, I'm not a city feller. I can already ride a horse, build a fire, chop wood and repair a roof."

"Uh-uh." Jillian shook her head. "No more roofs for this family. We call in a roofing company, or the deal is *off*."

"Okay, if that's your last word on the subject."

"It is."

"Then you'll marry me?"

Jillian lifted her left hand and admired the engagement ring she wore. "Of course. After all, we've already done most the work of being engaged. It's been announced in the newspaper. People have congratulated us. We even have an engagement party scheduled for next week."

"It would be a shame to waste all of that effort," Andy said solemnly.

"Waste not, want not, as my grandmother always says." Jillian smiled and kissed him again, pleased he'd been confident enough not to ask if she loved him the way she'd loved Michael.

Love couldn't be compared, because each person was different. She loved Andy and his son completely and wholly, and that love would just keep growing and growing. And maybe with time, they'd have more children to share it with. There was no question about it—she was the luckiest woman in the world.

TESSA SAT BY Bull Moose Lake enjoying the late afternoon sun and quiet.

The past several days had been frantically busy between the work to get everything ready for the engagement party and still cover the trips during the Fourth of July week. Then Clay's parents had arrived. From what she'd gleaned, they normally came up the first of July and stayed into August, but had decided to get there a few days early to take a larger role in preparing for Andrew's engagement party.

Tessa liked the elder Carsons, though she'd had little opportunity to speak with them. Laura Carson looked younger than her years and had a warm, energetic nature. Russell Carson was an older edition of his two sons and his manner reminded Tessa so much of Clay that her jaw had dropped. Clay's sister was also there, on a break from her postgraduate studies.

But with their arrival had come another concern—how would they feel about her?

The family had been eating their evening

meals at the ranch barbecue, but tonight they were having a gathering at Andrew's house. Clay had asked her to join them, but she hadn't felt comfortable about it, too aware that Renee had been responsible for Clay being seriously injured.

Nonetheless, warm satisfaction filled Tessa. Clay had hired three new guides on a provisional basis and was looking for more, so he'd asked her to lead as many of the short day hikes as possible while he observed how the new employees handled trips. In turn, it gave Andrew more freedom to take groups on overnight excursions.

Doing the day hikes meant spending less time with Clay, but his trust meant a huge amount to her.

Tessa sighed.

She wondered about fate and what her life might have been like if she had never met Clay Carson. It made her feel odd, but if she believed in fate, then maybe they would have met another way, regardless. It was a nice thought, one she would hold on to.

Her parents were on the road, leaving Javier in charge at Alderman Pools. Her own team was often called on to help clean up after a storm in the monsoon season and they'd been in contact a couple of times, just to touch base.

She closed her eyes and filled her lungs, drawing on memories of the stunning storms that crashed over the Sonoran Desert. The feel of the air, the wind blowing, water gushing down normally dry washes, lightning cracking across the sky…

The sound of footsteps jerked her into the present and she twisted to see Clay coming up the trail with Molly at his side.

"I see you're ready to repel unwelcome visitors," he said, his tone light as he gestured to her hand.

Tessa made a face and released her grip on the can of bear spray to give Molly a proper greeting. "I just don't want to be somebody's dinner. Speaking of which, I thought there was a big Carson gathering tonight."

"It doesn't start for a couple of hours. Were you thinking about the desert? You had a homesick look on your face."

Tessa shrugged noncommittally. "It's odd to think monsoon season has started down in the Southwest. The weather is so different here."

Clay sat next to her and Molly plopped down near the edge of the lake, plainly happy that life was getting back to normal. For the first time in weeks, she'd been going on trips with Clay, and she loved it.

"We may not have monsoons," Clay said, "but our dry thunderstorms over the mountains have their exciting moments, especially when they start fires."

"Ugh."

He grinned. "You'll probably prefer the Northern Lights. We start seeing them more often in August. My mom says they look as if someone is spraying liquid light across the sky."

"I'm looking forward to it."

A breeze ruffled the surface of the lake, blurring the reflection of hills and trees.

"How many new guides do you expect to need?" she asked. "I thought you were just going to replace Nadia and Grace, but you've hired three guides and are looking for more. Oliver is getting nervous—he doesn't want to work in the office for any longer than necessary."

"I expect to need all of them, along with Oliver. Gunther Computer Systems called a few days ago. They want a contract. We've been hammering out the details."

Tessa was thrilled with the news. "That's wonderful. What prompted it?"

"Our rescue of Aiden and Skeeter. Andrew sent the owner copies of the newspaper articles that Ruby Jenkins wrote. Trask Gunther is a dog lover, too."

"I knew that interview would raise your company profile," she teased.

"Getting publicity from a rescue makes me uncomfortable," Clay admitted. "That isn't why I'm a member of the ECSR. I would have told Andrew not to send the articles, which he knew, so he didn't ask."

"I'm glad he took the initiative. I wish I'd thought of it." Tessa stretched out her legs and wiggled her toes, thinking how strange it was to be enjoying herself so much. After her sister's death, it had seemed impossible that she'd ever be happy again. Yet she'd found peace. And somehow, she was certain that wherever Renee was, she was at peace, too.

"How are your folks doing?" Clay asked after a moment.

"Better. Actually, they'll be in Elk Point tomorrow. They left a few days ago to drive up here. It's the first time Mom and Dad have taken a summer vacation since I was a small kid. Summers are a busy time in the pool business."

"I hope they're coming to the barn dance. It's turning into an even bigger deal than we expected."

Tessa scrunched her nose. "I told them about it, but Mom isn't sure they should attend. I'm not sure about me, either."

"I don't see why not."

"My sister nearly got you killed," she reminded him. "Your parents won't forgive that quickly."

Clay lifted her hand and laced their fingers together. "My parents aren't holding anything against you or your family. In fact, they're unhappy with me for not insisting you spend more time with us."

Tessa drew a quick breath. "Why would that make them unhappy? I'm just a contractor."

Clay gave her a long glance, filled with humor. "You know that isn't true. They're hoping the party on Wednesday will be a double-engagement celebration. They firmly believe you're the only woman on the planet who could convince me to get married and have a family. And they're right, of course.

It's amazing how wise parents become at a certain point."

Tessa swallowed, trepidation and hope and a thousand other emotions flooding her heart. "I don't want to *convince* you to do anything you don't want to do."

CLAY LEANED OVER and kissed the curve of Tessa's neck. Her scent filled his senses.

"Bad choice of words," he murmured. "How about this? They know you're the only woman I would ever *want* to marry."

"Better. Not a lot, but a little."

"You're going to be tough to please. I like that. Maybe this will do it—my entire family knows that you're the only woman for me period. Full-stop. And I agree. There's no one else I would give up Montana and move to the desert to make happy."

Tessa's eyes widened. "You aren't serious."

"Completely and utterly. I love you, Tessa. Before you came, I'd forgotten how to dream, or even what having an imagination felt like. So I'll leave Andrew in charge here, and move to Tucson to start a new branch of Carson Outdoor Adventures. One that specializes in taking people into the desert and up into the mountain ranges around the city."

"No."

Clay shook his head. "I'm following you, no matter what. I'm too much in love to ever live without you again. I'll read and study and you can teach me about desert ecology while you create sustainable landscapes. We'll wow the world together."

"That isn't what I meant." Tessa threw herself against him and they tumbled backward, kissing and laughing.

When he could finally get his breath, he looked up at her. "Then what did you mean?"

"I'm staying in Montana. I love it here, too. It will take some adjustment, especially in the winter, but I have a few ideas about how to fit in. First off, I'm going to make Carson Outdoor Adventures a showcase for my abilities as a landscape architect."

"You are?"

"That's right. You're going to love my ideas. Everyone will want to hire me. We'll also have the best system to harvest rainwater in the entire country."

"So I'm losing a terrific outdoor guide, and gaining a prizewinning landscape architect." Clay threaded his fingers through her thick, silky hair and pulled her head down for another lingering kiss. Loving Tessa was like being set free and he would be grateful for every moment they had together.

"I'll still be a guide sometimes," Tessa said breathlessly when the kiss ended. "But I also want a fruit and vegetable garden, along with my own career."

"No problem. You can have as much space as you need and I'll have a contractor build a giant greenhouse. You'll have to decide which features you need, but do you think we can have one that doesn't look too out of place with the barns?"

IF IT HAD been possible, Tessa would have loved Clay even more for his suggestion. A greenhouse where she could grow plants and vegetables to her heart's content was just what she'd need on a cold, snowy Montana day.

"I'll do my best," she promised.

"Then there's just one more thing."

Tessa raised her eyebrows as Clay sat up and reached into his pocket. He took out a jewelry box. Her breath caught when he opened it. Inside was a lovely sapphire engagement ring.

"Tessa Alderman, will you marry me?"

"Yes."

They kissed again and she didn't think it was possible to be happier.

EPILOGUE

One year later

THE RANCH'S SECOND Independence Day party was in full swing, with revelers spilling out into the picnic and games area. Children who weren't interested in square dancing were having fun with the cornhole toss and other games.

Cars filled the parking lot and lined the road. A hayride shuttle helped transport guests who hadn't come early enough to get a convenient spot, or just wanted a ride in the sunset.

Tessa was cuddled with her husband on the office porch swing, close enough to hear the music and laughter, and far enough away to have privacy for kisses and whispered conversation. They'd enjoyed sharing the responsibility as party hosts, but had wanted a few minutes to themselves.

Clay's strong hand covered the small baby

bump on her abdomen. While it was early to expect any movement, he was determined to share the first flutters with her, if possible.

Though he still enjoyed taking groups out, particularly if she came along, he was staying home more and kept his weekly hours to a reasonable number. They'd visited Tucson several times during the off-season and he had become fascinated with desert ecology. And more cautious. His first scorpion sting had taught him a healthy respect for the arachnid.

The sound of water spilling over rocks by the porch lulled them both. The small stream at the base of the waterfall was surrounded by ferns and other growth. Tiny lights hovered, blinking on and off in a random cycle, looking like fireflies. They'd been created by a local artist, at Tessa's request. It was a popular feature and several businesses in town, along with private homeowners, wanted versions for themselves. Tessa had a long waiting list for her landscaping designs, both in Elk Point and back in Tucson.

She was going to continue working after the baby came and Aunt Emma had eagerly declared her availability for babysitting. She was going to be busy with Jillian expecting, as well.

"Tessa? Clay? I wondered where you'd gone," called Laura Carson from the path that led to the office porch.

"We're just getting some well-deserved rest," Clay said lazily.

Laura nodded. "Good. But folks are asking for you both."

Tessa kissed her husband's jaw and sat up. "Not to worry, there are still people I haven't had a chance to meet yet." She tugged Clay to his feet. "Come on, we have host and hostess responsibilities we're ignoring."

He walked ahead of them and Laura linked arms with Tessa. They'd become close over the past year. Russell was a great guy, too.

Her parents were on okay terms with the elder Carsons, but real friendship would take time. While Melanie and Chuck hadn't started a business in Elk Point, they'd bought a small house near the Carson Double C where they could spend part of the summer and stay on other visits. Clay's mother and father had thought it was a little odd, since they always stayed with their sons and daughters-in-law when visiting.

Tessa had understood and explained that

her parents were still coping with Renee's death and needed privacy, even when they were visiting family. Her reasoning seemed to have sorted out the matter.

Inside the patriotically decorated barn, Tessa saw her parents sitting with Andrew and Jillian. They hadn't been sure Jillian would make it to the party without going into labor, but she seemed to be doing all right. Little Derry was sitting on Chuck's knee. Tessa looked forward to introducing her own son or daughter to the sweet boy.

Tessa's father-in-law kissed her forehead. "How are you doing, hon? Not getting too tired, I hope."

"I'm fine."

"Maybe you should sit down," he urged, looking anxious.

"Laura warned me that you're a little over-protective."

He sighed and nodded. "Guilty as charged."

CLAY PUT HIS hands on Tessa's shoulders, drawing her against him as his parents joined a square dance. He felt like the luckiest man who'd ever lived.

With Tessa, he was whole. He couldn't even contemplate life without her. She had become his entire reason for waking up in the morning.

He still loved exploring the Montana wilderness, but he needed her more. And now he was going to be a father, something he'd never expected to happen.

"Is something wrong?" he asked, sensing a stillness in his wife. He turned her around and saw joy in her blue eyes.

"I may have felt the baby move."

Clay swiftly put his hand on her abdomen. Everything else seemed to fall away while he focused. Softly, like the first flake of snow falling in winter, he felt a movement.

Their child.

He looked into his wife's excited face, awe filling him. Tessa had filled spaces in his heart that he'd never known were empty, and now his heart just kept getting bigger.

"I love you," he breathed and kissed her.

* * * * *

*For more great romances from
Julianna Morris and
Harlequin Heartwarming,
visit www.Harlequin.com today
and check out:*

Twins for the Rodeo Star
Christmas on the Ranch

Get 4 FREE REWARDS!

We'll send you 2 FREE Books plus 2 FREE Mystery Gifts.

Love Inspired books feature uplifting stories where faith helps guide you through life's challenges and discover the promise of a new beginning.

FREE
Value Over
$20

HARLEQUIN SELECTS COLLECTION

Get 4 FREE REWARDS!

We'll send you 2 FREE Books plus 2 FREE Mystery Gifts.

FREE Value Over **$20**

Both the **Romance** and **Suspense** collections feature compelling novels written by many of today's bestselling authors.

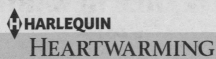

#383 BUILDING A SURPRISE FAMILY
Butterfly Harbor Stories • by Anna J. Stewart

Being nicknamed Butterfly Harbor's most eligible bachelor has taken Ozzy Lakeman by surprise! But he's more surprised by the town newcomer and single mom-to-be, Jo Bertoletti, a woman he can't get off his mind...or out of his heart.

#384 THE SECRET SANTA PROJECT
Seasons of Alaska • by Carol Ross

Travel blogger Hazel James has scheduled her holiday at an unexpected but much-needed locale—home. Major disruption to her peaceful Christmas: Cricket Blackburn, her brother's best friend and the love of her life she can't quite seem to get over.

#385 STEALING HER BEST FRIEND'S HEART
The Golden Matchmakers Club • by Tara Randel

Heidi Welch wants the house Reid Masterson intends to flip for a profit, which puts it out of her price range. Will they make a deal or take a chance on a friendship that has grown into love?

#386 A COWBOY'S HOMECOMING
Kansas Cowboys • by Leigh Riker

Rancher and widowed single mother Kate Lancaster needed help. But she'd never accept it from Noah Bodine—the man she was drawn to...and the man she blames for her husband's death.

Visit
ReaderService.com
Today!

As a valued member of the Harlequin Reader Service, you'll find these benefits and more at ReaderService.com:

- Try 2 free books from any series
- Access risk-free special offers
- View your account history & manage payments
- Browse the latest Bonus Bucks catalog